Also by Virginia Ripple

Toby's Tale

Apprentice Cat
Journeyman Cat
Master Cat

Malkin novellas

Secrets of the Malkin

Non-fiction

Fear Not! Discovering God's Promises For Our Lives
Simply Prayer

Apprentice Cat

ISBN-13: 978-1479249817

ISBN-10: 1479249815

Cover design by Virginia Ripple
Photo image courtesy of Eric Isselée/Bigstock.com

To my husband, who has always been
my biggest cheerleader and greatest supporter
no matter how strange my ideas might seem,
and
to my family, who believed in me and
were always there to give me great ideas

Chapter 1

The old mage shivered as the cold damp air worked its way through his robe. His torch sputtered and hissed as water dripped from the low ceiling. Edging carefully past an overturned sarcophagus, he wondered again if he should have told anyone else what they had planned. But who? He shoved the thought aside. He'd made assurances everything he and his companion knew would be found by the High Council. Now was not the time to second guess. Accomplish the mission. Wonder about should haves later.

He had studied the old maps of the High Council lower passages and compared them to the maps the Brothers kept of the city crypts. Somewhere there was a door leading from this crypt to one of the hallways just below the council chambers. Blast this dank vault. How was he supposed to see anything with his torch flickering so erratically? His aged hand slid across a crack in the stone wall. He traced it from floor to head height. This was the door. He pressed his ear to the cool stone. Were those voices?

"R'VELthay." He could hear them now. Two males.

"They captured him at a meeting."

"I assume you interrogated him."

"Yes. He was very informative. Of course, I made sure he was cared for after he'd answered all of our questions."

He heard the muted sound of cloth being pulled over fur. The old mage pressed his hands against the wall. Who? Was it Victor? Surely it wasn't Kiyoshi. The black and brown cat was a master at infiltration. His stomach tightened with the thought. He closed his eyes and prayed to the One that he was wrong. The mage opened his eyes. The cats on the other side of the wall had begun speaking again.

"How hideous."

"Gargantua Felis Asesino: The Great Cat Killer. A favorite pet of mine."

"A spider bite did this?"

"A sting, actually. I thought it fitting."

The torch fell to the ground as the old mage pushed away from the stone door and closed his eyes again, fighting the sting of tears. He drew in a deep breath. The musty, decay-laden air threatened to choke him. Foolish old man. They knew. They knew all along. He curled his hand into a fist, wanting to pound the wall. He blinked his eyes in the darkness. Keep it together. Still a job to do. He placed his ear back to the wall.

"What of his companion? Do we know where he is?"

"As a matter of fact, I do." The mage sucked in a breath, his heart beat loudly in his ears. He heard the soft sound of paws pacing toward the door.

"Right here."

The door scraped as it opened, spilling the old mage onto the floor. He looked into the yellow eyes of a large gray tom. Turning his head he saw the misshapen lump of fur the two had been discussing. He crawled to his old friend's side, the mottled black and brown fur unmistakable. He reached to touch the once silken body.

"I wouldn't if I were you."

Apprentice Cat

The old mage stared hard at the gray tom whose whiskers were splayed wide. He could feel the strain of the muscles in his jaw as he clenched his teeth. His vision dimmed to pinpoints, centering on the yellow-eyed cat.

"A single feather touch can rupture the victim's skin and cause it to expel an acidic fluid that would eat through metal."

The sound of a rough tongue on fur from behind caught the mage's attention. He turned to look at the large black tom near the crumpled body of his companion. The cat looked up at him.

"Quite a nasty experience, I would imagine."

The old mage stared at the sleek black tom across from him. The cat's piercing green eyes made the human's neck hair stand on end. Dragging his gaze away, he saw a wooden barrel behind the cat. The old mage looked further down the hall toward more barrels. He turned his head to see the other end of the passage. More barrels. His brows furrowed. He could hear the swish, thump of the cats' tails.

Cautiously, the human crawled toward the wooden drum nearest him, keeping the black tom within his sight. He reached out to touch the wood. He slowly brought his fingers to his nose, his eyes never leaving the black cat, to smell the fine black powder on them. It smelled like the residue leftover from fireworks. The black tom's eyes were twinkling, the cat's whiskers splayed wide. The mage's eyes widened as he realized what they were planning.

"You won't —"

"Get away with this? But I already have."

A piercing pain in his neck. He slapped a hand at it, flinging something large and furry against the floor. An orange and green spider scuttled away as it tucked its stinger back under its abdomen. The poison burned its way down the old man's arms. The room reeled. He crashed to the floor, gashing his head on the wall as he fell. His body began twitching. Too late. He'd come too late. The gray tom paced over to his master and sat down, gracefully wrapping his furry tail around his paws. Curiousity gleamed from their eyes. The black tom's tail swished back and forth as if he were watching a mouse he intended to pounce on.

"What will happen to him?"

"I'm not sure. I've never seen a human stung before, so it should prove to be interesting. Most likely he'll live, but his mind be will gone."

The black tom swung his head toward his henchman. His ears flattened.

"Most likely? This is not the time to experiment."

"Not to worry, master. Even if he still has more brains than a fool, no one will believe anything he says. I've made sure of that."

"You had better be correct."

The gray tom said nothing. He sat watching the old mage as his twitching grew less and foam began to ooze from his mouth. The man blinked slowly. He could hear the gentle sucking his eyelids made as they parted. The cats became blurry images.

"Then let us alert the High Council of this man's treachery." The black tom's voice sounded like it was coming from a long metal tube. As he watched the gray and black blurs slip out the catacomb door, he wondered if anyone would be able to decode the documents he'd left behind.

"Wrong. Do it again."

Toby grimaced, flattening his ears and wrinkling his

nose. It was a spell he'd done right a hundred times, but never when his mother was watching. She always made him as nervous as a field mouse venturing into the open during winter.

"Pulling faces will not make the writing appear coherently," she scolded, piercing yellow eyes never wavering in her scrutiny. "Again and this time concentrate."

Toby schooled his expression with difficulty. How he wanted to growl at her, make her understand that he knew "pulling faces" would not make the spell work any better. In fact, when he was alone, he could make any writing appear crisp, clean and in modern language without so much as a twitch of a whisker. Yet every time he tried to perform it for his mother the words would blur together until they formed a solid ink snake, which would then slither off the page, down the table leg and through the cracks in the floor.

Collecting his willpower, he stared at the complicated scrawls upon the page. He stretched out his mind to touch the first inked letter, pulling it into the air just above the time-worn paper. Satisfied that the first letter was stable, he drew the others to it one by one until every word was floating inches above where they had been. With great caution, Toby sent a tendril of will at the writing, hoping that this time the letters would cooperate and transform themselves into something at least resembling modern language.

The letters began to tremble, then slowly rotate. Toby spun more willpower into the process until the letters were spinning so fast they were little more than tiny balls of black. Just as it seemed the process would never cease, he felt the little snap that meant the letters were ready to be pulled into a new form. *So far so good,* he thought. It was further than he had managed the last time. With a quick twist of thought, he halted the spinning letters. The ink spread into long loops and flattened into miniscule blobs as it coalesced, becoming words that could be understood by any mage in the present time.

Just as the ink was settling back onto the page, there was a knock at the door. With the speed of a blue racer, the letters ran together and slithered off the page, down the table leg and into the cracks in the floor to join its predecessors. Toby sighed. A moment more and the words would have sunk into the paper. After that, only a reversing spell would have put them back into the form they had originally been in.

Toby chanced a glance at his mother. She looked steadily back at her only son, her whiskers clamped together in irritation, her ears swiveled outward. He knew that look very well. Without looking away, she twitched her tail at the closed door.

"Enter," she called as the door opened on its own.

"Oh," the startled housekeeper replied. "I'm sorry Mistress. I thought the Master had forgotten to remove the no disturbin' sign again. I was jus' on m' way out and thought I should pop in to check the firewood."

"No apology necessary, Mariam," replied the black queen, never taking her eyes from her son. "We were just drilling in the art of Transferring Ancient Glyphs, something young Toby needs practice in if he ever wants to be accepted into the King's Academy of Mages. Please go about your chore."

"Yes, mum. Won't be but a moment."

Toby stared resolutely at the scarred table, listening to the housekeeper bustle about the fireplace. He could feel his mother's eyes boring into his fur. He wished he could join the inky snakes in their dark crevices beneath the floorboards. The housekeeper was as good as her word and was gone moments later. She closed the workroom door on her way out, saying nothing as she left. He listened as the outer door leading to the street clicked shut.

He was alone with his taskmaster now. He waited. The clock on the mantle ticked the minutes by. She said nothing. He curled his tail tighter around his toes. Still she said nothing. He slowly hunched himself on the table, trying to make himself appear smaller. And yet the tongue lashing he was expecting did not occur. Steeling himself, he slowly looked up at the black queen. Yellow eyes pierced to his heart. The only indication that she was not a royal black statue was the rhythmic tapping of her tail tip.

"Well?"

Toby wasn't sure what answer she expected him to give. She growled in impatience, making him shudder. If she weren't his mother, he wasn't sure he'd escape with his fur attached if he said what he was really thinking. Even so, she had taken a clump from his hide on occasion, though certainly not without provocation. Toby worried that this might be one of those times whether he remained silent or not.

"Don't just lay there like a worthless dish rag. One interruption does not mean the lesson is over."

"Yes, Mother."

He sat up, turning toward the open book. Try as he might, though, he could not order his thoughts to make the writing on the page even begin to hover over the paper. His mother hissed. Toby didn't need to turn around to know what his mother looked like. Her ears would be flattened, her eyes slit in annoyance.

"Don't tell me you've forgotten how to begin."

"Of course I haven't. You just won't give me a chance. You never give me a chance. All you ever do is criticize."

The hair on the black queen rose along her sleek back.

She bared her sharp teeth, growling and raised a paw to cuff the orange tom. Toby stood his ground, waiting for the paw to fall upon his ears.

"How dare you speak to me that way," she hissed. "I'm your mother. I brought you into this world and I can take you out again."

"Then do it, mother, because obviously I can't please you."

"Maybe I should, you ungrateful whelp," she exclaimed, voice rising to a yowl.

They stood, staring at each other, fluffed for battle. The moments inched by in dreadful silence. The paw still hung in the air, ready to strike, yet never fell. Hair by hair, their fur flattened, though the air crackled with leftover anger. Toby turned and leapt to the open window sill. He glanced at his mother's reflection in the window pane. Her mouth was open, as if she were about to call him back. He didn't want to hear another sound from her. Without a backward glance, he jumped from the sill to the ground.

Toby landed between the hedges with a thud, not caring what creatures he startled. *She can be so unreasonable,* he steamed. *She knows I study every night until Master O'dorn comes home. What does she think I do? Look at the pictures and drool all over myself?* The orange tom stalked down the worn footpath toward the garden gate. He jerked his tail at the latch, which snapped open, then butted the heavy wooden gate with his head. It didn't budge. He slashed his tail to the side, making the gate slam open against the stonework fence. His ears flattened as he slunk past the rattling gate. This was Master O'dorn's prize herb garden and deserved his respect. He could hear his mother lecturing him about strong emotions and lack of magical control. He growled and snapped at

14

a dust mote floating past his nose.

Toby trotted to the huge oak past the gate, its trunk worn and scarred. As thoughts of what his mother had said to him rumbled and rolled through his mind, he vigorously clawed at the tree trunk, its bark completely gone as far up as he could easily reach. The way she had virtually accused him of being an idiot made his hair stand out in rage.

The bark-less trunk wasn't doing it for him this time. He needed something he could really get his claws into. He peered through the low branches, backing away from the oak. There, about halfway up, was the perfect branch, straight, solid and with plenty of bark to claw at. With a wiggle of his behind, Toby shot toward the tree, swarming up its length until he reached his destination. It was perfect. He set to work scratching with all his might. Eventually Toby was able to calm down. Logic began to inject itself into his thoughts.

She never actually called him an idiot. In fact, in a strange way, she seemed to be saying the exact opposite. Never once, in all the times she had drilled him at lessons, had she given up on him. He had given her enough reasons to believe he was incapable of doing even basic magic, but still she persisted. That didn't seem like the reaction of someone who considered her pupil stupid. Did it?

Perhaps I was being dull-witted. Toby sighed. The orange tom peered through the leaves, noting that fall would soon be here in the slight change of coloring. He lifted his nose to sniff the crisp evening air. Yes, fall was quickly approaching. The time for him to go to the academy would be very soon. With another heavy sigh, he put his head on his paws, flattening himself out along the branch. It was so obvious why his mother was in such a foul mood. Time was growing short and he had yet to display any real abilities. Add that to the problems Master O'dorn seemed to be having in the Council and it was enough to wear any cat's patience thin.

Toby peered down at a lower branch where a bird's nest lay empty. He had watched in interest as the little sparrows had built it, then hatched their young. He wondered what it was like for the hatchlings to snuggle together while they slept and be taught how to hunt worms. How did their parents react to their failures? To Toby it seemed they didn't mind because the little birds soon learned how to hunt for themselves. Too soon, they had flown away to begin families of their own.

The little family was nothing like his own. His mother had spent a portion of her time each day teaching him to hunt when he was a kitten. That had been almost as miserable an experience as learning magic was from her now. He chuckled as he remembered her frustrated expression when he had mistakenly caught Master O'dorn's bedroom slipper rather than the mouse he had been chasing.

She had said nothing, only given him that same look she'd bestowed upon him earlier today and stalked away. When Toby's father had returned home that night, she recounted the entire episode. When his father had laughed, the black queen had hissed at him and told him that if he thought it was so funny, he could be responsible for teaching his son the difference between rodents and footwear. She then stalked from the room.

Toby asked why his mother hated him and was relieved when his father had explained that Adele didn't hate him. She was just angry that things weren't going the way she wanted. After that, the two tussled until Toby began to yawn and stumble from fatigue. He fell asleep listening to his father's rumbling purr. It hadn't been long after that that he had caught his first mouse, which pleased his mother immensely. Now he wished all it would take was catching a mouse to make her happy.

The sound of a coach arriving at the front gate brought Toby out of his reverie. He glanced at the sundial across the garden. The shadow had inched its way nearly a quarter down the sundial's face, making Toby flinch as he realized how long he'd been in the oak. His mother would be even less pleased with his behavior now. He could just hear her accusing him of sulking.

The orange tom heaved himself up and turned around to climb back down the tree. Waiting any longer would do no good. He was in for it whether he went back into the house now or later. Dropping the last few feet, Toby turned toward the gate and slowly paced back down the footpath. The sound of the front door closing made him prick his ears forward. He wondered if Master O'dorn was home for the evening or if it was another patron hoping the Master had a cure for some minor ailment. He was about to jump to the open workroom window when he heard voices. Toby sat behind the hedges to wait.

"He's head-strong, worse than his father," complained Toby's mother.

"Toby is a good cat and you know it, Adele," Master O'dorn said. At the mention of his name, the orange tom's ears pricked up. He stared intently up at the open window, imagining his mother pacing the workroom table as Master O'dorn sat in his rumpled old chair.

"Oh, I know he's a good cat. I just wish he'd apply himself to his lessons. What if he doesn't get chosen, Clarence, what then?"

"If Toby isn't accepted into the academy it won't be

because he can't do magic. It will be because there just isn't a suitable human to partner him with."

"But how do you know that? How can you be sure? I've never seen him do more than the simplest spell. The only thing I know he's good at is reading and remembering his history lessons. That's not going to be enough. I remember how hard it was going through the academy, how some of the teachers made it so much more difficult just because I didn't have the advantage of a private tutor. If I can't help Toby shine, then I've failed him."

The pain in her voice was new to Toby. She didn't talk about what her time at the academy was like except to remind him time and again of how there were always more cats than humans hoping to get in and to admonish him to study hard because it wouldn't get any easier. He tried to imagine his regal mother as a young apprentice who was mistreated by teachers and students. The image wouldn't stay. His mother had always been a self-assured, commanding presence in his life.

"Adele, my dear friend, that was a long time ago. Your son is a wonderful masterpiece. I know you haven't seen him do much magic, but I have. Trust me when I tell you that he is quite capable."

"I wish I could."

"Could what? Trust me or believe in your son?" the mage asked, a smile in his voice.

"You know, I'm not sure which. It's difficult to believe in something you never see, even when your most valued friend assures you it's real."

"And yet you are a master cat, able to see the end results of a spell before it is more than a few jumbled words and assorted herbs. How is it that you fail to see what your son can do?"

"That is a very good question. I feel like a miserable failure. I'm his mother and I know I should be able to believe in my son simply because he's my son, but I just can't do it. Why is that?"

"Do you really want to know what I think?"

"I wouldn't have asked if I didn't."

Toby could imagine the reproachful look she was bestowing on the master mage, eyes slitted, whiskers clamped together.

"Well, my dear," Clarence began, obviously ignoring Adele's reproving attitude, something the orange tom thought must come with having been friends for so long. "I believe what you are seeing is your past fears reflected in Toby's seeming inability to do magic. You fear that your son will have to endure the same pain you endured and so you push him much harder than any but the most ruthless teacher at the academy. Toby is terrified of disappointing you, which translates into failure after failure during your lessons. Fear feeds upon fear."

Toby held his breath, waiting for the feline eruption he was sure would come. The only sound being made was by the lark in the garden, its melody contrasting sharply with the nervous tension in the tom's body. Minutes passed. Finally, Toby heard his mother's gentle sigh.

"I suppose you're right... as usual."

"Ah, well, that's one of the perks of being a master mage," joked Master O'dorn. "But seriously, Adele, I believe you really must have a good chat with your son. Perhaps if he understood where you are coming from he might begin to excel in his lessons with you."

There was a long pause. Toby began to wonder if he

had somehow missed the sound of the workroom door opening and closing when his mother spoke again.

"I love my son, Clarence," she said in a low, impassioned voice.

"I know, Adele —"

"That's why I can't tell him."

There was another long pause. A squeak of springs made the young cat imagine Master O'dorn leaning closer to Toby's mother.

"Are you sure?"

"I'm all he has. I have to be strong… for him."

A moment more passed and then Toby heard the click of the workroom door opening, followed by the soft thunk as it closed. He sat and stared at a digger beetle working its way between the packed earth behind the hedges and the gray stone walls of Master O'dorn's house, his mind trying to work through the conversation he had overheard. Was his mother right? If he couldn't do what she demanded of him, how could he expect to do what his teachers asked him to do? They wouldn't all be as easy to work with as Master O'dorn. He shivered as he considered the possibilities.

Chapter 2

Toby turned his attention to watching for the coach, trying to ignore the stony presence of his mother. The silence between them stretched uncomfortably. He stared across the street at the neighbor's gray rock fence, watching as the sunflowers danced in the light fall breeze, their bright yellow heads bobbing a good cat stretch above the weathered stone.

Colorful maple leaves scooted along the brown cobbled street. The orange tom flicked an ear as a lazy fly buzzed around his head searching for a place to land. The quiet was stifling. If he could have conjured the coach at that moment, he would have. Adele shifted beside him.

"I wonder what is taking that coach so long?"

Toby glanced at her to find that she seemed as fidgety as he was. He had mixed feelings about that. On the one hand, it was nice to know he wasn't the only one wishing to get on with things. On the other hand, he was a little disturbed to think that his mother was so eager to see him gone.

"Oh don't look so taken aback. You know I hate good byes."

He watched a beetle crawl over a clump of dried grass protruding in the cobblestones at the edge of their path, he wondered what had caused his mother to dislike saying goodbye so much. Rummaging through his memories, he noted that there was a marked decline in her liking of good byes from the day his father disappeared. It made Toby wonder if she somehow blamed herself for his father's disappearance.

"Toby, did you hear me? Your coach is coming."

The sharp tone of his mother's voice startled the orange tom out of his memories. He shifted his gaze down the street where the coach was steadily approaching. It looked the same as the one his father had taken the day he disappeared, from the two black horses to the square box-like structure perched on the large round wheels. Toby couldn't be sure, but even the driver looked like the same man, an overlarge round-brimmed hat sunk low on his head. His faded overcoat rippled in the light breeze. A long whip stood erect by his side. The coachman deftly pulled the coach to the curb as he slowed the horses to a stop.

"Toby, look at me," his mother commanded. Gathering his wayward emotions together, he steeled himself to look into her eyes.

"Your father would be the first to tell you that you earned this right. Mourning him on the eve of your impending selection is wasted energy better used in reviewing past lessons."

"I know you're right, mother, but—"

"No 'buts'. You are your father's son... and you are mine, as well. You were born to this. It is time you took your place among the Cats."

"Cum along, cat," hollered the coachman, his voice as brittle as the fall breeze. "I don' git paid extree t'wait fer no maudlin' goo' byes."

The scowl Toby's mother gave the coachman would have cowed any ordinary person, but the man was unfazed. Looking back at her son, her eyes softened for a moment. She stretched forward to give his right ear a quick lick.

"Be strong, my son," she whispered. She backed away, then, and sat down again. Her stern demeanor returned. Toby's tongue seemed glued to the roof of his mouth. Shouldn't he say something? Maybe something profound? Even a thank you might have been appropriate, but the words stuck in his throat.

When he hesitated for a moment longer, his mother gave him a small magical nudge toward the coach with a twitch of her tail. Toby got to his feet and trotted to the coach's open door. Pausing again, he looked back at the regal black queen sitting motionless on the pathway, the only hint that she was more than a statue in the movement of her fur in the crisp fall breeze.

He glanced up at the coachman, noting that the man was about to say something rude if he delayed any longer, then leaped into the dark opening. The orange tom barely had enough time to pull his tail in behind him before the coach door slammed shut. It was as dark as Master O'dorn's root cellar, but thicker. Toby wondered if he could reach out and slice through it with his claws.

Before he had more than a moment to wonder about the inky darkness he was knocked from his feet as the coachman urged his horses into a quick trot. *So much for a leisurely ride to the academy,* thought Toby.

Picking himself up, he glanced around the coach's interior. There was a small window in front of him near the ceiling, the curtains pulled nearly closed. A sliver of warm sunlight tried vainly to illuminate the inside of the coach, but only managed to cast a weak glow over the area where Toby stood. As he stood on the floor waiting for his eyes to become more accustomed to the unusual darkness, he sniffed the air to help get his bearings. A strong smell of rusty iron and marigolds hit his nose, making him sneeze in surprise.

"Blessings, little cat." Toby jumped, his hair standing on end, feet splayed and claws extended to aid in a quick flight. The voice chuckled. Embarrassed, Toby quickly pulled himself into a dignified sitting position and gave his ruff a quick lick.

"My apologies for startling you, little cat," said the deep voice. "I had forgotten how dark this coach is when one first enters."

"No apology necessary, sir," answered Toby. He turned to face where the voice was coming from. Squinting, he attempted to see who the voice belonged to, but the darkness was impenetrable. Not wanting to be considered rude by staring, the tom turned around to find the seat he assumed must be across from the voice's owner. He found the same darkness on the other side as well.

"Let me give you some light to find your way by," said the voice. "No need to stumble around this tiny coach trying to find a proper seat."

From the darkness slid a dragon's head cane, glinting in the narrow shaft of light from the window. The cane's owner caught the edge of the curtain in the mouth of the snarling silver dragon and quickly pulled it aside, the curtain rings rasping in protest. Bright sunshine beamed into the coach. Toby squeezed his eyes tight against the sudden brightness. He squinted just enough to find the seat the voice had indicated was nearby. It was thankfully in shade, which would give him time to adjust to the lightened interior without looking like a mewling kit.

"Thank you," Toby said, leaping to the proffered seat. He took a moment to knead the padding into a slightly softer place, turned around once and lowered himself into a comfortable position, tucking his front paws beneath his chest and wrapping his tail around himself.

"You are very much welcome, little cat," said the owner of the voice. Although the other side of the coach was still shadowed, the light from the window made it much easier for Toby to see the man sitting across from him. He was well-groomed, his dark hair swept back and his anchor goatee precisely trimmed. Toby had seen other noble men and women at a distance, usually by peeking into Master O'dorn's receiving room, but this was closer than he had ever considered he would get. He found it rather unnerving. He was in the middle of wishing he knew a spell to make himself transparent when the man spoke again.

"I'm sorry, My Lord, but I didn't quite catch what you said," Toby replied in embarrassment. He was beginning to feel like that was all he did, embarrass himself.

"I asked your name. It seems rather rude of me to continue to address you as 'little cat' in such close quarters."

"My apologies for not introducing myself, My Lord. My name is Toby."

"Think nothing of it, Toby. And since you were kind enough to give us your name, allow me to introduce myself. I am Fedelis Arturo, Gravin of Hielberg County and this is my companion Chivato."

He motioned to a large dark mass on the seat beside him. Toby tried to imagine what it could be. The ruler of a county was usually a magician of some power, so it made sense that Gravin Arturo would have a master cat companion, but the dark mass didn't resemble anything more than a pile of clothes. The man scowled at the creature when several moments had gone by without movement.

"Chivato, my friend, would you not care to welcome

our guest?" asked Gravin Arturo, a slight growl to his voice. A pair of slitted yellow eyes slowly opened halfway and gazed for a long moment at the orange tom across the coach. The large tom yawned wide, exposing sharp fangs.

"Welcome."

He stretched out a sleek gray paw, closed his eyes and returned to ignoring everyone. Gravin Arturo gave a long-suffering sigh and shook his head.

"My apologies. I'm afraid Chivato is in a less than civil mood today."

He turned back to the orange tom. Silence stretched between them as the gravin studied Toby, something Toby wanted to do himself, but felt would be rude. The man's gaze bored into young Toby's orange pelt until the cat began to wish once again for a vanishing spell.

"Forgive my rudeness, but that is a very unusual color for a cat. Might I ask if it's natural?"

"Yes, sir. I was born this color," Toby replied, hesitant to go into detail.

"Your color clearly didn't come from your mother, assuming the queen who saw you off was she, and I thought I knew every unique tom in the city. Tell me, who was your father?"

Toby gulped. What should he say? His mother had made it clear that wanting to enter the academy and not being noble was unacceptable to many. After all, had he been noble he would be the same color as his parents. He wouldn't deny who his father was, but to name him would be to spotlight his middle class status. Or would it? Did the gravin know Victor? His mind raced for an answer.

"Oh for the love of Faust, Arturo," growled the large gray cat, rolling onto his back to stretch. "Your passion with genealogy borders on obsession. Who cares who fathered young Toby. He obviously has the qualifications to enter the academy or he wouldn't be in this coach."

Toby glanced from Chivato to the gravin, who looked as if he had swallowed something sour. A cold silence fell on the coach with only the creak of the wheels to be heard. The big gray tom curled back into a ball and closed his eyes. The gravin stared at the passing scenery through the small window, lightly tapping his cane with an index finger in time to the gentle swaying of the coach.

Toby closed his eyes to mere slits and decided to take advantage of the uneasy silence to study his surroundings. The coach's interior was cleaner than he had first thought, though well-worn. The cloth beneath his paws was nearly worn through, the straw used as padding just beginning to show. Tiny dust moats drifted in through the window to float and sparkle in the sunlight. A faint scent of lilac hung in the air. Toby opened his mouth to taste it. He instantly regretted taking such a deep breath as the lilac scent was overpowered by the smell of wet metal. A coppery tang sparked across Toby's tongue, reminding him of hunting mice with his father. The pungent aroma of marigolds assaulted the young tom's nose, mixing with the metallic smell in Toby's mind.

No sooner had Toby inhaled, than he began sneezing. As sneeze after sneeze crashed over his small body, he began to wonder if the smell would ever leave his nose so he could breath again. He stood and began backing up step by slow step, instinct making him try to get away from whatever was making him sneeze. As his rump collided with the wall he was wracked by three rapid-fire sneezes. Suddenly the smell disappeared, taking the sneezing fit with it. Toby blinked watery eyes at his companions. Gravin Arturo and the big gray tom stared back, eyes wide. Afraid the sneezing fit would return, Toby took a small, hesitant breath. When nothing happened, he took a deeper breath and let it out in a grateful sigh.

"My apologies, good sirs," Toby began, sitting back down on the padded seat. "I'm not sure what happened. One moment I was enjoying the scent of lilacs and the next I'm trying to sneeze away the overpowering smell of marigolds and wet metal. Perhaps we passed a large garden of the flowers as they were being irrigated. I must be allergic to that particular flower."

The gravin exchanged a look with his cat. In unison, they turned to stare at Toby. The young tom felt like he must have sprouted fairy wings the way the duo looked at him. The uneasy silence seemed to stretch forever, making Toby want to fidget. He managed to keep all but his tail tip still. He jumped when Gravin Arturo cleared his throat to speak.

"I'm afraid it is we who should apologize, young Toby," the gravin said. "You see, I suffer from a stomach ailment and the remedy requires certain ... potent ... ingredients such as a large amount of marigold flowers and a thimble of copper. I would imagine the reason the smell was so strong to you is because I prepare the remedy myself with Chivato's aid."

"In other words, little cat," Chivato said, "You just received a double dose of a particularly strong scent."

Something in the way the gravin had said the word potent made Toby want to let the subject drop. He had been around Master O'dorn and his mother while they were working often enough to know even the strongest of medicinal magic left little, if any, residual smell on the person preparing it. However, he didn't know if that were true for a person who prepares and takes his own remedy. Either way there had been something about that smell that made the orange tom decide against asking any questions.

"Ah, yes. I'm sure that explains it," Toby replied.

He glanced out the window, hoping to discern how much further it was to the academy. Unfortunately, the only thing he could see was blue sky and the top of an occasional maple tree. He thought longingly of the windows over-looking Master O'dorn's garden, almost wishing he had stayed home instead of chasing a dream that may or may not see fruition. He sighed as he looked back down at his paws.

"There are steps hidden in the wall," said Chivato.

"Pardon?"

"If you wish to see out the window," the gray cat explained, as if speaking to someone of little intelligence, "there are steps hidden in the coach's wall for those lacking height."

Toby stared blankly at the wall under the window. As far as he could tell it looked like any ordinary wall. The gray tom snorted, uncurling himself with liquid grace and flowing onto the floor. Chivato paced to the wall beneath the window.

"Rev EALTH est EPS," murmured the gray cat, touching a delicate paw to a knot in one of the boards making up the coach's wall. With a gentle hiss the board slid downward, revealing a hidden compartment. Chivato took two steps back and sat on his haunches, curling his fluffy gray tail around his paws. Entranced, Toby watched intently as thin wooden steps levered themselves out from the wall and into the shape of a miniature stairway. The steps seemed suspended in air, but Toby was quite sure, if he knew the correct spell, he could make the magic cords binding the stairs together appear.

"May I?"

"Certainly," replied the gray tom.

Although he wanted to dash up the stairway in his excitement, he managed to climb it at what he hoped would be considered a sedate pace. At the top step he stretched to try to see out the window, but the best he could see was a lot of windowsill and a little beyond. At first he was disappointed. The knot to access the stairway had been just at the edge of a cat's reach, so whoever had put them there had considered the need of felines to see outside and yet the stairway itself was just short of the height a cat would need. He was about to ask about the difference when it dawned on him that there was likely a way to make the stairway taller.

"May I increase the height a bit?" Toby asked, hoping the other cat's opinion of him would raise a bit.

"Of course," the tom. "They would be useless if one couldn't choose how tall they needed to be."

"Leng THENTH eSTAIRS," the orange tom commanded before Chivato could offer the correct incantation.

The step he was sitting on gave a little shudder, then began to rise slowly and smoothly upward. Toby waited patiently as more of the passing scenery came into view. They were traveling through a wooded area, the trees huddling together along the roadway like close friends engaged in one enormous group hug. Sunlight filtered down through the colored leaves, lighting patches of the dry grass in hues of gold and casting other areas into shadow. The cool fall breeze sliding past the moving coach caressed Toby's sensitive nose and tugged gently at his whiskers. The smell of drying leaves and moist earth tickled his senses.

The young tom closed his eyes to better enjoy the scent of fall. Somewhere nearby a crop of corn was ready to be harvested. He could almost see the dry leaves, torn away by a previous wind, being tossed about above the cornstalks like some fine lady's scarf set loose upon the breeze. Somewhere else was a small orchard. The scent of ripening apples drifted past, filling him with memories of the cook's delicious apple tarts. Under it all was a hint of manure, signaling to Toby that far ahead was a stable offering sanctuary to a large number of horses. *I wonder if that's the academy's stable. I think I remember Master O'dorn mentioning having to borrow one of their horses once.*

Something touched the tip of Toby's ear. Assuming it was a fly, he flicked his ear. The annoying thing became more insistent, pressing down on his ear. The orange tom was about to murmur a spell to repel the irritating insect when he heard a soft clearing of a feline throat behind him. Suddenly it dawned on him that he had forgotten to say the incantation to stop the stairs.

"ENdl ENGthen," murmured Toby, his skin feeling hot and prickly.

"I think I can smell the academy's stable from here," Toby reported, trying to hide his faux pas. "I suppose we'll be arriving there shortly?"

"That would be a good assessment," answered Chivato. "If you perform magic as well as you detect smell, you should find yourself at the top of your class... if you're chosen to be apprenticed, that is. You do understand that there is a very good chance you may not be chosen?"

Toby turned to descend the stairs, carefully jumping from step to step, careful not to trip and fall on his nose. He could feel both the gravin's and his companion's eyes on his fur, waiting for him to respond. He quietly paced to the knot in the wall, said the incantation to shorten and replace the stairs, then pressed the knot with his paw. As the cover clicked into place, he made his decision.

"Yes, sir," the orange tom answered, turning to face the

large gray cat. "My mother made me well aware of the difference in number between the many cat hopefuls and much fewer human initiates. All I can do is my best and leave the rest to the wisdom of the head master mage and head master cat."

"A good answer," replied Gravin Arturo, nodding sagely. "I believe Master Chivato is correct. You will most certainly be top among your peers, should you be chosen."

Toby nodded politely to the gravin in thanks, then silently walked to the seat he had previously occupied and jumped. Chivato resumed his seat as well, though he did not return to his nap. The travelers spent the rest of the ride to the academy talking of mundane things, much to Toby's relief. The scent of manure continued to grow stronger as time passed, slowly being enhanced by various other smells Toby had never encountered, smells he decided must be attached to the academy.

"Ah, it seems our young friend has indeed a very good sense of smell," the gravin exclaimed, leaning just a bit for a better view outside the coach. "I can just see the academy tower over the trees. We should be arriving in just a few moments."

The coach gently shifted as it turned a corner. Maples and oaks gave way to a continuous line of weeping willows. At least, that's what Toby thought they were. The elongated leaves on the wispy, draping branches looked similar to the willow tree near Master O'dorn's gazing pond in the herb garden, but the color was wrong. The leaves on the willow at the gazing pond always turned a brilliant yellow during fall. These trees had bright blue leaves. As the breeze stirred the willow branches, Toby could see the underside of the leaves were a paler shade of blue.

"What unusual trees," Toby murmured.

"A rare species of willow," Gravin Arturo said. "They were a gift to the school from my predecessor. Dragon Willows grow thick in our county and are rarely seen anywhere else in the world."

"I'm familiar with the properties of the common varieties of willow tree. May I ask what differences there are in such a rare tree?"

"Generally speaking, there are very few. Aside from the color of its leaves in fall, the only real difference is in the potency of its various parts used in spelling. An immature tree is three times more potent than the common variety."

"How interesting," said Toby. "Your trees must be in high demand, then."

"Indeed they are. Dragon Willow trees are rarely ever sold; however, we do make a tidy sum on the exporting of their leaves and bark. Of course, import and export taxation does cut into our profits."

"Unless one skirts the laws and bends a few rules, that is," added Chivato.

"One could do that, yes," replied the gravin, scowling at his companion, "but as gravin to Hielberg I will not, under any circumstances, bend the rules and be accused of aiding the practicing of the shadow arts."

"I never said you should." The gray tom yawned. "I was merely stating the fact that some might consider doing so."

"Why would circumventing paying import and export taxes get you accused of aiding a shadow arts practitioner?"

"Besides the obvious illegality of not paying one's taxes," answered Gravin Arturo, "Dragon Willow parts are in highest demand among those who practice the shadow arts, due to its potency."

"Really? I didn't think willows would be a component of any shadow spell."

"You will find, young Toby, that there are those among us who can twist the most benign spell into the most vicious curse. All it takes is a little learning and the will to create an outcome which serves only one's own desires."

"Sir, may I ask how you learned about the shadow arts?"

"Why might you want to know that?" The gravin's scowl darkened as he leaned forward and looked at Toby. The orange tom shrunk in on himself. Toby's mind whirled with explanations for his question, explanations that became more ludicrous with each new one.

"Faust's bargain, Arturo. Must you see inquisitors at every turn?" growled Chivato. "Young Toby is just another curious hopeful wanting to get a head start." The big gray tom looked at Toby, eyes slightly narrowed.

"Y-yes," Toby stuttered. "M-master O'dorn said my curiosity equaled my ability to do magic, that it was a good thing. I apologize if I offended you in some way."

The man eased back against the wall. The silence pressed down on Toby. For once Toby was grateful for his mother's explosive temper. At least it had prepared him remaining still and enduring uncomfortable situations like this. The gravin nodded as if he'd made a decision.

"Once again I'm afraid I am the one who should apologize," he said, placing both hands over the dragon's head cane. "I find I must be vigilant in what information I give out because of the precarious situation in the council and my county's highly visible trade in Dragon Willow. As Chivato rightly accused, I have begun to 'see inquisitors at every turn.'"

"That's understandable, sir," replied Toby. He hesitantly sat up straighter, deciding not to ask any more questions. He could hardly wait for the coach to stop at the administration building to let him out.

"It may be understandable, but it is inexcusable. To answer your question, I learned *about* the shadow arts in school. I've learned much more since becoming gravin, mostly to stay ahead of the shadow marketers who buy magical items in bulk at a discounted rate legally, then sell to shadow art practitioners at an inflated price. Every bit of information I've gained has been used to stop the marketers from profiting with my county's goods."

"Unfortunately," continued the gray tom, "there are those in the council that believe any knowledge of the shadow arts is dangerous and have begun, if you'll excuse the phrase, a 'mage hunt.'"

Toby mulled over what the duo had said. It seemed strange that the council would be trying to eliminate anyone who knew anything about the shadow arts if that knowledge was the only thing keeping the marketers in check. But why would the gravin and his companion lie? He didn't want to ask any more questions, but curiosity was burning in his mind.

"May I ask a question?"

The gravin gestured that Toby could ask away. The young tom collected his thoughts and tried to choose his words with care.

"Does the academy teach the shadow arts or did you learn about it on your own there?"

"I took an elective course on the history of magic that speculated on how the shadow arts have affected our knowledge and use of magic today. Now, while I detest repeating myself, I find myself compelled to ask you again, why do you want to know that?"

"Well, sir, I was just wondering how the council could be "hunting mages," as you say, when the academy openly teaches about the shadow arts."

"That is very astute thinking, my young friend. In fact, that is partly why I am here. Apparently some of the council members are attempting to pressure the head master mage into discontinuing the courses teaching anything about the shadow arts. I–."

Chivato cleared his throat.

"We, that is," continued Gravin Arturo, glaring at his companion, "are on our way to the Academic Council to lobby in favor of keeping the courses open."

The coach slowed to a stop in front of a large red brick building. Toby could see the twin towers rising toward the bright blue sky, their white crowns like grasping claws trying to snatch the occasional puffy cloud. He assumed it was the administration building and breathed a silent sigh of relief when the coach door slid open.

"I see we've reached your destination, young Toby. It was a pleasure to meet you."

"It was a pleasure to meet you, too, sir," replied Toby. "I hope your meeting ends well."

The orange tom flicked his tail in farewell and lightly jumped to the floor. As his paws hit the cobbles, he took a deep breath. A multitude of new smells danced around his nose. In the distance he could detect several animated conversations taking place. The cobblestone path he stood on led to the double-wide heavy wooden doors of the administration building, its twin towers now clearly evident as mere decoration. Toby flicked his ears back as he heard the coach door sliding shut.

"A very clever cat," said Gravin Arturo, his voice muffled by the thin door.

"Yes, very clever. We must keep an eye on him."

The creak of the coach's wheels as it was pulled away to its next destination startled Toby. He wasn't sure why, but the conversation he'd overheard didn't comfort him at all.

The sun had just begun to creep across Toby's flank when he was jarred awake by the ringing of a hand bell. It sounded as if it had been crafted from second-rate metal and then been beaten about by an exuberant toddler.

"Rise and shine, you vermin," bellowed someone in the doorway. Toby blinked the dark figure into focus. The owner of the voice was an adolescent tuxedo tom only a few years older than Toby. The tom strode into the room, chin high, tail straight.

"M'festus," admonished a petite white she-cat, stepping around the tuxedo tom with dainty paws, "just because we are second years it does not give us the right to oppress those who are seeking to be apprenticed."

"Whatever," growled the tom, flicking his tail.

The she-cat paid no attention. She sat slightly in front of and to the left of the tom, making it obvious to Toby that she was in charge. The orange tom glanced around at his fellow hopefuls to see if any of them noticed. If they did, not one of them gave it away. With the exception of a couple, each cat sat perfectly still, as if they had trained to pose for a master artist rather than to become apprentice cats. Toby tried not to show the worry that began to settle into his fur. His mother had warned him that most of the hopefuls would have had the best tutors money could buy. It looked as if she were right. Shoving the fear aside, Toby concentrated on what the she-cat was saying.

"Good morning, hopefuls. My name is Lilith and this is M'festus. We will be your counselors while you are here. I'm sure you're all anxious to begin your orientation immediately, but I'm also sure most of you ate very little last evening and will be suffering stomach rumbles before long."

As if to illustrate her point, someone's stomach growled. Lilith's whiskers splayed in amusement. M'festus scowled at the gathered cats. He seemed ready to swat the hopeful whose stomach had growled, but was unable to locate the offender.

"It seems I was right. Well then, let me briefly explain what will be happening from now until your first orientation session. You'll begin orientation today just after breakfast, which you'll take each morning in the dining room on the main floor of this building. The stairs at either end of the this hall will take you to the main entryway. The door to the dining room is between these stairs."

"The other door is obviously the exit and if you go through it you'll find yourself outside instead of getting in line for food," M'festus added snidely. The she-cat gave him a look Toby's mother would have been proud of. Unfortunately the tom was either too dense or too cocky to notice.

"When you finish," continued Lilith. "You are to take your dishes to the dish washing room window at the back of the dining room and then proceed to your designated orientation classroom. You'll find a list posted to the right of the entryway door with your name and finder incantation word. The finders are color coded to your class. If at anytime you get lost on campus, please do not hesitate to ask an apprentice, master or grounds keeper's aid for assistance.

"Getting lost, however, is no excuse for missing orientation. Those who miss any part of orientation will have penalties assessed to their final evaluation–"

"Which will keep you from being chosen," interrupted the tuxedo tom.

"Which *may* keep you from being chosen," Lilith corrected, glaring at the tom. M'festus glared back.

"The only thing that *will* keep you from being chosen is getting into a fight." The white she-cat continued to glare at the tuxedo tom as she spoke, then turned her gaze back to the gathered cats.

"This will be your sleeping quarters for the duration of orientation," Lilith continued. "You are encouraged to consider the bed you have chosen and the surrounding area to be your personal nest. We want you to feel as comfortable as possible during what can be the most stressful week of your academic career. If at any time you need assistance with settling in, please don't hesitate to see either M'festus or myself. You are dismissed."

M'festus gave one last scowl and quickly turned his back on the gathered cats, walking out the door ahead of Lilith. The she-cat closed her eyes for a moment, took a deep breath, then left behind the tom. Toby watched her until her tail slipped out of sight around the door frame, then looked around at his fellow hopefuls. Some were busy tidying up their nests. Toby glanced at his nest. As far as he could see there was nothing to tidy since he'd brought nothing with him, unlike a few of the others. Those not trying to shove belongings into manageable heaps were already forming little groups and heading down to breakfast.

It was apparent that Toby would not have been welcomed in most of the little groups since they were made up of cats from noble households. Some of the other groups looked to be made of cats devoted entirely to the intellectual side of magic or those who were here because they were forced to by a parent. Toby didn't think he could keep up a steady conversation with the smart cats and wasn't keen on listening to the endless complaints of a cat who would rather be elsewhere.

"Excuse me," said a timid little voice by Toby's ear. Toby turned to see a small gray and white patched tabby. The tabby tom looked too young to be amongst the hopefuls, too young and very nervous.

"Yes?" When the little tom shrunk in on himself, Toby made a mental note to speak softly to this particular cat.

"Was there something you needed, friend?" he asked.

"Well, sir," began the patched tabby, "I was wonderin' if I could come to breakfast with you."

Toby blinked in surprise. He'd never been called sir before. He wasn't sure he liked it. It brought to mind images of some of the arrogant nobles that would stop by Master O'dorn's cottage expecting the aging mage to drop everything to serve them. He looked back at a group of cats leaving for breakfast. *They looked a lot like them,* he thought. *If they're anything like those nobles, I know I don't want anything to do with them. But who does that leave?*

"It's okay, sir. I can see you'd rather eat with them. I'll see if someone else would like to have breakfast with me."

"Wait," Toby called to the little tom as he started to slink away. The little gray and white tabby looked back, a small glimmer of hope flashed in his eyes.

"What's your name, friend?"

"Terence."

"Well, Terence, I think it would be nice to have breakfast together. That is if you still want to."

"Yes, sir," Terence replied. The little cat wriggled, then his eyes widened. Toby could feel the embarrassed heat coming from the gray and white tom. He hid a smile of amusement.

"Alright, then, let's head down. And please, call me Toby."

"Yes, sir– I mean Toby."

The duo headed for the door. Toby couldn't help noticing that his new friend's coat was fluffed out and he was walking proudly, stretching to seem as tall as Toby. The tip of Toby's tail twitched with pleasure. He glanced sideways at Terence. The little tom purred.

"I hope they have tuna," said Terence. "Momma used to snatch a tuna from the fishmonger every chance she got when we lived on the docks."

"Didn't her master mage buy it for you?" asked Toby, shocked at the thought of a mage's cat stealing.

"Momma didn't have a master mage. She said her family was too poor to even think about sendin' her to the academy."

Toby suddenly felt ashamed. At least his mother hadn't been forced to steal for them to survive. In fact, compared to Terence's family, Toby felt like he had grown up among nobility. He wasn't exactly sure what to say next. Thankfully, Terence seemed unaware of Toby's sudden discomfort, and continued to chatter on about other things he was hoping for at the academy.

The two new friends padded down the worn wooden stairs. Toby occasionally uttering a noncommittal grunt whenever Terence paused. Listening to the little tom was almost like trying to hear every note played in a symphony by every instrument. Toby had tried to keep up with him, but before they arrived at the first landing he decided it was impossible.

Half way down the stairs the aroma of fried bacon, fresh roasted peanuts and creamed peas drifted up to caress the orange tom's nose. It seemed an odd combination for breakfast, though the tom figured finding any combination that made sense when feeding such a diverse group of felines would be a challenge at best. Under the tempting smells he caught the tantalizing scent of fish. Toby took a deep breath and let the image of a large yellow-finned fish with a blue stripe down its side dart through his mind.

"Looks like you're in luck," Toby said, interrupting Terence. "Unless my nose misleads me, we'll be breaking our fast on tuna today."

"Really? How do you know that?"

"I can smell it."

"You can smell it?"

"Sure. Can't you?"

"No," said Terence, lifting his nose to better sniff the air. "I can smell the bacon and... I think I smell some kind of nut, but that's it. How do you do that?"

"Do what?"

"How do you smell things so far away? Is it some kind of spell? Is it something I should know how to do? Do you think–"

"Terence," Toby shouted. He instantly regretted shouting when the little tom shrunk in on himself.

"Terence," he said, "It's not a spell. I can just smell things better than most cats. I guess I was born that way."

"Really?"

"Yes. Really."

"So it's not somethin' you can teach me?"

"No. It's not something I can teach you."

"And you're sure it's not somethin' I need to be able to do to get accepted?"

"As far as I know, getting accepted into the academy is based on magical abilities and not strange things you're born with."

"Oh. Okay."

The two cats proceeded toward the dining room doors in silence. A muffled buzz grew as they approached, erupting into a racket when they pushed past the doors to get into line. It seemed every cat in the room was wailing to be heard. Toby flattened his ears, trying to dampen the volume.

"Wow," he called to his little friend. "It sounds like every cat in the nation is here."

"This is nothing," Terence yelled back. "You should hear the din at the market on fresh produce day."

Toby didn't think he wanted to be anywhere near the market on fresh produce day if the noise was worse than this. The duo trotted to the rear of the breakfast line. Toby stretched on his hind legs to see how far away the buffet was. The line stretched around the wall of the dining room to the front, nearly the entire length of the room. He could just make out the cats getting their food. Toby sighed.

"Looks like we're going to be very hungry by the time we get our food. I just hope there's enough time to eat it before we need to be in class."

"I just hope there's enough food. I've never seen so many cats in one place before."

"Neither have I. My mother told me there would be a lot more cat hopefuls than humans, but I never could have imagined this."

As the line slowly snaked its way toward the buffet,

Toby took the opportunity to look over his surroundings. Four ceiling to floor windows lined the opposite wall, giving the only illumination to the room. Beyond the windows was a stunning view of the academy's garden. If Toby hadn't known it was fall, he would have been convinced spring had already arrived. The garden was filled with herbs in full bloom. The indeterminate shade of brownish-red carpet worn to threads in the high traffic areas looked dull and pathetic next to the bright yellows, purples and reds of the flowers outside. Several long tables with benches were arranged to maximize the number of occupants the dining room could comfortably hold.

When they finally made it to the buffet, Toby was intrigued by the set up. A set of cat-sized stairs led to a wooden ledge just high enough for a cat to easily see what goodies were available. Each food was clearly labeled, which was a really good thing considering some of them looked identical. *That would be a nasty surprise*, Toby mused as he noticed two pans of a brown meat-like substance. One was labeled chicken. The other rat'ler. *I'd hate to have my mouth all set for chicken only to bite into a tough bit of snake hide.*

The noise level was quickly diminishing as the hopefuls left to find their way to their orientation classes. The two cats hurried to fill their plates. Toby nearly sent his bit of omelet flying over his ears as he tried to make his next selection while magicking the egg goody onto his plate. He mentally cursed himself for losing his concentration, then continued as quickly as he dared.

There were only a few hopefuls left in the dining room when the two toms sat down to eat. Neither cat took the time to engage the booster seats, afraid they would be late to class, and took only a little longer in eating. It wouldn't do them any good to choke on breakfast. As they dashed for the dishwashing room window, plates whizzing behind them, Toby wondered what his breakfast actually tasted like. He vowed to wake sooner and hurry down to eat tomorrow. The duo raced out the dining room doors and paused just long enough to find their names on the roster in the entryway.

"GOO d'LORis," said Toby, turning toward the door. Nothing happened.

"GOO d'LORis." Again nothing happened.

"Oh great," he cried. "I can't even get a simple finder incantation to work for me."

"Let me try mine," said Terence. "TE n'der GRAHshus."

They waited for something to happen. The entryway stubbornly remained the same. The toms looked at each other. Panic was beginning to set in. They were going to be late. Being late meant having penalties added to their final evaluation. Penalties on their final evaluation could mean not being chosen. Toby felt like howling in frustration. He'd just arrived and already he was behind. He caught sight of a white cat trotting by and turned to see Lilith heading for the entryway.

"Wait," he called. They ran to her.

"Could you help us, please. We can't seem to get our finder incantations to work."

His skin warmed. From the heat coming off his little friend, he guessed Terence felt the same. A finder incantation was one of the most basic of beginner spells every magic cat learned. Having to ask for help with one made Toby feel like an idiot, but that was better than being late to class.

"Well," said Lilith, "I'm really not supposed to help you with spells and such..."

"Please, ma'am," Terence begged.

"We know how to do them," Toby added. "It just isn't

45

working like it's supposed to."

"You really know how to use them?" She looked at them through her eye whiskers. The image of Master O'dorn looking over the top of his glasses at him, eyebrow raised, flashed through his mind. He blinked the image away, glancing at Terence. The young tom was dancing from foot to foot.

"Yes, ma'am. You think of what you want to find, say the incantation and concentrate really hard."

"And you have to be as specific as you can when you think of the thing you want to find."

"Hmmm... I think I have an idea," said Lilith. "I can't help you with your incantation, but maybe I can help you get it to do what it's supposed to do. Follow me."

The she-cat flicked her tail to open the double doors and the toms trotted out on her heels. She stopped two tail-lengths outside the entry. If Toby hadn't been watching her closely, he would have run into her. Terence did run into him.

"Sorry," he mumbled.

"Okay," said the she-cat as she turned to face them. "Try saying your words again."

The toms looked at each other. How could it make any difference to go just a little further away and say the incantation? Lilith whipped her tail to and fro, ears flattened.

"Just try it."

The toms looked dubious. The she-cat rolled her eyes.

"I'll explain in a minute."

"GOO d'LORis," Toby said. A bright green arrow suddenly appeared in front of him, hovering just at chest level.

"That's what I thought." She looked at the toms with some satisfaction. "Apparently, no one told you about the dampening fields inside each of the common buildings."

"Dampening field?" asked Toby.

46

"Yes, a dampening field," Lilith said, her tone bordering on what one would use to explain something to a small child. Toby looked at Terence to see if he had any better idea of why there would be a dampening field on the common buildings. The young tom's expression was as confused as Toby's was.

"Look, I could go into the details, but that would make you later than you already are. Suffice it to say that the fields keep any disagreements from getting out of hand."

"You mean it's like a big bouncer at a pub that'll throw you out if you start kickin' up dust," said Terence.

"Huh?"

"Something like that," replied Lilith with a smile. "You two better get going."

"TE n'der GRAHshus." A bright green arrow appeared in front of the young tom. "I'll explain it on the way to class. Come on."

The little gray and white cat ran in the direction the arrow pointed, leaving Toby to hurry behind. Toby wasn't sure he liked the feeling of being in the dark, though he figured it was likely to happen a lot while he was at the academy.

"The field," he called, catching up to the young tom. "You were going to explain."

"Oh yeah. Basically it does just what Lilith said, it keeps things from gettin' too big to handle– magical things."

"I'm still not sure I understand."

"Let's say you get in a fight with another student."

"Okay."

"Now let's say that someone throws a magical punch."

"A what?"

"You know," coaxed Terence as they careened around a corner and up the stairs to a large brick building with lots of windows, still following their green arrows. "The magical equivalent to clawin' someone's ears off."

"Oh."

"Anyway, let's say he throws some magic at you. The dampenin' field gets between you and the magic. No harm done."

"I see. So the dampening field keeps students from taking out their anger on each other magically."

"Yep."

"How did you learn about that?"

"Spent some time as a bar cat. Chased vermin out of the food stores. Overheard the owner tell a customer one day that he got tired of havin' to repair holes blown out in his walls whenever some mage got mad 'cause his food was a little slow in arrivin'. He got someone to put a dampenin' field on the pub."

"Wow."

"Yeah. Cost him, too. Had to get a loan to pay for it, but he said it was worth every penny."

The duo took the stairs to the classrooms as fast as they could, sliding around the corner on the polished wood floor as they reached the top. They stopped to catch their breath just outside the room the finders pointed to. They could hear a female voice through the door. Toby looked at Terence. He saw the dread he felt mirrored on the young tom's face. Taking a deep breath, Toby gently flicked his tail at the door. The door opened just wide enough for the two cats to slip in. The voice didn't pause. No one seemed to notice they had entered. Quickly they found seats in the back row squeezed between the door and the building's chimney.

"Nice of you to join us, gentlemen," the tortoiseshell feline at the front of the class said without turning around. "I hope being late to class won't become a habit."

Every eye in the classroom, save the teacher's, turned to stare at the latecomers. Although Terence shrunk as low as he could, Toby kept still, looking only at the teacher. His heart beat fast until everyone was facing the front again.

"Now then," continued the she-cat, "if you'll all turn your attention back to the board I am quite sure you may well learn something new."

Thankfully the rest of class went by uneventfully. Toby was beginning to enjoy the tortoiseshell feline's dry sense of humor and her way of turning even the most tedious bit of learning into something more engaging. Before he was aware of it, it was time to dismiss for lunch.

"Ladies and gentlemen, please be sure to be *on time* when we resume or you may miss the campus tour," the she-cat looked pointedly at Toby and Terence. A few cats snickered. Toby's skin heated in embarrassment again. He managed a small nod to the teacher. He wasn't sure, but he thought he saw a look of satisfaction cross the she-cat's face.

"You are dismissed."

"I really don't want to be late again," whispered Terence.

"Me either. I say we hurry to the dining room and see if we can get closer to the front of the line this time."

"I'm with you."

The two raced to the dining room. By the time they made it they were panting, but the run had been worth it. This time they were half-way to the buffet before the dining room began to fill up. They hurried through the line, gobbled down their food and raced back outside. The doors hadn't even closed before they said their finder words. So it was the rest of the day.

By the time the duo wearily climbed the steps to their sleeping quarters, Toby was beginning to wonder if being chosen could possibly be worth the amount of running he'd had to do. Not only that, but he had yet to taste any of the food he'd eaten. It seemed to have gone straight from the plate to his stomach without so much as touching his tongue.

"Do you think it gets any easier," asked Terence.

"I hope so."

"I haven't run so much since living behind the fish market. Even the fur between my toes hurts."

"I know what you mean. Mother told me there would be a lot of going from one building to another, but she never mentioned having to run. Then again, mother has always been an early riser. She was probably already on her way to breakfast before the second years even began their speech."

"Your mother sounds... sounds...," Terence began, squeezing his whiskers and scrunching his eyes.

"Driven?"

"Well, that wasn't exactly what I was going to say, but yeah."

"She was. Her family wasn't noble enough by some cats' standards, so she had to work hard to stay ahead. She graduated with honors."

"I think I can understand what she went through."

Toby suddenly remembered what Terence had said about his own family situation and wished he'd kept his mouth shut. It didn't seem fair that the little tom would have to work so hard just to be taken seriously. And yet the gray and white tabby seemed more than up to the task. Toby hoped Terence would be among those chosen. *At least I'd have one friend already*, he thought. *If I have to face three years here with just those stuffed noble cats I think I would sooner go back home or petition to be a loner like father*. The thought of his father called up a loneliness that never seemed to fade. He wished for the millionth time that he knew what had happened to the big black tom.

"I was thinking," said Terence, breaking into Toby's gloomy thoughts, "do you think it would be okay if I switched nests with one of the cats nearest you?"

Toby focused on his little friend. In the lamplight he looked even smaller than he had during the daylight. He wondered if Terence wanted to be close because they were friends or because he was feeling homesick. Maybe a little of both. In the end he figured it didn't matter. He needed the companionship too.

"I don't see the harm in asking."

"Could you... I mean, would you..." Terence began, his voice almost a whisper.

"Actually, I was thinking maybe I should switch with someone near you," Toby said, pretending not to hear the little tom's request for help. "Your nest is closer to the door. I think if we're closer to the door then maybe we can get a head start on tomorrow. What do you think?"

"That sounds like a great idea." Terence's tail quivered.

"Great! Why don't you go ahead and get settled in while I find someone to switch with."

Switching nests turned out to be easier than he thought it was going to be. The she-cat next to Terence was more than happy to exchange when she discovered Toby was near a handsome oriental short-hair who was apparently among the hopefuls in an attempt to stay in the country. Or so the she-cat had said. Toby thought the tom had more likely spun the tale to gain more female admirers. Either way Toby won since he now had the nest next to his new friend.

By the time Toby had helped the she-cat lug her belongings to his old nest, he had gone from being tired to staying on four legs by willpower alone. He quickly settled into his new nest, hoping the dawn was further off than he suspected.

"Thanks, Toby," mumbled the little tom. His gentle snores told the orange tom that his friend was fast asleep. *Your welcome*, thought Toby, curling into a comfortable ball. Before he could think anything else, he was asleep.

When the tuxedo tom arrived to rouse the hopefuls, Toby was already awake. He stretched and yawned, ignoring M'festus' usual rude comments, and waited to hear whatever instructions the cat counselors had to give for the day.

"Some of you may be anxious about today's class as you will be demonstrating your abilities to do magic," said Lilith. "While the Masters will be watching you closely, please understand that they do not expect you to perform each and every spell flawlessly."

Toby felt the tension in the air ebb ever so slightly. The rest of the instructions were little more than a repeat of the directions they'd been given the last two days: be late and have it affect your final evaluation, do well and earn a bonus that would be applied to the same evaluation. Toby wondered if the second years had been told to repeat themselves or if they honestly believed it was necessary.

The first half of the class Master Meredith, the tortoiseshell queen who had been instructing them from the first day, led the class in basic warm-up spells.

"This is kit stuff," growled a brown tabby in front of Toby. "I cut my teeth on harder spells than these."

"You disagree with warming up?" asked the master cat.

"No, Master," the brown tom said, obviously surprised at being heard. "It's just that my tutor always made me work on spells befitting an apprentice from the beginning of our sessions."

"I see. And might I inquire as to the name of your fine tutor?"

"Lord Master Derwin Midland," answered the brown tabby with pride.

"Ah, yes. Derwin Midland. A fine enough student, but not very creative. He was rather too fond of finding fault in other students' spellwork while neglecting to pursue anything outside his comfort zone. I'm sure he gave you his speech on what constitutes real magic versus... how did he put it?"

"Common street magic," mumbled the tabby.

"Yes, thank you. Common street magic. I'm afraid poor Derwin was not very adept at making the leap from history to magic or he would have discovered many great Masters have adapted common street magic to the higher magics with fantastic results. Something I hope each of you learn to do."

The master cat fixed each student with a piercing yellow-eyed gaze. Toby felt bad for the brown tom, who was staring at his own paws. He imagined the tom was as embarrassed at being singled out as Toby had been every time he'd failed to do a spell his mother had told him to do.

"Now, as I'm sure there are others of you who do not understand why we are doing such basic work, let me shed some light on it. I know many of you come from noble households, but have any of you paid close attention to the musicians employed for your master mages' great feasts? What is the first thing they do after unpacking their instruments?"

"They play the House Song," answered a yellow she-cat near the front.

"Our master mage has them play His Lady's favorite melody," rumbled a large gray long-hair tom.

"In our Noble House," said Reginald, a white angora, "they play the Hielberg County Anthem."

As the discussion continued, Toby fished through his memories for the evening his little family had listened to a performance given by some traveling minstrels. He remembered the musicians sitting down to play and the most awful cacophony coming from the various instruments. He had covered his ears and mewled. When his father asked what was the matter, Toby had asked why they had come to hear such terrible musicians.

The memory of his father's deep chuckle and rumbling purr made the young cat stare with drooping whiskers at his paws. Slowly he recalled the black tom's explanation of why the minstrels didn't seem to be able to play what sounded like real music to him as a young kitten. Blinking the melancholy away, Toby raised his eyes to the master cat patiently listening to the student's shouted answers.

"Master Meredith," called Toby. "I think I understand what you're teaching us. It's the same lesson my father taught me when I was a kit."

The room got quiet. Toby felt the weight of everyone's gaze, some hostile, some just curious. It was no secret that he was not from a noble house. Master Meredith nodded for Toby to continue.

"After unpacking their instruments, good musicians do a few warm ups before playing anything resembling real music."

"Good," said the master cat. "Can you take it one step further and explain why they do warm ups before playing anything else."

Apprentice Cat

"The warm ups help their fingers remember what to do," said Toby. The class snickered.

"An interesting way to say it, but you're correct. Would you care to explain to the rest of the class what you mean in a way they may understand?"

Toby warmed at the implied compliment. He tried not to notice the growing hostility of his peers, but it was difficult not to in the sudden oppressive silence. A quick glance in Reginald's direction made it quite clear that the white cat thought Toby was becoming more than an annoyance. Toby quickly looked away, refocusing his attention on the master cat.

"Playing music is like working magic in that each lesson builds on previous ones," Toby explained. "If you warm up with the earliest lessons, then by the time you get to the difficult magic you don't have to think so hard about the steps you already know how to do. You can concentrate on just learning the new stuff instead."

"Excellent," said Master Meredith. "Your father was a great teacher."

Toby nervously licked his ruff. Having the master cat's praise felt wonderful, almost as good as impressing his father. As the master cat called the class back to what they had been doing before the brown tom's interruption, Toby chanced a look around at his classmates. Reginald spared him one last glare before turning his attention back to the lesson.

The brown tom, however, nodded ever so slightly. Toby took it to mean the brown tom was impressed and at least a little grateful for the explanation. Terence beamed with pride, as if he had come up with the explanation himself. The rest seemed content to simply return to the lesson at hand.

The rest of the morning was uneventful. The class broke for lunch with Master Meredith's reminder to be ready to have their performances evaluated during the second half ringing in their ears. Toby and Terence headed straight for the dining room, discussing differences and similarities of the warm up spells as they went.

"So you think you're exceptionally smart, don't you," growled a voice in front of them. Reginald sat, barring the door to the common, with a pair of massive Russian blue cats.

"I suppose you think you deserve a place in the academy because your *Daddy* taught you a few tricks."

"No. I believe I deserve a chance to receive an apprenticeship in the academy because I studied hard."

"We've had the best tutors since kittenhood. What makes you think a simple commoner could possibly have learned enough to even begin to have a chance at an apprenticeship?"

A crowd had begun to gather around them. Some had obviously taken sides already, choosing to sit by the cat they supported. Others hung about on the sidelines. Of those Toby noticed a few were eager just to see a fight.

"Seems to me," Terence jumped in boldly, "you musta been asleep in class or you would've heard what Master Meredith said about one of your so-called best tutors."

Toby would have liked to chime in with the agreeing growls around him, but thought better of it as he watched Reginald. The white tom's tail tip tapped steadily as he gazed around at the gathering cats, stretching to see those coming up behind Toby and Terence. It was almost as if he were looking for someone in particular. The orange tom considered the white cat's words. Hurtful, yes, but nothing more. As more cats joined the crowd, the tom's whiskers splayed wider.

Toby sat quietly going over his options. He could follow the advice he'd overheard from his father one night: walk away or turn the tables, except neither alternative looked promising. The gathering of cats had almost doubled in size. Reginald now had six cats sitting with him, each determined to block his way to the dining room. The crowd around Toby and Terence seemed set on making sure there was a fight.

"Oh look," taunted one of Reginald's group, "It seems our parents were right. Commoners haven't any more brains than a mouse."

"Indeed," joined another, "He can't answer the question himself so he has his little sparrow parrot the instructor. How amusing."

"Make it talk again, Reginald," purred the she-cat Toby had traded nests with. "I do so find it entertaining."

Terence tensed to spring at the nearest tormentor. Toby gently laid his tail across the young tom's shoulders. Terence looked at his friend with the question of "why not" burning in his eyes. The orange tom looked pointedly at Reginald. The white cat hadn't said another word. He was staring at them, his whiskers splayed and eyes narrowed in triumph. Terence relaxed. Toby sighed inwardly. He couldn't blame the little gray and white cat. If he hadn't listened to his father's stories he might have attacked Reginald himself. That, he decided, wasn't going to happen.

He wouldn't fight, but walking away didn't look possible, either. *So that leaves what? The only way past those cats was to try pushing them away from the door and that will land me right into a fight.* He couldn't remember his father mentioning being in the same situation. *Perhaps someone from history,* he thought.

Toby ignored the continued taunts as his mind raced through memories of old texts. In a flash he remembered something from an ancient religious text: a man who didn't fight, but didn't surrender either. By the end of the story, the bully's friends had left him. Toby had no noble ideas that Reginald's groupies would desert him anytime soon. However, if he stood his ground and made no aggressive moves, he figured he might be able to wait them out. Eventually they would get bored or they would have to give up because class would begin. He knew that, if nothing else, that would end it because every one of them wanted a good evaluation.

"Haven't you anything to say?" asked the she-cat, her tail lashing.

"Perhaps he thinks he's the strong, silent type," taunted another cat.

"More like he's slow witted. It's been awhile since you asked your question, Reginald," said another. "Maybe you should ask him again, but use small words so he can understand."

"My friends have made some interesting points, Toby," Reginald said. "You appeared to have some brains about you in class, but now you have nothing to say? Could it be that you agree with me?"

It pained him to stay silent, but he was determined not to react. Terence uttered a soft growl and nothing more. Reginald's groupies snickered. Several cats, the ones hoping to see a fight, left, muttering that the scene was becoming a bore. Slowly the crowd thinned. Reginald's group allowed them to filter through to the commons. Eventually the only ones left outside were Toby, Terence and Reginald's small group.

"Come on, Reginald," coaxed the she-cat. "Why should we stay out here with the riff raff and miss what I'm sure will be an excellent lunch?"

Reginald cast one last disdainful look at the duo, then

accompanied the she-cat in. The twins followed close behind. Toby breathed a sigh of relief. He'd managed to keep his cool, but he hadn't been sure how much longer he could have sat there pretending to ignore the group's taunting.

"Do you think it's over?" asked Terence.

"Not a chance."

"Yeah. Didn't think so. Looks like bullies come from all classes."

"Looks like."

"So what do you want to do about lunch?"

"Good question. By the time we make it through the line it'll be time for class."

"I guess we could share what I saved from supper last night."

Toby scrunched his brows. Leftovers? When did Terence have time to beg the kitchen staff for leftovers? The orange tom thought back through the day. No, they'd been together the whole time. He cocked his head at the little cat. The little tom ducked his head, staring at his paws.

"I know it's not exactly right to take food from the dining room, but... well... when you grow up bein' hungry all the time, you learn to take what extras you can."

Toby blinked. As he considered the little cat's words. He smiled.

"I was just wondering how you managed to save any with the dampening field on the common buildings."

Terence looked back at his friend. His shoulders relaxed and he sat straighter, his whiskers splaying in return.

"That was simple. A lot of mages and cats don't know that you can make magic work inside the field if you're outside it. I just moved my leftovers from the dish washin' room to my nest as soon as we left the buildin'."

59

"Clever. Care to enjoy your leftovers back in the class-room?"

"It would be a pleasure." Terence gave a mock bow.

As the duo turned to retrace their steps, Toby caught sight of a tortoiseshell cat rounding the corner, heading in the direction of the Administration Building. He thought it might have been Master Meredith. Whoever it was, Toby was sure the cat had been witness to the entire scene with Reginald.

Master Meredith entered the classroom just as the tower bell chimed the hour. She glanced in Toby's direction, but said nothing. The orange tom was left wondering if she had indeed seen his altercation with the white cat. Lost in his confused thoughts, Toby almost missed what the master cat was saying.

"For this half of the class you will be paired with another of my choosing to perform a spell you most likely have never seen before. After you have succeeded -- or failed," she said, pausing to look closely at each of them, "We will go over your performance. I will be watching closely for cooperation and skill." The master cat quickly paired the hopefuls and placed a sheet of paper with the spell they were to perform in front of them.

"There's no title," said the black and white she-cat Toby had been paired with. "How are we supposed to know what we're doing?"

"Master O'dorn has a few spells like this in his really old books. Mother says that when you look at the ingredients and read through the incantation you can usually get a good idea what's supposed to happen."

"Have you ever done anything like this?"

"Mmm... not exactly, but..."

Toby read through the incantation. Nothing stuck out as odd or particularly difficult. The she-cat pushed in close, making it difficult to see the writing past her whiskers. He glanced toward the group of cats walking toward the shelves of ingredients, then back down at the page. The she-cat shook her head and turned toward Toby.

"Perhaps we should gather the ingredients first."

The young tom looked back at his partner and blinked. "Why not?"

They trotted to the shelf lined wall where a large number of magical ingredients were stored. Several other cats had decided to do the same thing, so it was difficult to find anything without having to push someone else out of the way. Toby waited patiently for another cat to move while the black and white she-cat danced from foot to foot beside him.

"Why don't you just push in front?" she hissed.

"Because that would be rude. Besides we're not in a race to see who can finish the spell first."

"Yeah, but —"

Toby shook his head. He was not going to let impatience get the best of him. He'd had plenty of experience with doing unfamiliar magic before he was completely ready and was not in any hurry to singe his fur again. The last time it had taken several weeks for his whiskers to grow back.

"No. We'll wait our turn."

The she-cat growled in protest, but settled in beside him to wait. She could have gone ahead and tried to butt in except that there were too many bottles with unknown ingredients for one cat to look through alone. Quicker than Toby expected, there was room for both he and his partner to maneuver. They wasted no more time locating the ingredients they needed. As they proceeded back to their table, Toby glanced around the room.

"Take a look at the others," Toby whispered. "I think we don't need to worry about competing with anyone else on the same spell."

"What makes you say that?"

"Well, unless the teachers have intentionally put the same magical items in a number of different shaped bottles, it seems to me that we're all working on a different spell."

"You're right," exclaimed the she-cat in a hushed voice. The pair began putting the bottles in order of use. Toby read over the incantation again.

"You know," murmured the she-cat as Toby picked up the first bottle in his mouth. "I don't agree with what Reginald's cronies say about you. I think you have more brains than a mouse."

"Fanksh," said Toby, his answer muffled by the bottle as he tried to pry the cork loose.

"Here. Let me do that."

Toby put the bottle back on the table and stepped aside. With a flick of her tail, the she-cat popped the cork out. It sailed across the room, bounced off the closed window, ricocheted off the cauldron of another pair and landed on the floor at Master Meredith's feet. The master cat blinked. She bent down and gave the cork a delicate nudge in their direction, which sent it floating back to their table.

"Please try to be more careful next time," she said and went back to observing the others in the class.

"Whew," Toby's partner said. "I just knew we'd had it."

Toby nodded in agreement. He glanced at the pair whose cauldron they had accidentally pinged, hoping the errant cork hadn't caused problems with their spell. The pair had their heads bent over the spell sheet, seemingly unaware that anything had happened. Next to them, though, Reginald glared down at them. Toby felt his stomach tighten. He sent a quick prayer to whatever cat god would be listening that no one would be able to claim foul if their spell didn't work for some reason. He turned back to his partner.

"Let's get back to work."

Toby glanced at the white tom from the corner of his eye. Reginald bared his fangs, then went back to working with his partner. The orange tom sighed. They added their ingredients to their cauldron, taking care to add the exact amounts called for. The brew began to turn milky white just as they neared the part calling for the incantation to be said over it.

"Do you think it's supposed to look like that?" asked the she-cat.

"I don't know. There's nothing here saying what it's supposed to do," said Toby, putting a paw on the bottom of the spell sheet.

"Do you want to say the incantation or should I?"

"You can do it if you want to."

"Okay. Here goes nothing. CayMO flahg."

A tiny puff of pink smoke drifted from the liquid, but nothing else happened. The pair looked at each other. The orange tom scratched at an itch in his ear. According to the spell sheet, one of them was supposed to drink some of it. Toby saw his own hesitancy in the she-cat's face.

"Well, since you said the incantation, maybe I should drink it?"

"Are you sure? I-I could do it," stammered the she-cat.

"No," Toby said, feigning confidence and scratching his itching ear again. "I'll do it. It's only fair."

Toby leaned over the cauldron. The milky substance

bubbled. It smelled faintly of spun sugar, the kind Master O'dorn had brought back from a fair he'd visited while away for a Council Session. Toby sneezed and scratched his ear again. *Well, it's now or never. I hope it tastes as good as it smells.* Closing his eyes tight, he quickly lapped up some of the liquid. It tasted nothing like spun sugar. In fact, if Toby had to describe the taste, he would have said it tasted like something one would scrape from the bottom of a shoe. He tried not to gag.

"Anything?" asked the she-cat.

"Other than craving something to get the taste out of my mouth, nothing," gasped Toby, scratching his ear with more vigor. The itch seemed to have worked its way in deeper. *I hope I'm not coming down with ear mites. What a wonderful impression that would make.*

The black and white cat sat down, wrapping her tail around her toes. Her whiskers drooped and her ears flattened.

"Hey," Toby said, "Let's take a second look–"

Suddenly Toby felt like an army of fire-breathing ants were crawling through his fur. He nipped at his right flank. Spun. Nipped his left shoulder. He tried shaking furiously to rid himself of the sensation, but only succeeded in making himself dizzy. Within moments, the sensations disappeared. The only thing remaining was the itch in his ears. Toby sighed in relief. He could live with the itch, irritating as it was, but the other would have driven him mad. As his partner came back into focus, he noticed she was staring at him, mouth open wide.

"That has some kick," Toby said. He shifted from foot to foot, forcing his whiskers to splay.

The she-cat continued to stare at him. Toby realized the room was very quiet. He looked around. Everyone had stopped their work and were staring at him. Reginald's whiskers were splayed wide as he leaned over to whisper to his partner. They both shook with silent laughter. Toby looked back at his partner.

"Why is everyone staring at me?" he whispered.

"You're pink," answered the black and white she-cat.

"And glowing," said a voice at his side.

Toby turned to see Master Meredith sitting calmly beside him. He barely caught the slight whisker twitch that betrayed the master cat's desire to laugh. Looking down at his paws, he discovered they weren't exaggerating. If anything, they had understated his appearance. He had become a furry pink star in the middle of the classroom. *A furry pink star with a gawd-awful itch.* He wanted to claw at his ear, but, given the circumstances, decided it would make everything look worse.

"This isn't what's supposed to happen, is it?" he asked.

"Not exactly," answered the master cat. "Do you know where you went wrong?"

Toby looked over the spell again. They had put in exactly the amounts of each ingredient called for. They had stirred the correct number of times. The itch grew more insistent. Toby gave his ear a quick swipe, glancing at the master cat. She seemed to dismiss the action. Toby sighed inwardly and returned to reading the spell. As he re-read the incantation he realized what had gone wrong.

"We did everything exactly as the spell dictates, except I think we had the inflection wrong for the words," he said.

"You think? When working magic," said Master Meredith, "you'd best be certain."

"I'm certain that's what went wrong," Toby corrected. "Could we try again?"

The master cat measured the pair through a slitted

gaze. Toby fought the need to claw his ear to ribbons. He could hear his partner's rapid breath. It was becoming difficult to think. It felt like the itch was alive and digging deeper into his ear with every passing moment.

"Since you're certain it was the incantation that was done wrong..." The master cat paused to give each of them a stern look. "I will reverse the spell to that point and allow you to try again. As for the rest of you please continue your work."

"Thank you, Master Meredith," breathed the pair.

"Don't thank me yet. You may find that your spell is still incorrect. Rev EARsay tuGIV enPOIN."

The master cat walked away to another set of students. Toby looked down at his paws. They were orange again. With relief, he noticed that the terrible itch was gone as well.

"Okay. I think it's fair to say that unidentified incantations are not my strong suit," said the she-cat.

"That's okay. I had a hard taskmaster that made sure I would never forget how to decipher the proper inflection in any incantation." Toby thought back to those lessons. His mother had drilled him in incantations until he had the words chasing him in his nightmares. At the time he had thought she was being unreasonable.

"In that case," said the she-cat, "I think you should say the incantation and I'll drink the potion. Seems only fair."

"It's a deal. CAYmo FLAHG."

The black and white she-cat took a deep breath. Quickly she lapped up some of the potion. She looked up at Toby. He watched carefully, waiting to see if she reacted as he had. Nothing. He looked back at the spell sheet. He was sure he'd said it correctly this time. He looked back at his partner – or more precisely where she had been. He gasped.

"What?" said the empty space where his partner had been.

"You've disappeared," he exclaimed.

"Really?"

"No. Wait. You're still there."

"Obviously," said the she-cat. "I can still see myself." The air shimmered for a moment. Toby thought she had turned in a circle to get a better look at herself.

"Yeah, but I can't."

"You can't?"

"I can sort of see you when you move. It's like looking at the heat coming off a rock in summer. But when you stand still you completely disappear."

"Oh that's too rich."

"It would seem, young Toby, that you were correct," said Master Meredith as she walked past them. "And, seeing as you have passed this exam, you and your partner are free to go."

"Excuse me, Master Meredith," called the invisible she-cat to the master cat's retreating back.

"Yes?" She turned to look back at the pair.

"Um... Would it be possible to... it's just that..."

Toby could feel the embarrassed heat coming from his invisible partner. It dawned on him what she was trying to ask.

"Master Meredith, the spell doesn't include a reversal incantation," he said.

"Ah, yes. Rev EARsay t'SPIL."

In an instant the black and white she-cat was visible again. She looked at Toby, her eyes wide in question. When he nodded, tension drained from the she-cat's posture and they turned their attention back to the master cat. Master Meredith

flicked her tail toward the door in dismissal. As the pair trotted toward the door, the orange tom glanced over his shoulder at Reginald. His eyes were narrow slits and his whiskers
were clamped tight. The white tom's tail lashed. Toby's fur
rose along his spine as he considered what the tom might do.

"Thanks for covering for me," whispered the she-cat
when they entered the hallway. The orange cat looked back
at his partner.

"No problem. That's what partners are for."

"Yeah. Right." The pair walked down the hall in silence.

"Toby," the she-cat said as they exited the building.
She stared at him for a long moment. The orange tom began
to wonder if Master Meredith had missed something when
she reversed the spell the first time.

"Good luck," said the she-cat. She blinked once and
walked away.

Chapter 3

The next morning saw them all plodding to the Lesser Hall after breakfast.

"This is it, then. The last day," said Terence.

"The last day," repeated Toby. The words hung between them. It felt as if a thunderstorm should have been brewing overhead. Instead a pale fall sun was doing its best to warm the cloudless blue sky. *At least its chilly. I don't think I could stand it if it was a perfect day.*

"What are you gonna do if..."

"I'm trying not to think about it."

"Yeah. Sure. But what if... you know..." The little tom stopped in the middle of the packed dirt path. Toby sighed.

"I suppose I'll apply to become a loner like my father," he answered. "*After* I glue my fur back on where Mother is sure to claw it off."

"You can do that?"

"Do what? Glue my fur back on?"

"No," said Terence. Toby heard the soft scrape of the little cat's claws on the packed earth. The young tom's pupils widened as he stared at the orange tom.

"Apply to become a loner. I thought loners were just cats whose mage had died."

"That's usually the case, but Father said that's only because being a loner is a lot harder."

"How?"

"Well, for one thing, there's no one to balance your magic, so if something goes wrong it goes really wrong."

"I never thought about that."

The friends rejoined the line of cats heading toward the Lesser Hall. Toby gave the little tom a sidelong glance.

"Then there's if you run into trouble. There's no one to back you up."

Toby could still hear his mother arguing with his father the night before he left for his last mission. They'd been just outside the closed bedroom door, thinking he was fast asleep. He didn't think either one of them ever knew he was listening. It was one of the rare nights his mother had snuggled close to him as they slept. The young tom wondered what trouble had caught his father.

"Now *that* I understand," said Terence, breaking into Toby's memories. "I saw a cat face down a whole gang once. Got away, but lost a good chunk of tail doin' it."

"That's more or less how Father put it. You can win, or at least get away, but you'll probably lose something in the process. He also said there's a lot more to learn, special classes you have to take."

"Sounds like a lot of work."

"Yeah, but what's the alternative?"

"You gotta point. It's not like either one of us has a rich family to crawl back to. The only way I know to survive if you're not a master cat is to run a fortune-telling scam or join a gang as its protectorate cat. I don't think I could hustle strangers or curse someone just to make them pay the gang to make the curse end."

"I thought cats who could use magic, but didn't become master cats or loners, could find work with local apothecaries," said Toby.

Terence stopped. Toby looked back at his young friend. The tom's eyes were wide. His tail whipped back and forth. The orange tom was bewildered at the sudden change. Shaking his head, Terence continued walking toward the Lesser Hall.

"Someday you need to visit the city. The apothecaries are scam artists. They don't want cats who can do magic unless they're willin' to work an angle that puts money in their pockets. Those cats are nothin' more than slaves."

Toby shivered. Terence's future seemed bleak if he wasn't chosen. *I wish there was something I could do for him.*

The din in the Lesser Hall from all the feline voices drove Toby's dark thoughts into the background. The duo made their way up the stairs to a bench near the back. The orange tom looked around. Near the ceiling were bas-reliefs in white marble depicting scenes from ancient history. The sky blue walls were peeling in places and the wood floor showed the passage of years, worn thin by the footsteps of hopefuls and students alike. A faded maroon curtain hung over the stage. The room had all the charm of a great lady in her declining years attempting to hold onto the ghosts of the past.

Toby watched as cats and humans filtered in. He noted with interest how similar the two species were, each sitting near those who were most like themselves. It wasn't easy to tell by appearance with the felines, but the human nobles were instantly identifiable. Even in his finest robes, Master O'dorn would have looked like a peasant farmer next to some of the younglings in their bright colors and fine fabrics.

It wasn't just in their finery that Toby saw a difference. The way the nobles walked and talked set them apart as well. It seemed to the orange tom that each one of them must have smelled something foul. Or perhaps that they found every-thing around them beneath them. Whatever the reason, the noble born humans held their noses just a little bit higher than the others.

"If you will all take your seats, please," said a bald man, striding to the center of the stage.

He stood straight and tall with a piercing gaze that made Toby want to pay close attention to whatever the man said. His long nose added to his regal bearing. Everything about him, from his severe black tunic and breeches to his black master's robe said this was a man to be respected, a man who would tolerate nothing but the best from his students. Behind the imposing man paced Master Meredith. She grace-fully leapt to a stool beside the man and sat. Toby instantly made the connection.

"Master Meredith is—"

"the head master cat," breathed Terence, finishing To-by's startled sentence.

"Trust, ladies and gentlemen," said the man, his rich baritone pleasantly reverberating off the walls. "Trust is what makes a partnering work. It is not, as some would have you believe, a matter of blood bearing. Neither does it have to do solely with training. Levah TAH teh."

Before Toby could blink, Master Meredith shot into the air. She sat calmly on nothing, hovering at eye level to the head master mage.

"I think we would all agree that a fall from this height might hurt, but it isn't likely to cause injury. However — RAH zeh."

Master Meredith zoomed to the ceiling. She yawned and curled into a comfortable ball, one paw outstretched. She looked for all the world as if she were settling down for a nice nap in her cozy nest.

"At this height, should I lose my concentration, Master Meredith would be spending a well-earned vacation in the hospital."

"If it's all the same to you, Master Jalen, I would rather vacation in sunny South Felaydial," called the head master cat.

"Indeed," said Master Jalen, smiling.

"History teaches," he continued, "that even the most careful partnerings head masters make can end disastrously, and usually it is due to a break in or a lack of trust. I urge each of you to consider carefully the case of Master Hecktor Ribaldy and Master Kiyoshi. Each had unique talents that complimented the other the likes of which we haven't seen since."

Toby noticed a young human male begin to fidget in his seat. Several of the other human hopefuls turned to look at him. Although Toby wasn't adept at reading humans, it seemed to him that the other hopefuls disapproved of this single human more than any of the others. He looked no different than any of the other less-than-rich humans. In fact, judging by his clothing, Toby estimated the boy was middle class just as Master O'dorn was.

"No one could have foreseen the break in the bond between Master Ribaldy and Master Kiyoshi. Countless individuals have done their best to uncover what madness could have crept into Master Ribaldy's mind, why he attempted to destroy the High Council during Session. It was a sad day of loss, a great mage to insanity and a great cat to death."

The room was silent. Not even the shuffling of feet or whisper of fur upon the benches could be heard.

"It is for this reason that the academy is very selective. There are two main reasons you may be turned away. You may not be ready for a career in magic, either for lack of maturity or basic experience.

"For the other reason you need only look around you. The ratio of felines to humans is indeed considerable. Although it would be nice to believe, as a human, you are guaranteed a place in the academy simply because there are so few of you, I must restate the importance of careful partnerings. There are more feline hopefuls to choose from, but that does not mean there is one suited to be partnered with you."

The human Toby had been watching squirmed again. He was slowly sinking lower in his seat.

"Magic must be balanced to work properly. Each of you, human and feline, can perform spells on your own. If you couldn't, you wouldn't be here. However, the more difficult the spell, the more training and effort it takes for a lone mage or cat to perform. After today, those of you who are partnered will become one half of the equation. You will learn how to reach your own potential and to balance your partner's unique abilities."

Master Jalen looked around the room at the eager hopefuls, seeming to assess them. The orange tom glanced up at Master Meredith. She looked as if she were napping, but Toby didn't believe it for a moment.

"Master Meredith," called the head master mage, "would you care to inform the hopefuls of what they should expect during the final interview?"

The head master cat stretched and yawned, then sat up to peer down at them. It was a little awkward to crane his neck up at the tortoiseshell, but Toby was determined not to miss even a whisker twitch.

"During your final interview this afternoon you will be asked some very hard questions. We encourage you to take this time during your extended lunch break to consider why you want to become a master mage or cat and what you could contribute to the world by doing so."

"Very good. Are there any questions?" asked Master Jalen.

"What about final evaluations?" asked one of the cat hopefuls. "Will we get to see them before the partnerings are made?"

"Excellent question. Yes, you will receive your final evaluations at your interview. If you have any questions, or would like to explain your reasoning behind a course of action, that will be the time to do it. Are there any other questions?" asked the head master mage, looking around the room. Tension crackled in Toby's fur. He knew they all had questions, but no one asked. The sounds of fidgeting began to grow.

"In that case," said the man, clapping his hands together, "You are dismissed."

The orange tom followed his friend down the stairs behind the other cats. Neither said anything. They made their silent way to the Common and waited quietly in line for lunch. Some cats were talking and carrying on as if nothing had changed, but most were just as silent as the two friends. Toby wondered again about Terence's future. He felt helpless.

The duo ate their lunches lost to their own respective thoughts. Terence's nervous chatter had ceased. Toby glanced over his food at his friend, noticing how tightly the little cat's whiskers were clamped. *I want to do something for him so bad, but what if I just make things worse?* Toby licked his ruff in agitation. *This must be what it feels like to be caged.* The orange tom looked morosely out the window at the false spring garden, his thoughts whirling and spiraling like dead leaves in the wind. Between one thought and the next he felt a tiny puff of air on his ear. He flicked it in surprise and looked out of the corner of his eye to see what had caused the sensation. Hovering inches away was a brightly colored miniature dragon. Toby nearly had to cross his eyes when he looked at it, it was so close.

"Excuse me, sir," said the little dragon in a chiming bell-like voice. "Master Meredith requests your presence in her office for your final interview."

With a minuscule bow, the dragon popped out of existence as suddenly as it had appeared. Toby blinked. He'd seen a few dragons working in the library when the hopefuls had taken their tour of the grounds, but he knew very little about them except that the academy employed them for various tasks. He wondered just what they were paid.

"Good luck," said Terence.

"Thanks. You, too, if I don't see you before your interview. I'm sure you'll do great."

Toby hoped his friend couldn't hear the emptiness he felt in that last sentence. He wanted to claw himself for doubting. Terence had shown intelligence and skill Toby hadn't been sure was there when they'd first met. *But the head master is right. There are so few humans and no guarantees Terence would be a good match for any of them. For that matter, who says I would be?*

The orange tom let his thoughts sink deeper until he had almost convinced himself he would never be accepted into the academy. *What am I doing?* He could almost feel his mother's cuff across his ears. If she could hear his thoughts she would have surely disowned him. He had trained hard all his life. He was the son of a master cat, one paired to a master mage on the High Council, and a loner highly trusted by the same council. He had every reason to believe he would become either an apprentice or a loner in training.

He'd reached the head master cat's office door. Toby stood looking at the solid wood. Doubts still wiggled in his mind as he lifted a paw to scratch at the worn wood. Master Meredith had told them to ponder what each of them would be able to contribute to the world if they became a master cat. He had no idea how to answer that. What could he, one little cat, hope to accomplish in his lifetime that would affect the rest of the very big world?

He was still standing there, paw raised to scratch at the door, when it suddenly opened. Toby peered into the dimly lit interior. Sitting on a large wingback chair was the head master cat. She looked as steady and calm as ever, the roaring fire in the nearby fireplace adding orange and red highlights to her tortoiseshell coloring.

"Would you care to come in so we can begin your final interview?" she asked.

"Oh. Sorry. Yes," stammered the young tom, suddenly aware he was still standing in the hall.

He trotted to the small stool standing in front of the head master's chair. Leaping gracefully to the seat, Toby settled down to face his interviewers. Lilith reclined on a leather footstool near the fireplace. M'festus sat stiffly in a straightback wooden chair on Master Meredith's other side. The single window behind them was covered by a heavy drape, keeping out the chilly fall day and leaving the office darkened save for the light from the fire.

"Thank you for joining us, young master Toby," said Master Meredith. "Let me explain how the interview works before we truly begin." The head master paused for a moment. Toby dipped his head politely to indicate he was listening.

"First we will go over your evaluation. You may comment at any time on what has been said in it. Once you feel comfortable that you have had your say regarding your performance in orientation, we shall proceed to the actual interview. I will allow the second years to each ask a question. I will then ask a final question. Everything said here will be recorded for the head master mage and I to review this evening before tomorrow's partnering ceremony. Do you have any questions about what we will be doing here today?"

"No, ma'am."

"Very well, then. Let us begin."

At a flick of the head master cat's tail, a sheaf of papers rose from a monstrous, cluttered desk. A fountain pen rose to hover over a larger stack of papers on the desk as the smaller stack floated to a small table beside the wingback chair. There were only four or five sheets in all. Toby wasn't sure if that was a good or a bad thing.

Master Meredith leafed through the papers, informing him that he had gained high marks for his knowledge in basic history and abilities in performing basic spells. She went on to inform him that he had shown unusual patience for his age and had shown some beginnings of leadership qualities. Toby was starting to feel his worries had been for nothing when the head master cat pawed another page from the small pile. It was a list of his shortcomings. Besides being tardy, though it had only occurred the one time, Master Meredith expressed the concern of allowing another cat to proceed with a spell when he believed it had been performed incorrectly.

The gentle scritch scritch of the pen worked its way into the young tom's thoughts, making him want to twitch his ears and bite at non-existent fleas. Each pen stroke seemed to punctuate his failings and, although Toby did his best to explain his reasoning, in the end he felt like everything he could say sounded like an excuse. He tried to gauge the head master cat's reaction, but she was as unreadable as ever.

"Young master Toby, are you satisfied with your evaluation?" asked Master Meredith at last. "Do you have anything you would like to add?"

"No, ma'am."

"Then let us proceed to the interview. Lilith?"

Toby's heart trip hammered in his chest. His mind raced to guess what question the white she-cat would ask. Her blue eyes stared steadily into his.

"Toby, why do you want to be a master cat?"

Nothing like asking the hardest question first. The orange tom considered telling the three interviewers that he could make a larger contribution to the greater good by becoming a master cat, then decided not to. It seemed so rehearsed, something anyone interviewed might say because it was the most commonly held idea.

In truth, he had never really thought about why becoming a master cat was so important. It was what his parents wanted him to do and until now that had been a good enough reason. He had been born to magic, but did that mean he had to become a master cat? He thought about the histories and myths he had read. Was every hero a master cat? It had always seemed so, but was that only his perception?

He sat staring at the fountain pen poised above the paper on which it had been recording their meeting. Whatever he said would be written down, made permanent. Who might read it in the future? How could what he said now make a difference to someone later?

In a flash he saw Terence as he would be if he weren't

apprenticed. He imagined him starving and frightened, huddled in some dark alley waiting for a gang to decide what to do with him, the little gray and white cat's fur long ago dulled and matted. Toby's gut twisted at the thought. Could he make a difference for cats like Terence? He turned his eyes back to Master Meredith.

"I want to become a master cat to make a difference in the lives of other cats who believe their only alternative for survival is to join a gang or become a slave to a scam artist."

"A noble cause," said M'festus, his lip quirking in a sneer. "Perhaps you should join a temple instead."

The head master's whiskers clamped together, but she said nothing. The tuxedo tom looked smug, his tail tapping a slow rhythm against the chair leg. Toby opened his mouth to reply. He shut it again and looked back to Master Meredith.

"May I reply to that, head master?"

"You may, but keep in mind that your reply will be recorded and discussed with Master Jalen, and may affect our decision."

"Thank you, ma'am. I'll remember that." The orange tom turned to look M'festus in the eye. He took a deep breath, allowing his thoughts a moment to order themselves.

"Temple cats do a lot to help the less fortunate. I admire them. But, a temple cat would have difficulty influencing the leaders of our kingdom or this academy. As a master cat I would be able to become a part of the Council or the Board of Regents or, at the very least, to have access to the brilliant thinkers on the Council and the Board.

"As a master cat I believe I could help cats and humans who can do magic, but who aren't able to be partnered. I believe there has to be a way for them to make an honest living using the skills they've learned and I believe as a master cat I can help make it a reality." Toby watched as M'festus's eyes narrowed.

"That is, indeed, a noble idea, young master Toby," said Master Meredith. "M'festus, would you please ask your interview question?"

The tuxedo tom took a moment to lick his shoulder.

"Tell us, Toby," purred the black and white tom, "why you believe you should be chosen over a cat of noble blood."

Toby looked at his paws. What could he say? Did he deserve to be apprenticed? He'd seen the way many of his classmates had treated those they thought beneath them: pushing past them to be first in line, the cutting looks, the whispered jokes. The orange tom shuddered to think how cats of the Lower Districts would be treated if the nobles were left to do all the magic.

"I believe any cat, be he noble or common, deserves the chance to reach his potential. If I were a master cat I would use my abilities to encourage balance between noble and commoner, so that each may reach out to their own, or across the invisible boundaries, without fear."

M'festus gave a soft growl, but otherwise said nothing more. Toby endured a heartbeat more of the tom's fierce yellow gaze before looking back at Master Meredith. He willed his skin not to shiver. The tuxedo tom was still glaring at him. He could feel it. Toby forced his attention to focus on the head master cat. *One more question. Then it's completely out of my paws.* He took a deep breath and shifted from paw to paw. The young tom resettled into a slightly more comfortable position. He was ready.

"Young master Toby," said the tortoiseshell cat, pausing, "How would you handle working with someone who holds you and everyone you hold dear in disdain?"

The logs in the fire shifted, sending a shower of sparks onto the hearth. Toby watched them fall and fade away. He felt his hopes fade with the question. He'd challenged the very ideas many of his fellow hopefuls held dear, but he hadn't needed to cooperate with any of those who thought he was beneath them. He thought back to his confrontation with Reginald and his groupies. That was certainly not about cooperation, just survival. *Was that Master Meredith I saw,* he wondered again.

"I have to be honest," Toby said. "I'm not sure what I would do."

M'festus looked smug. The orange tom felt his hopes slide further away. If the tuxedo tom was happy, it surely could mean nothing good. He turned toward the head master cat who leaned forward and stared at him with narrowed eyes.

"I try to decide the best course of action before I say or do anything. I think I would do the same if I worked with someone who hated me. I would hope to gain their respect in the end or to at least avoid causing problems."

As the head master cat continued to watch Toby, the pen fell silent. The fire crackled and popped. The orange tom blinked, trying to thing of more to say but couldn't.

"Thank you for answering our questions, young master Toby," Master Meredith said. "If you have nothing to add then you may go."

Toby dipped his head to each cat in turn. He was about to leap to the floor when Terence's face flashed to mind. Did he dare?

"Master Meredith," said Toby. The head master cat turned toward him, eyes wide. The sheaf of papers she had been about to send back to her cluttered desk paused in midair.

"Yes?"

Toby took a deep breath to gather his courage. He was pretty sure what he was about to do, although not forbidden, was definitely frowned upon. Even so, if he didn't say something now he knew he'd forever regret the missed opportunity.

"I'd like to recommend a hopeful for loner in training status if he's not chosen for a partnership," he said in a rush. "His name is Terence. I've had a chance to get to know him well over the week and I know he would add fresh understanding to what we know."

"This is highly unusual, Toby," said the head master cat, "but..."

She gave the young tom a narrowed gaze that made him feel as if he had suddenly become a new object to be studied closer. With a satisfied nod, she flicked her tail to set the papers back in motion.

"We will keep your recommendation in mind. You are dismissed."

Toby let out a sigh and gratefully leaped to the floor. As the door shut quietly behind him, he said a little prayer to whatever cat gods were listening that he and Terence would both be moving into the academy rooms come tomorrow.

Toby watched the sunlight creep across the floor. Today was the day. Either he would be moving into permanent academy quarters or he would be among those waiting in the chill fall air for a coach. Sleep had been elusive. He'd managed to doze a little but that was all. He heard the soft pad of paw steps at the door.

"Good morning, ladies and gentlemen," came Lilith's

soft voice.

    The orange tom looked toward her. He'd expected another morning of being insulted by the black and white second year, but he wasn't with the she-cat this time. The rest of the cats in the large room rose to their feet without so much as a stretch or a yawn. He glanced at Terence. The little gray and white cat held his head high, a look of determination in his eyes. Whatever thoughts he'd had during the long, sleepless night, Toby could see he'd come to a decision, though what that decision was he didn't know.

    "As you know, today is the end of orientation. You will be allowed this morning to collect your belongings and move them to the outer room of the Commons. After the partnership ceremony, apprentice cats may return to move your belongings into your permanent quarters. All other hopefuls may..." Lilith looked around the room, ears at half-mast, whiskers clamped together.

    "All other hopefuls," she continued, "may take their belongings to the Administration Building. The city coaches and House carriages will pick you up there to take you home. Everyone is welcomed to attend the celebration after the partnership ceremony. There will be a calling mirror set up in the outer room for those who need to arrange to be picked up at a later time so you can enjoy the celebration."

    The second year stood in the doorway a little while longer. Toby tried not to shift in the awkward silence, tried not to wonder who would be staying and who would be leaving. The older cat turned quietly and left. Hopefuls began packing their belongings away. Toby glanced around his nest. There was nothing there that was his. He looked over to Terence. The gray and white tom stared back.

    "Wanna go get breakfast?"

"Sure."

Together they trudged down the stairs to the dining room. Toby didn't think it was possible, but the room was even more quiet than yesterday. He looked around to see only a pawful of cats scattered across the large room. A few were having hushed conversations.

"It feels like we're at a funeral," whispered Terence.

Toby nodded. It was a good description. He looked at his friend. Reflected in the young tom's eyes Toby saw his own thoughts. A funeral for someone's hopes and dreams. They just didn't know whose yet. He looked away to the large windows. The bright spring colors made him feel worse.

"That's what I'm gonna do," said Terence, "if I'm not chosen."

Toby stared at his friend in confusion. The gray cat motioned to the windows. They gazed out the window together. Try as he might, Toby still couldn't figure out what his friend meant.

"I'm goin' to learn how to garden like that. Then I'll set up shop somewhere and sell what I grow to the mages and apothecaries who can't or just don't wanna take the time to garden."

"That's a great idea," lied Toby.

It wasn't that it was a bad idea, really, but to his knowledge no cat had ever grown a garden. For that matter, Toby had never heard of a cat owning a business. Yet, hadn't he himself told Master Meredith and the second years in his interview that he wanted to help cats like Terence find a way to make an honest living? *Am I being hypocritical?*

"How do you plan on doing that?" he asked.

"I don't know that yet."

Toby's ears flattened to half-mast, wrinkling his brow.

"What I mean is I haven't figured out all the details," Terence said quickly. "The first thing I'm gonna do is try to get hired here as a grounds keeper. From there it's just a matter of learning all I can learn."

The orange tom asked Terence about what he'd like to grow and where he'd like to start his business. They discussed Terence's dream until it was time for lunch, walking around the campus to see what the academy grounds keepers were doing. Toby came away impressed. Terence had said he hadn't figured out the details, but as far as he could tell the little tom had thought it out pretty well. His ideas sounded very creative to the orange tom and he thought again of the recommendation he'd made. Master Meredith had said they'd keep it in mind during their review. He hoped it made a difference.

They were in the midst of a lively discussion of how to maintain the temperature in a greenhouse bubble when the deep sound of a bell resonated in the dining room. Conversations ceased as everyone's attention focused on the brass colored dragon, about three times the size of the messenger Master Meredith had sent to Toby, hovering just inside the doors.

"The head masters request the presence of all hopefuls in the Lesser Hall for the partnership ceremony," called the messenger dragon in a voice that reminded Toby of the big bells in the church just beyond the amphitheater. The dragon bowed once and disappeared with a loud pop.

There was a moment of silence, then the room exploded into excited chatter. Cats streamed from the dining room across campus to the Lesser Hall. Toby sneaked a peek at the ceiling, almost expecting Master Meredith to be there. When the orange tom found a seat and turned back to the stage he found the head master cat perched on a tall stool next to a podium in deep discussion with Head Master Jalen. They looked as if they were still deciding the partnerings. Behind them were seated several master mages and master cats Toby assumed were academy instructors.

The orange tom watched them with some fascination, wondering what they taught. Their expressions ranged from intent interest in the hopefuls filing in to complete boredom. As he studied each in turn, he realized there were two more cats on the stage than mages. At first he thought their partnered master mage might have been late, but then he noticed that neither one was seated near a chair as the others were. In fact, the stools they sat upon stood slightly apart from the others on the stage.

The longer Toby watched the two cats, the more interesting they became. Although their posture said they were bored with what was going on, their measuring looks said differently. Their gazes swept over the cat hopefuls, never once landing on the humans in the next section. The charcoal gray tom reminded the young cat of his father. The older cat's broad shoulders spoke of an amount of physical training the others on stage lacked. His father had taken time out of each day to practice fighting moves, as well as doing other physical feats to strengthen his muscles. He'd said that, as a loner, sometimes his missions required brute strength rather than magical finesse.

He looked at the silver tabby she-cat seated beside the tom. While she wasn't broad like the tom, she was no less athletic in build. Toby could easily imagine her running long distances without tiring and slashing and dodging with a quick grace others would envy. Loners? He was fascinated. He leaned over to draw Terence's attention to the unusual cats.

"If I can have your attention," called Master Jalen.

Toby sat back. The room fell quiet. Toby glanced toward the section of seats roped off for the newly chosen. Compared to the number of hopefuls gathered, the section seemed minuscule. Toby's stomach felt like it had caterpillars wriggling around in it in some kind of mad dance. He looked back to the stage.

"As your name is called, please take your seat as partners and remain until the ceremony is completed."

Toby held his breath and waited. Name after name was called. Toby closed his eyes and flattened his ears, the cat equivalent of crossing one's fingers, and prayed to whatever cat god would listen that he would be chosen soon. The head master cat called his name. Toby nearly raced to the middle of the floor, facing the remaining humans. Who would it be? The chubby girl with the golden curls? Or perhaps the tall lad who, by the appearance of his ill-fitting clothes, looked like he'd put on a sudden growth spurt? Toby waited impatiently, tail tip twitching, scanning the humans.

"Tarah Nichole," called the head master mage.

A tiny red-headed waif of a girl stepped forward from behind the tall boy. She looked hesitantly at the orange tabby and then back at the head master mage. It was quite apparent that this young lady did not think Toby was a fitting companion. Anxiety squeezed the blood from Toby's heart. He turned his head to look at the head masters.

Master Meredith was pointing at the list of humans with a delicate white paw and whispering something to Master Jalen. Try as he might, Toby could not decipher what the head master cat was saying. Master Jalen nodded gravely. Clearing his throat, he looked back at the young hopefuls patiently waiting in the center of the room.

"I'm sorry, Tarah. It seems that my eyes were playing tricks on me," he said with a gentle smile. "You are to be paired with Dulcinaya."

Toby watched a sleek chocolate point Siamese pace forward with measured steps. The young girl smiled. The tension in her tiny frame melted away as she curtsied to the elegant cat. Dulcinaya returned the curtsy with a little head bow. Toby watched them walk away. Like two genteel ladies, the human and cat walked to the newly chosen section and gracefully lowered themselves into their seats.

The young girl had seemed so glad to be partnered with any cat other than him. He looked behind him at the cats waiting in hopes to be partnered, then at the group of humans left. Toby's heart sank as reality dawned. His odds of being chosen were rapidly decreasing. He hunkered down and began to slowly back toward the rest of the waiting cats.

"Toby, please do be still," scolded Master Meredith.

Toby froze. Turning her head back to her companion, she whispered something else as she continued to point to the list of humans. Master Jalen bent to read what his companion had been pointing at. Tapping the tip of his nose with a forefinger, he frowned as he read on. With a sharp nod, he looked up at the remaining hopefuls.

"It appears we have only one partnering left. Before I call the final names, I want to encourage those of you here who will not be entering the academy this season to return in a year. At this present time, while you show potential, it is clear that you are not quite ready to be admitted to this school. We do, however, look forward to seeing you next fall.

"Now, without further ado," continued the head master mage, "the final partnering is Lorn Ribaldy and Toby."

Toby scanned the remaining humans. Which one was

Lorn Ribaldy? There, at the end of the line, a young boy had his eyes scrunched closed and his fingers crossed at either side of his face. It was the human Toby had noticed at the partnerings lecture. As they made their way to the last open seats, Toby wondered if it would be the loners turn to announce their selections.

"Congratulations to this year's apprentices," said Master Jalen.

There was a smattering of polite applause. Toby looked at his friend. Although his whiskers were clamped tightly, he held his head high. The orange tom wanted to yowl at the unfairness. He looked at the two cats he suspected to be loner instructors. Without a backward glance they leaped to the stage floor and walked to the exit. His hopes crashed as he watched their tails disappear beyond the curtain.

"We would like to extend an invitation to everyone to enjoy this evening's celebration, which will be in the academy Ballroom. Thank you all for coming."

Toby didn't think he'd be able to enjoy anything anytime soon. As the new apprentices were herded from the hall to collect their things and move them to their permanent quarters, he glanced one last time to his friend. The little gray cat was waiting patiently at the end of the line to leave the hall by the opposite exit. Toby knew the look of determination on the young tom's face. He was going to put his plan into action. As the orange tom edged out the door he wished his friend luck.

"Do you want to stop by the building you were staying at first or should we stop by mine first?"

"What?" asked Toby, startled from his melancholic thoughts.

He stared up at the boy he'd been trotting beside. He wasn't very tall by human standards, though not short. He was neither muscular nor skinny. His brown hair was cut the same as many other humans Toby had seen. The boy's eyes were nearly the same shade of brown as his hair. In short, the orange tom would say his apprentice mage was entirely unremarkable.

"I asked if we should go to your building or mine first," repeated the boy.

"Sorry," said Toby. "I didn't bring anything."

"That's probably just as well," said the boy, turning toward the Common Building he'd stayed in. The partners walked on in silence. Toby's thoughts flicked back to his friend. *Stop it! Terence is a resourceful cat. He'll be fine.* The orange tom looked up at the young mage beside him. *I've got other things to think about.*

Lorn's shoulders drooped as he shuffled to a stop. The young man sighed, looked down at Toby for a moment, then looked back toward the Common Building. The tom followed his gaze to a mound of luggage near the door. At first he wondered why the human hopefuls had piled their belongings together. Then he noticed each piece matched in color and design. As he studied the miniature mountain he found they were all embossed with a purple bird. He looked back at the mage.

"My mother helped me pack," Lorn said with a grimace.

"Oh."

The partners stood considering how to move the numerous bags and trunks. It would take an entourage of servants to pack them from the Common Building to the Apprentice Quarters half-way across campus. Toby knew how to float objects, but he'd never attempted anything larger than a book roughly the same size as himself and only slightly heavier.

"I don't suppose you know how to float things," he said.

"Nothing bigger than a fountain pen... without it exploding, that is."

Fantastic. This day just gets better and better.

"In that case I guess we carry what we can and see if we can find someone to help us with the rest."

Lorn hoisted two large satchels down from the top of the pile while Toby carefully pawed a medium-sized carry-all out from the edge. It was a little bigger than anything he'd managed to float before, but he thought he'd be able to manage it. He was in the process of concentrating on what he wanted to happen when he caught a better look at the purple bird he'd noticed before.

"Is that a purple duck?" he asked, looking up at the young mage.

"Yes," Lorn answered, another sigh following. "Mother is very fond of the ridiculous thing. She's had it embossed and embroidered and woven into everything we own. She wanted to have our horses branded with it, but Father drew the line at that."

"I'm not very familiar with human heraldry," said Toby, doing his best to stifle a laugh. "What does it mean?"

"In short? The purple to signify high magical status, the duck to identify us as persons of many resources."

"Are you? Related to someone of high magical status, I mean."

Lorn snorted, contemplated the mountain of luggage and added another, smaller satchel to those he planned on carrying. He hoisted everything into his arms then turned toward the orange tom, obviously expecting him to pick up the carry-all. Toby quickly murmured the levitation incantation and followed his new companion as he set off for their new living quarters.

"It depends on who you talk to. Mother would say yes. Father would say no."

"So why does your mother say you are if your father says you're not?"

"Mother has never doubted Uncle Ribaldy's innocence. Father, though, would rather disown him."

The partners paused in front of the three buildings designated as Apprentice Quarters. Three identical pack-dirt paths led to each dark gray stone building. Two well-manicured bushes flanked each of the three iron-banded dark wood doors. Nine darkened windows stared mutely at the partners from each three story building. A brightly colored banner was the only differing thing between them. Toby looked hopefully at the mage. He'd been so wrapped in his thoughts about Terence's future he hadn't paid attention to what the head master had said after the partnerings were announced.

"I take it you weren't listening either," Lorn said.

"Sorry. Any ideas on how to find out which building we're in?"

Lorn chewed his lower lip and scowled at the center building. His face brightened a moment later and he whispered an incantation Toby wasn't familiar with. A bush in front of the building on the left burst into flames. The orange tom flattened himself instinctively, ready to flee, the hair along his back a spiny ridge. The carry-all thunked to the ground, missing the tom's foot by an inch.

"Sorry about that," mumbled the boy. "Happens sometimes when I use the finder incantation. Good news is I know which building we'll be calling home for the next three years."

Toby slowly pulled himself into a sitting position. He cast a sidelong glance at the seemingly unremarkable mage he'd been partnered with and wondered again what cat god had found it humorous to throw them together. Still, he surmised, there had to have been something in Lorn that had made the head masters decide he was a good candidate for apprenticeship in the academy. He gave his ruff a quick lick to help settle his thoughts.

"Well, now that you've found the building shall we go find our rooms?"

Lorn nodded. With only half a thought, Toby levitated the carry-all and started toward the building. The grounds keeper dragons were already busy putting out Lorn's accidental blaze, their voices chiming like miniature bells. Toby hazarded a glance in their direction and decided most of what the small dragons were saying was not complimentary in the least. He wondered just how many times sometimes had been this week.

"Maybe I should find our rooms," Toby said as they passed the smoldering bush.

"That might be best." Lorn tried to shrink past the irritated dragons.

It took a few moments for their eyes to adjust to the dimness of the entryway. A wood stairway stood before them, a long hallway to the right of it. Neither had been lit well. Toby peered down the hall to see slightly darker shadows to either side, a small lantern just to one side of each. He assumed the shadows were doors to six separate living quarters. Looking up the stairs, the orange tom surmised the second and third floors were similar.

He hoped his luck was going to get better as he said his finder incantation, wishing the green arrow to direct them to one of the main floor rooms. His hopes sagged as the bright green finder pointed up the stairs. They fell flat when he discovered the arrow was leading them on toward the last room on the third floor. Toby watched Lorn struggle with the door latch while trying to keep his luggage from falling out of his grasp. The orange tom sighed.

"May I try?"

Lorn gave the door handle one last jerk, nearly dropping everything in the process. Toby waited patiently as the young mage juggled the luggage back into place, then stepped to the side. He took a moment to check the securing of the floating carry-all. The last thing he wanted was to look as inept to his new partner as Lorn had to him. He studied the door handle. It was a curious handle with a thumb-sized lever attached to the side of a curved handle. It made sense to Toby that the lever needed to be depressed to lift the latch. *So why didn't Lorn do that? Surely he could see you can't just turn the handle.* Satisfied that he understood the mechanism, the tom focused on the process and flicked his tail at the door.

The lever depressed, the handle turned, the door shuddered. It didn't open. He tried again. The door stubbornly remained shut. His fur grew hot with embarrassment. He'd been positive he could open the door.

"Now what?" asked Lorn.

Toby relaxed. At least Lorn wasn't going to be difficult about it. Unfortunately that didn't make a difference in the matter at hand. They were still on the wrong side of the door.

"Need some help?" asked a cheery female voice from down the hall.

The partners turned to see a girl, perhaps a year or two older than Lorn, walking toward them. Her dark curls bounced in time to her step. The black framed glasses she wore made her look slightly owlish. Trotting daintily beside her was a small calico she-cat. Stepping to the door, the girl quickly depressed the lever, turned the door handle and gave a hard shove. The door popped open.

"I had this room during my apprenticeship," said the girl, waving them into the room beyond. "Door's great for taking out your frustrations, but it's a real pain when you're in a hurry."

"Or carrying an armload of luggage," said the little she-cat as she snagged the young woman's trouser leg.

"Here, let me help you with that."

The older mage reached to take the two satchels Lorn had tucked under his arms. He pulled away. The girl gave him a smile and a small nod, reaching once again for the luggage. This time the young mage yielded them to her outstretched hands, returning a tentative smile.

"My name's Alie. This is Dora."

"Pleased to meet you," said the little calico, dipping her head respectfully. "Shall we enter?"

"After you," said Alie, nodding the partners toward the door.

The room was dark, the only source of light coming from the space between the shutters on the window and a doorway at the back. Toby could smell just a hint of various herbs under the overpowering smell of cleaning agents. A modest fireplace sat next to the door at the other side of the room. Bookcases and shelving for magic supplies faced the wall opposite the window. In the middle of the room sat a large, scarred table of unfinished wood. The legs were as thick as Toby was long, the top as thick as he was wide. It was, in the young cat's estimation, the perfect table for Lorn – indestructible.

"Welcome to your new home," said Alie. "Your bedroom is back there. It's rather drafty in the winter, but the fireplace has a nifty sliding door on the front and back, so you can adjust which room gets all the heat."

Lorn nodded. Toby leaped to the table top. He waited patiently as his partner surveyed the workroom. He wasn't sure why the young mage had yet to say a word. The silence grew more awkward with each passing moment. Toby rolled his eyes. Obviously it was going to be up to him to make their introductions. He opened his mouth to speak when Lorn turned and made eye contact with Alie.

"My name is Lorn and this is my partner, Toby. It is a pleasure to make your acquaintance."

"Oh there's no need to be so formal," Alie said and chuckled. Dora ducked her head, politely hiding her amusement.

"I'm sorry. I just–" The boy's face turned scarlet.

"Let's see. You're upper merchant class, right?"

Lorn's eyes widened. He nodded his head.

"Your father knows the value of money and believes in working hard, playing fair? Your mother plays the Lady of the Manor?"

The young man nodded again. Toby was fascinated now. He'd heard that some humans had the gift of reading others, but he'd never given it much credit.

"You grew up being told you must be polite and use formal greetings with anyone older than you or of a higher social class. Am I right?"

"Are you a Reader?" whispered the young man.

"We prefer Gifted Intuitive Telepath, if you please," the young woman said, frowning and putting her hands on her hips.

"Oh. I-I-I didn't know. I'm sorry."

The girl's mouth twitched. Dora turned to nip at her flank. Toby was reasonably sure the young she-cat wasn't after a flea. Both females seemed to be trying very hard to keep a straight face.

"I think she's teasing you, Lorn."

Alie began laughing. The little calico she-cat leaped to the table beside Toby. Her whiskers were splayed wide in a cat grin.

"Hoo boy," the young woman exclaimed between laughs. "I'm sorry. I just couldn't help myself. You looked so awe-struck."

"But–. You said–."

"Better tell them how you did it, Al, or they'll never believe another word you say," chirped Dora.

"It's pretty simple, really. I'm a Journeyman Liaison to the High Council and the Merchant Guild, so I could tell by your clothes that you're most likely from a merchanting family. Nearly every merchant I've met believes in hard work and being fair, though a few will slit your purse strings if they can." The delicate she-cat made a face as if she smelled something foul.

"Anyway, once I guessed that much, it wasn't difficult to deduce from the matching luggage that your mother likes to play Lady of the Manor and — is that a purple duck?"

"Unfortunately, yes," said Lorn. "Please don't ask."

"I see. Anyway it was easy to guess from all the clues why you reacted like you did."

"Yes. And it doesn't hurt that my mage's favorite pastime is solving puzzles," said Dora. Alie shrugged.

"Well, if there's anything else I can help you with, let me know."

"Actually," Toby said, giving Lorn a sidelong glance, "we could use some help getting the rest of Lorn's things up here."

Alie's eyes widened.

"There's more?"

Toby nodded and looked pointedly at his mage. The boy slumped and shuffled his feet.

"Mother helped me pack."

The girl nodded and cast a sidelong glance at her companion.

"Say no more."

Moving Lorn's luggage from the Human Commons to their new residence was a lot more pleasant with Alie and Dora helping. Dora showed Toby a trick to floating some of the heavier items. After Lorn burnt a hole in one of the larger bags, though, they all agreed he should just carry the other things. Before Toby realized it, it was time to make their way to the celebration. Suddenly all the fun he'd been having seemed empty. Terence wouldn't be there, he was sure of it. Toby closed his eyes and tried to will the sadness away.

"Ready to go?"

"Yeah," murmured Toby.

The brightly decorated ballroom did nothing to lift Toby's spirits. The upbeat music clashed with the gloomy thoughts oozing through the young tom's mind. He watched as several gaily clad nobles twirled past in an intricate dance. The lights bounced off their bejeweled clothing, leaving sparkles in front of Toby's eyes.

"Hey, there," said a familiar voice behind the orange cat. Toby twisted around, not believing his ears. Blinking the small gray and white cat into focus, Toby couldn't stop the purr that burst from his chest.

"Terence! I thought you wouldn't—"

"Come to the celebration because I wasn't chosen? Nah. Mama didn't raise no fool. Where else am I gonna get food like this?"

"I'm so glad you came. I didn't think I'd ever see you again."

"Oh you can't get rid of me that easily," said the little tom. "I'm a street cat, remember? I've always got a plan or two tucked in my fur."

"I guess I should have figured that out when you said you are going to become the first garden cat," Toby replied, his whiskers splayed in a wide cat grin. "By the way, have you put your plan into action yet?"

"I got somethin' even better."

"Really? What could be better than becoming the first garden cat ever?"

"A loner-in-training."

"You're kidding. That's great. I thought — when you weren't called up – I mean –"

Terence chuckled.

"I guess someone aroun' here has a lot of pull 'cause I was on my way to wait for a city coach when this big gray tom named Chivato walks up to me an' says someone wants a word. I thought I was in deep manure 'cause on the street a tom that big usually works for a Boss."

Toby held his breath. His heart beat faster and his paws went numb. It seemed like someone had added three times as many lit candles in the room as the young cat's pupils widened. As he listened to Terence's story he saw a slender man in purple velvet pacing toward them. In the man's shadow stalked a large gray tom.

"So this Gravin Arturo heard that someone had recommended me for loner-in-training and wanted to sponsor me. Even said he'd give me a job when I reach journeyman status. Talked the loner instructors into givin' me a spot in the classes on a... what was it they called it?"

"I believe the words you're looking for, young master Terence, are 'provisional basis'," said the man in a deep, rich voice.

"Yeah, provisional basis. That means if I do good they'll re-evaluate my performance and I can complete the training."

"Provided he continues to show progress, that is," said the man.

"Toby, I'd like you to meet my sponsor, Gravin Arturo."

"I was pleased to hear that you were chosen. The academy can only benefit from it."

"You know each other?"

"I had the opportunity to get acquainted with young master Toby during a coach ride to the academy. An excellent sense of smell, as I recall."

"Gravin Arturo, a pleasure to see you again."

"And I'm sure you remember my companion Chivato." The gravin waved his champagne glass in the gray tom's direction. Toby dipped his head to the tom.

"Toby," purred Chivato. "I'm so glad you were chosen, even if it is, like our young friend here, on a provisional basis."

"Excuse me?" blurted Toby. The orange tom thought his heart had stopped. His sight narrowed to the large gray tom in front of him.

"Oh. I'm sorry. I thought you knew." Chivato's eyes widened. His ears swiveled outward. He looked up at Gravin Arturo. Toby looked up at the nobleman, too. The man's gaze softened.

"I'm afraid that's what we heard," said Arturo. Toby looked back at the gray tom. Chivato nodded toward a group of mages.

"It seems," he said, lowering his voice, "that there are some who do not think cats of lower status should be allowed in such a prestigious school as this."

Toby watched the group of mages. They were laughing. One glanced his direction and raised his glass. Toby felt a soft tail fall gently over his shoulders. He turned to see Chivato watching the group of mages beside him.

"Perhaps that is why you were partnered with Lorn Ribaldy," he murmured.

Chapter 4

Reginald stared across the room at Toby. Chivato had placed a fatherly tail across the young tom's shoulders. The white cat's fur bristled. It wasn't right. Being chosen was an honor. How could a cat from the Middle Districts, a commoner, ever understand the subtleties of such a relationship? Reginald stared at the orange cat who had somehow impressed his own mentor. The gray tom looked at him. Reginald lowered his eyes. He could hear the clink of glasses and rustle of robes. Laughter rang from across the room. It all made his stomach feel sour. He stared hard at the floor. A set of gray paws entered his line of sight.

"You don't agree with the selection."

The white tom looked into Chivato's yellow eyes.

"I thought blood mattered."

"It does."

"Then why were they chosen?" Reginald nodded toward Toby and Lorn, his tail twitching.

"They passed the tests and are compatible, would be my assumption."

"But they aren't noble. Doesn't that count for something?"

Chivato cocked his head to the side and stared at the young tom for several minutes. Reginald began to fidget.

"You feel strongly about this."

Reginald licked his ruff. Did he speak out of turn? He looked back at the large gray tom.

"Father says it's the commoners being brought into high positions that caused the problems in the High Council." The white tom glanced at Toby and Lorn again.

"I think he is right."

"I see. Your father is a very proud cat, one worthy of a seat on the High Council."

"Yes, but he won't have one, will he?" Reginald glared at the orange tom and his companion.

"Unfortunately this is true. Master Ribaldy saw to that before his insanity was uncovered."

The white tom wanted to hiss. Another common partnering. What right did a commoner have to say who could or couldn't be appointed to the High Council. And, once the King passed judgement, nothing could be changed. Ribaldy and his partner had been a worm in the King's ear.

"Flatten your fur, son. You'll draw unnecessary attention to yourself."

Reginald looked around. No one was looking at them, but the gray tom was right. This was a celebration, not a dueling arena. Slowly his fur began to lower. He took a few calming breaths, remembering the ritual exercises his tutor had made him practice until he wanted to snarl. Finally he was able to get his temper under control.

"Forgive me, Master Chivato."

"There is nothing to forgive. You are a loyal son. It is only natural that you would feel your family's slight so keenly." The gray tom studied Reginald. The silence between them was punctuated by more clinking of glasses, more laughter. The young feline could hear Chivato's tail thump rhythmically on the floor.

"If you want to earn back a spot on the High Council for your family, perhaps I can help."

Reginald's eyes widened.

"How?"

Chivato leaned forward, closing his eyes to slits. The young cat leaned closer, afraid to miss a single word.

"As you know, Master Ribaldy was working closely with a loner before he was captured. That loner was young Toby's father. My companion and I suspect Toby to be part of a scheme the traitor set in place to remove key members of the High Council. We need someone here at the academy to maintain a watchful eye on him."

The young cat glanced over at the partners. They were in deep conversation with a young woman and her calico she-cat. Reginald thought he remembered seeing them at the High Council last time he and his father had visited Master Chivato. If they were connected to the council, then Toby very well could be part of a conspiracy. Who knew how far this conspiracy had leeched into the Council. That orange pest needed to be watched.

"I could do that."

Chivato leaned back, giving the young cat a considering look. He shook his head.

"No. It would be too risky. Forget I mentioned it."

Reginald swung his eyes back to the older tom. His paws prickled with the need to convince his mentor that he should be allowed to have this mission. The young cat stepped forward, his eyes wide with excitement.

"But you said this could help my family. I can do this."

Chivato closed his eyes and sighed as his head drooped to his chest. The older cat's whiskers were clamped tight, his ears flattened to half mast.

"If anyone discovered what you were doing, it would mean humiliation for your family. I could never ask one of my House to suffer their title being stripped simply to satisfy my curiosity."

The gray cat's voice cracked. Reginald could imagine the heart ache the gray tom was feeling at the very idea. *He was there when they chose someone else for the High Council. That's what he's remembering. I know it. But I could change that if he'll just help me.*

"But what if you're right? What if Toby is a spy for Master Ribaldy? I would be a hero. I could bring honor back to my family."

The gray tom cocked his head, looking at the ceiling.

"True. That would put your father in a better light as far as the High Council is concerned." Reginald held his breath. Chivato looked back at him. The tom's whiskers slowly spread into a cat grin.

"Are you sure you're up to such a task?"

"Yes."

With a nod, the older tom stood and motioned the young cat to follow him.

"Well, then, let us discuss how you might go about this counter-spying adventure, shall we?"

They were late again. Toby jumped onto a stool at the back of the classroom as Lorn dropped into the seat next to him. This was becoming a habit, one Toby didn't like. The first week of classes had been much like orientation. Hurry to be first in line for meals. Swallow food un-tasted. Race to class. Repeat. Of course, racing along next to Lorn was like running with a turtle. Toby supposed the young human was as quick as anyone of his species, but it was painfully clear to the orange tom that four legs would always be faster than two. Master Meredith glanced at the two as they took their seats, continuing her lecture without so much as a pause. An hour later class dismissed with the chiming of the noon-time bell.

"Toby. Lorn," called the head master cat. "Master Jalen and I would like to have a word with you."

Toby tried to ignore the snickers of passing students. His skin grew hot. A quick glance at Lorn revealed his skin turning pink. Master Meredith slowly followed the students as they made their way up the stairs toward the exit. She waited at the door until every student had left except Toby and Lorn.

"Follow me, gentlemen."

Through the hall, down the stairs and out the building, the partners followed the head master cat. Not a word was spoken. Toby's imagination played scene after scene through his mind of what his mother would say when he arrived home in disgrace. Although he'd sent her a letter letting her know he'd been chosen, he'd left out the part about being on a provisional basis. He also hadn't told her who his mage was. The door to the head masters' shared office opened as they arrived.

"Good day, gentlemen," said the head master mage. "Please sit down."

The partners seated themselves in the two straight-backed chairs facing Master Jalen, who sat behind his large ornamental desk. Master Meredith landed lightly at the head master's elbow. They stared silently at the partners as the fire in the fireplace crackled and popped. Toby's fur felt too thick and hot.

"Do you know why we've called you here?" asked

Master Jalen.

Lorn fidgeted. Toby could feel his skin growing hot again. He stared at his paws, his whiskers clamped tight.

"Well?" prompted Master Meredith.

"We've been consistently late to class," murmured Toby.

"That is accurate—"

"Oh please, sir, madam," blurted Lorn, scooting to the edge of his seat and gripping his hands together. "It's my fault. I get everything ready for first class the night before, but I always seem to forget something the next morning and have to go back for it. Toby could easily run ahead to class without me, but he refuses to. I've tried to make him. Really I have."

Master Jalen raised a hand to cut the boy off. He looked at Toby.

"Is this true?"

"In a sense, yes, sir."

"Would you care to explain what that means?"

"Well, sir, Lorn does get everything ready for first class the night before, just as he said. And we do have to go back for something nearly every time. Lorn has tried to convince me to go ahead and go to class, but it just doesn't seem right. We're partners. Partners are supposed to work together at all times. If I went to class without Lorn then that defeats the whole purpose of putting us together in the first place, doesn't it?"

Master Jalen gazed at the two youths sitting before him. He turned to Master Meredith, who cocked her head slightly. It reminded Toby of how his mother and father often sent silent messages to each other through that secret parental look. With a small nod, Master Jalen turned back to the apprentices.

"Although we don't approve of your unfailing tardiness, that is not why you are here."

"It's not?" they asked together.

"No," said Master Meredith. "It's not."

"Before we begin, I must warn you that what we are about to discuss is highly confidential. It's not something to be spoken about beyond this room. Is that understood?"

"Yes, Master Jalen," they agreed.

"Good." The head master mage leaned back into his wing-back chair. "Meredith?"

"Last spring your father, Toby, was ordered on a special mission. How much do you know about that?"

"Not much. It had something to do with my father being sent on an information gathering mission by the High Council because he was a loner. I remember mother being very upset and them arguing about why he had to go, but that's about it."

"As I thought. And you, Lorn, how much do you know about your uncle's situation?"

"Situation? You mean his treachery, don't you?"

"Some would say it was treachery, yes," said Master Jalen. "However, we do not believe that to be the case."

"What? I don't understand."

"First things first, Apprentice Lorn. Please, tell us what you know," said Master Meredith.

"Father said Uncle Ribaldy went crazy while working on one of his schemes and tried to blow up the High Council while they were in session. If Master Kiyoshi hadn't stopped him we'd be out not just a grand master mage, but the entire governing body as well."

"And what does your mother say?" asked Master Jalen.

"She says Uncle Ribaldy was working on a secret mission for the High Council and was set up somehow. She thinks someone on the High Council is covering it all up."

"Your mother is very astute," said Master Meredith.

"Mother?"

"Excuse me, head masters, but what does this have to do with us?"

"Toby, I understand you recently talked with Gravin Fedelis Arturo and Master Chivato on your coach ride to the academy. Do you remember what it was you visited about?" asked Master Meredith.

"Gravin Arturo was on his way here to lobby for the shadow arts classes to be kept. He said his county was having problems with illegal dragon willow trading and that there was a "mage hunt" going on. He got very upset when I asked him about it all."

"That would be expected given the gravity of the situation," said Master Jalen. "Did he mention what county he is gravin of?"

"Hielberg County, sir."

"And did he say anything about knowing your father?"

"No, sir. He seemed anxious to find out who my father was, though."

"Did you tell him?"

"No, sir. Master Chivato told him that he was being nosy, so he stopped asking questions."

Toby watched as the head masters gave each other that look again. He glanced at Lorn who seemed as confused about everything as he was.

"It seems we may still have time," said Master Meredith.

"Indeed, but how much?" asked Master Jalen.

"At this point there's no way to know. All we can do is go ahead with the plan and pray."

Master Jalen made a noncommittal noise, staring off

into the space just to the right of Master Meredith's whiskers. The head masters sat unmoving, each lost in thought.

"Excuse me," said Toby.

The head masters jerked their gazes toward the orange tom as if they'd forgotten the apprentices were still in the room.

"May I ask why Lorn and I are here?"

"You are here because we believe you can be of service to your King and country," said Master Meredith.

"Us? How?" asked Lorn.

"I'm afraid, gentlemen, that we must ask you to do something that would normally be asked of fully trained masters."

"Or a loner," added Master Meredith. She regarded Toby with an intense gaze.

"We need you to gather information."

"What kind?" asked Toby.

"Anything on the shadow arts market in Hielberg County. It won't be easy, but we think you two are our best choice based on your families' histories and your own unique skills."

"Unique skills?" inquired Toby, glancing at Lorn. He wasn't sure accidentally setting hedges on fire and exploding homework counted as a skill.

"Apprentice Lorn," said Master Jalen, pointing at the young mage, "unless you use magic, which I strongly urge you to refrain from until you've gained more control, you seem completely average. Yet in orientation you displayed a keen sense of understanding how seemingly dissimilar pieces of information fit together to make a complete picture."

"You, Apprentice Toby," the head master continued, pointing at the orange tom, "have the same ability to find similarities in dissimilar information. You also have a unique ability we believe you inherited from your father."

Toby looked from Master Jalen to Master Meredith. He thought back to what he could remember of Victor. Nothing stood out as unusual. He blinked in confusion.

"Toby, do you remember what you had for breakfast on the first morning of orientation?" asked Master Meredith.

"I think it was some tuna and creamed peas."

"Do you remember how you knew tuna was on the menu?"

"I could smell it."

"Precisely when did you smell it?"

"While Terence and I were on our way downstairs. Why?"

"As I recall, Terence said you were only about half-way down the stairs when you told him you could smell the tuna."

"Terence?"

"It seems you made quite an impression on the young tom. During his final interview he made a point in mentioning that you had said having a good sense of smell wasn't a requirement for admission to the academy."

"A good sense of smell? I don't understand."

"Toby, you don't just have a good sense of smell," Master Meredith said. "Your nose is exceptional, just as your father's was. In fact, based on your reaction to the incorrectly spelled potion during orientation, I would hazard a guess that you share the same magical allergies as your father."

"I'm sorry. I still don't understand."

"You can sniff out bad magic, Toby," said Lorn. "Is that it Master Meredith?"

"Very good, Lorn. That is correct."

"I think I see where you're going, ma'am. Toby and I

can find answers to your questions because we have connections and we're less likely to be seen as an enemy. Who would suspect two apprentices, right?" asked Lorn.

"Indeed," answered Master Jalen with a slight smile.

"If we find someone or something involved in the shadow arts market a quick sniff and Toby'll know because of his allergies, right? So all we have to do is sneak around a bit, ask a few questions and there you have it."

"Something like that," said Master Jalen.

"Hold on," Master Meredith admonished, turning a sour look upon her chosen. "This is a very dangerous mission we're asking these young ones to take on. They need to know what could happen."

Master Jalen's expression darkened.

"Meredith is right. This isn't a simple game of strategy, boys. The person or persons responsible would be just as likely to kill you as an adult."

"In fact, that is exactly what we believe happened to Master Kiyoshi. I believe you are both aware of a species of spider called the Gargantua Felis Asesino."

The apprentices nodded. A shiver ran down Toby's back as he remembered the lecture his father had given him about the Great Cat Killer's ability to kill a feline with a single sting. It was the last lecture he'd ever received from Victor.

"It seems that is what killed Master Ribaldy's companion. We believe it might also have been used to cause your uncle's current madness."

Lorn sat back. His face suddenly pale. Toby's tail fluffed to twice its normal size.

"Is that what happened to my father?" he whispered.

"We don't know that for sure, Toby, but that is most likely," said Master Meredith. The she-cat's gaze softened.

"If there were another way, son, we would gladly choose it. As yet no other options have arisen."

Toby looked at Lorn. The young mage stared back, his brown eyes wide. Could they do this? Toby thought about the courage the large black tom must have mustered to jump into the coach that had taken him to his death. Toby watched as similar emotions played across Lorn's face. Lorn's mouth hardened into a grim line. Toby narrowed his eyes in silent agreement.

"We'll do it."

Toby sat rehearsing what he was going to say to his mother. He'd put off calling her since orientation, but now he had no better option if he wanted more information on his father's mission. With a sigh, he stared into his reflection and recited the mirror call incantation. The image wavered like a rippling pond. When the ripples cleared Toby could see Master O'dorn's receiving room with its shabby chairs. Mariam was scrubbing the worn floors.

"Hello," he called.

"Master Toby," squeaked the housekeeper, dropping the scrub brush as she spun around. "You gave me a fright."

"My apologies, Mariam. Would you happen to know if my mother or Master O'dorn are available?"

"Th' Master's workin' with Mrs. Tucker agin, but I'm sure the Mistress is about. Would you like me to fetch her?"

"No need for that," replied Toby, thinking his mother was never fetched for anything. "If you could just tell me where she might be I'll switch mirrors."

"I believe she's in your family nest, sir."

"Thank you, Mariam."

"Your welcome, Master Toby, and congratulations on

being 'prenticed."

Toby nodded, then turned his attention to moving the mirror call down the hall to the mirror just outside the family nest. He pictured the tarnished brass frame hanging from the dark wooden walls. It was always slightly cockeyed. Slowly he sent out tendrils of willpower through the mirror he faced until he felt them catch on the frame he wanted to use as an anchor. The mirror rippled again. He concentrated, sending more will toward the other mirror. The image was beginning to clear. His mother's stern gaze stared back at him. Instantly the image evaporated and he was looking at himself again. He groaned. As quickly as he could, he re-called the mirror in Master O'dorn's receiving room and asked Mariam to tell his mother he was calling from the public mirror.

"It's a wonder you were chosen," scolded Adele as she paced to the mirror. "Given the scant information you included in your letter I wasn't sure you had been. Really, Toby, a letter?"

"I'm sorry, mother, but things have been chaotic here."

"As if I don't remember what it was like as an apprentice: running from the Commons to the classroom and back until you managed to drag yourself half-asleep to your room. I trust you're managing to stay on top of your studies, at least."

"Mostly," murmured Toby.

"Mostly?"

Toby cursed himself silently. His mother's ears were just as sharp through the mirror as in person, it seemed.

"Yes, mother, we've had a few late starts. Nothing to worry about."

"I suppose. They do give apprentices more leeway than hopefuls, but that's no reason to start being lazy."

"Ummm. About that... I'm not exactly fully apprenticed yet."

"What do you mean: not exactly fully apprenticed yet?" Adele asked, her eyes narrowing.

"Well, I've been chosen, yes, but it's… ummm…"

The queen's tail tapped rhythmically as she waited. Toby looked down at his paws. He could hear the gentle scratching of the housekeeper's scrub brush. *Just get it over with.* The orange tom took a deep breath.

"I'm on provisional status," he said in a rush.

"Provisional status," repeated his mother, enunciating each syllable. She sat, tapping her tail, glowering at the young tom. Toby sat motionless. Several moments passed. Suddenly his mother seemed to deflate. She closed her eyes and sighed.

"I guess provisional status is better than nothing. Were you at least partnered with someone who could help you improve your magic?"

"Not exactly."

"Oh, Toby," Adele said, shaking her head. "Who?"

"Lorn Ribaldy."

In a flash his mother looked twice her normal size. Her eyes glowed. Mariam, who had been studiously ignoring them, hastily dropped her scrub brush in her bucket and scurried out the door. Toby was thankful for the solid mirror between himself and Adele.

"That traitor's nephew? How could they?" she stormed. "It's sabotage. That's what it is. If he's like his uncle he couldn't magic himself out of a woodshed let alone carry the weight of being a master mage."

"Mother," said Toby, watching her pace stiff-legged in front of the mirror.

"Why would they do such a thing after what that snake did? I'll just have to speak to someone about this."

"Mother," he said a little louder.

"No. I can't do that. No one would listen to me. Master O'dorn. Yes, he can talk to someone at the High Council. They know what happened. Surely they wouldn't want a Ribaldy at the academy."

"Mother," shouted Toby.

"Don't worry, son," Adele continued, turning to sit and face the orange tom. "I'm sure we can fix this."

"Mother, please. There's nothing to fix."

"Toby, you don't understand. You can't trust a Ribaldy."

"Lorn isn't his uncle."

"Can he do magic?"

"Sure," he temporized.

"By that I assume you mean he can do magic, but not very well."

"Something like that."

"Toby, do you know why Master Kiyoshi was partnered with Hecktor Ribaldy?"

"Master Jalen said it was because they had unique talents that complimented each other."

"That's putting it nicely," growled Adele. "Master Jalen has always down-played the differences between master mages and master cats, especially in their case. The truth is Master Kiyoshi kept Hecktor from blowing everything to kingdom come with his wild experiments."

"Oh."

"Yes. Oh. And now you're partnered with his nephew."

Toby wasn't sure what to say. He couldn't tell his mother about the exploding homework or how things Lorn had carefully laid out for class at night went missing every morning. He didn't want to broach the real reason for the call now. Asking about his father's disappearance after his mother's outburst seemed like asking for trouble. Yet, he needed that information. Bracing himself for more ranting, he decided to steer the conversation in the direction he needed.

"Actually, mother, I didn't call to talk about Lorn. I wanted to ask you a question about Father."

"What about your father?"

"I wanted to know about the mission he went on before he disappeared."

"Why do you want to know about that?" asked Adele, voice low, ears flat to her head.

"I was just curious," answered Toby, trying to look innocent.

"Curiosity is a bad thing. Forget it. You need to concentrate on your studies so you can become a full apprentice."

"But—"

"Leave it *alone*, Toby." The image of his mother shattered, leaving the young tom staring at his own reflection again.

Toby and Lorn were racing to the Commons for lunch the next day when he spotted Master O'dorn exiting the Administration Building.

"You go ahead. I'll see you in class," he shouted to Lorn, turning to intercept the old mage. The orange tom raced toward his old friend.

"Master O'dorn," said Toby as he skidded to a halt beside him.

"Apprentice Toby, what an unexpected surprise." The master mage smiled.

"I'm glad you're here. I need to speak with you."

"I suspected as much. Young cats don't usually rush to

meet me on a whim."

"I'm sure you've heard about my conversation with mother."

The old mage nodded. Toby wondered what his mother had said. Master O'dorn's smile was sympathetic.

"Did she ask you to come here?"

"Yes, she did."

"So you've spoken to the head masters?"

"Yes, I did."

"Does that mean Lorn and I won't be partnered anymore?"

"Is that what you want, Toby?"

The young tom cocked his head to the side, wondering what it would be like to be partnered with a mage who didn't blow things up and randomly set things on fire. Things would certainly be simpler. Still, he and Lorn had a connection, a shared mystery they both wanted to solve.

"No."

"Are you sure? You realize how much more difficult it will be to move beyond provisional status with a mage such as Apprentice Lorn."

"I know, but I think Lorn and I can be a good team. Once he starts focusing on the lessons at hand and stops trying to twist them before we've learned how, that is."

"If he's anything like his uncle, that's not likely to happen." The man gazed into the sky, a smile quirking his lips. Toby waited for him to reply. Master O'dorn looked back down at the young cat when Toby cleared his throat.

"Did you know Master Ribaldy well?"

"Well enough."

"Mother didn't cast him in a very favorable light."

"That is because she blames Hecktor for your father's

disappearance."

"Is he to blame?"

The old mage gazed down at the young tom in silence. A light breeze tugged at the master mage's cloak and ruffled Toby's fur. He stared up at the old man, willing him to say something. He gestured for Toby to walk with him toward a bench at the coach stop.

"In a way, yes."

"But there's more to it, isn't there? Mother was furious when she found out I'd been partnered with Master Ribaldy's nephew. I know it was more than just her worrying about me being held back by a second-rate mage. She was scared. Why?"

"Tell me how much you know about your father's secret mission," said Master O'dorn, easing himself onto the stone bench. Toby leaped up beside him.

"I know he was sent by the High Council to gather information about something. Mother was very upset about it all."

"Upset is a mild way of putting it. Your mother was beside herself. She didn't understand why the High Council chose Victor out of all the possible loners and partners available."

The old mage sighed and rubbed his forehead between his thumb and fingers. Staring past the surrounding buildings, he folded his hands in his lap. Toby waited patiently.

"I wanted to tell her, but he swore me to secrecy," he murmured. The master mage looked down at the young cat. His eyes glistened. He reached out a trembling hand and stroked Toby's head.

"Your father was a very special cat. Brave and loyal beyond anything I'd known. It was his idea to go on the mission, not the High Council's. They needed someone to gather information on a particular ring of shadow arts marketers. They were going to send partners, but your father talked them around to sending him instead. He reasoned a loner would attract less attention and could get in and out before the criminals knew what he was doing."

Toby gaped at the man. All this time he'd heard his mother's side of the story, that the High Council didn't respect loners, that they considered them to be dispensable.

"Why didn't he tell her?"

"For the same reason you aren't going to tell her you've been given a special mission."

He felt his fur fluff. His heart began beating rapidly. How had the old mage found out?

"Relax, little friend," said Master O'dorn. "It is simple deduction on my part. Since you are not a cat prone to seeking abuse, there could be only one reason you would risk your mother's wrath on the very same question you now ask me."

The young cat opened his mouth to explain, but shut it again when the old mage motioned for him to be silent.

"I won't ask and I don't wish you to tell me. Whatever the reason for this mission, I trust your instincts as I trusted your father's. Now, what more can I tell you?"

"Do you know where father went or who he contacted?"

"He was sent to Hielberg County. I'm afraid I don't know who he may have contacted once he was there. You see, the High Council agreed that the details of such a dangerous mission shouldn't be known by everyone. Instead we decided that only the loner going and a single representative should be privy to all the information until the ring was brought down."

"And that representative was?" the tom asked, barely

breathing.

The master mage gazed down at the young cat in silence. He was reminded for a moment of his mother. The partners had worked together for so long it seemed they now could imitate the same stern expression.

"Toby," he said, "Just so you know, I was here on council business, not on your mother's."

A coach rounded the corner and made its way up the road toward them. The old mage levered himself off the bench. They watched quietly as the coachman deftly executed the circle turnabout and pulled the coach to the curb. As the driver slid the door open, Master O'dorn shuffled toward it. Toby took a step after the human.

"Master O'dorn, who was the representative?"

The man paused with his foot on the step. Turning, he fixed the orange tom with a piercing gaze.

"Master Hecktor Ribaldy."

The old mage swiftly pulled himself into the coach's interior. The door slid shut and the coachman urged the horses into motion, leaving Toby frowning.

Toby hurried to the head masters' office before the morning bell had rung. When the door swung open, he entered to find Master Meredith alone. She seemed to be in the middle of writing.

"Have a seat, Apprentice Toby," she said without looking up. The scritch scritch of the pen continued. Toby occupied himself with reading book titles from the shelves across the room. Nestled amongst histories and incantation books were a group of well-worn, leather bound tomes that looked vaguely familiar.

"Have you read them?" asked Master Meredith.

Toby jumped, nearly falling off his stool. He shook his head and licked his ruff, trying to cover his embarrassment. Ignoring the prickle of heat around his neck, he looked into the head master's eyes.

"I noticed you peering at those," the head master cat said, nodding toward the old books. "I wondered if you've ever read them."

Toby turned to stare at the old books.

"I'm not sure. They look familiar, but I can't read the names on the spines."

"Those are the Books of the One. Only a few copies exist outside the Temple."

"Is one of them called Moriel? I remember reading a story about a man who refused to fight and refused to give in. It was in that book."

"It seems your memory is as good as your nose. You are correct. The passive resistance parable is in Moriel."

"It's a good strategy, don't you think?" asked Toby. The image of a tortoiseshell she-cat leaving the scene of his altercation with Reginald burned in the tom's mind.

"Perhaps. Its basis lies in another of the books, Lemuel. It's a guideline followers of The One call The Priceless Measure."

"Wasn't that mentioned in Moriel, too?"

"Very good." The master cat waved her tail in an arc from the books toward herself, capturing Toby's attention.

"Now, as much as I enjoy engaging in religious conversations, I am sure you did not come here this early for that. What have you learned so far?"

"Not much. My mother and Lorn's father refused to talk about it. I asked Master O'dorn if he knew anything, but all he could tell me was that father volunteered to go and that

Master Ribaldy was the only member of the High Council who knew specifics about the mission."

"We thought as much since no one else seems to have any information. What else?"

"Lorn's mother wasn't much help either. She says it's all a huge injustice and starts to cry every time Lorn tries to ask her anything. She did mention that the High Council confiscated all of Master Ribaldy's things."

"Unfortunately we are well aware of that, too," said the master cat, flicking her tail at the paper she'd been writing on earlier. "This is our third attempt to legally obtain Master Ribaldy's notes on a lecture he was to give this semester."

"May I ask what he was going to talk about?"

"I think he called it "The Benign in the Shadow Arts." He was one of the most knowledgeable masters on how shadow arts practitioners twist curses using ingredients we use for healing." The master cat's eyes strayed to the fireplace where new wood stood ready to burn. The tortoiseshell stared intently at the wood for a moment, then whispered a spell. Flames appeared with a whoosh, settling into a cheery pop and crackle. Master Meredith turned her attention back to Toby.

"He promised it would be very enlightening."

For a moment, the young tom was reminded of his conversation with the gravin and his companion. A ripple ran from his shoulders to his tail.

"Based on what Gravin Arturo said, I can see why you're having trouble getting those notes from the High Council."

"Indeed." The tortoiseshell she-cat stared intently at Toby, making his fur twitch. He wondered if his mother had learned how to do that from the head master cat.

"Have you seen much of Terence lately?"

"No. Between classes and everything else I haven't had a chance."

Guilt pricked at the orange tom's skin. His paws itched to take him to his friend's room. He still felt odd when he thought about the young cat being sponsored by the gravin and his companion. Shivers ran the length of Toby's body as he remembered the overheard conversation between the two.

"Perhaps it is time you had a visit with your friend. Have him introduce you to some of his teachers."

"Okay," said Toby hesitantly. "Is there anyone in particular I should meet?"

"I think you'll find the secret missions instructors have many interesting stories. In fact, if I'm not mistaken, they were classmates with your father."

"I'll be sure to do that. Thank you."

The head master cat nodded and began sorting through a stack of papers on the desk. Toby waited to see if there was more Master Meredith would say. She continued to ignore him. Taking it as a dismissal, Toby hopped down from the stool and made his way to the door.

"Be sure to tell Master Antwan and Master Natsumi I said hello," said the master cat without looking up. Toby nodded and continued out the door.

The mid-morning bell rang signaling the beginning of second class. The orange tom scrambled down the stairs to race to class. He was going to be late again, but this time he wasn't wondering how many more times he could be tardy before his provisional status would be revoked. His only thought was how to meet with Terence.

Chapter 5

Toby located his friend during lunch sitting alone at a table near the back of the Commons dining hall, a large book open beside him. The young gray and white tom looked as if he were trying to burn a hole through the pages of the book by thoughts alone.

"That must be a very interesting book," chirped Toby.

Terence turned his head sharply toward the orange tom. At first the little cat glared at him, then recognition dawned. Whiskers splayed in a wide cat grin as the young cat patted the table to indicate Toby should join him. Toby leapt gracefully to a seat opposite his friend and said the incantation to make it rise.

"It is. I'm readin' about how we cats have made life better for everyone."

"Is that for one of your classes?" asked Toby between a mouthful of food.

"No. It's somethin' Master Chivato thought I might like."

"Oh. I'm surprised you have time for extra reading. I figured you'd be as busy as we are running from class to class."

"I am," snapped Terence.

Toby's eyes widened. He looked closer at the young cat. Besides having a dull coat, his friend was thinner than he'd been in orientation. A glance at the plate beside the book showed little evidence of being touched.

"I'm sorry. I didn't mean you aren't busy."

"No," said Terence. "I'm sorry. I'm just tired. That's all. There's so much to learn. I feel like I'm drownin' in books sometimes. Then I get asked to do extra readin' and, it's interestin' and all, but it's more readin'. I have to read it 'cause they're sponsorin' me and I gotta do what I can to impress them. You know?"

"Believe it or not I do. Mother was like that, too. She set regular studies and tasks for me, then she'd ask me to do a lot of extra work on top of it. It was like she was trying to find my breaking point or something."

Terence smiled again. Toby relaxed.

"Actually, I was hoping to take your mind off studying for a little bit."

"What do you mean?" Terence asked, eyes narrowed, whiskers suddenly clamped tight.

"I was wondering if you would show me around the loner-in-training side of campus," Toby said. "Maybe introduce me to a couple of your teachers?"

"Why?"

"My father was a loner, remember? He went to this academy, too. I thought maybe I might learn something about him from walking where he did."

Terence stared at Toby. The orange tom began to wonder exactly what Terence had been reading and how many other things Chivato had said to make the little gray and white tom so suspicious.

"I only remember a little about him from when I was a kitten."

"From the way you talked in orientation you remember a lot," Terence said sharply, still glaring at his old friend.

"I remember the lessons and the family things, yes, but I want to know what father was like before he and mother were mates. Mother says I'm just like him. I want to know how."

Terence glared on in silence. The conversations around them seemed louder as he waited. With a huge sigh, the little cat closed his eyes and relaxed again. He looked down at the open book again.

"I really should finish this," he said.

"We can always do it another time. If you need to study, then I understand."

The gray and white tom continued to stare at the open book. Suddenly he snarled at it. Flicking his tail, he slammed the book closed and looked up at Toby.

"No. I don't know when we'll have more time than now. Besides, I miss talkin' to you."

"Me, too."

The friends leapt down and floated their plates to the dish washing room. Terence carefully floated his book beside himself. As they left the Commons, Toby glanced sideways. He caught a whisker twitch from Terence.

"Still moving your leftovers?"

"Not usually, but I was lookin' forward to that meal."

Together they trotted toward the loner side of campus. As they walked, Terence chattered on about what life was like as a loner-in-training. Toby could almost believe his young friend was still the same little cat he'd met in orientation.

"Do you know Master Antwan and Master Natsumi? Master Meredith said she thought they were classmates with father."

"Yeah. I do. They're my favorite teachers."

"I don't suppose we could meet them today, could we?"

"I'm not sure, but we could take a peek into their office. Wanna race?" asked Terence. He catapulted away, his book flying behind him.

"Wait," yelled Toby, scrambling to catch up.

Terence careered around a corner and flew up a set of stone stairs. Toby barely caught sight of the little cat's tail as it disappeared through a narrow swinging door. The orange tom spared only a moment to wonder where Terence's book had gone before he barreled through the door and slammed into a charcoal gray shoulder. It felt like running face first into a fur covered suit of armor.

"Toby," hissed Terence. "Over here." Toby righted himself quickly and slunk over to his friend. The large tom eyed them coolly.

"Explain yourself, trainee," said the tom.

"We're sorry, Master Antwan. I was showin' Toby around the loner trainee side of campus."

The massive tom gave each young cat a hard stare. Terence lowered his head. Toby did the same. He concentrated on the large gray paws a foot away. They reminded him of his father's.

"Carry on, but slow down."

The massive paws padded toward the door. Toby realized his chance to ask the tom about his father's disappearance special mission was headed in the opposite direction.

"Master Meredith said to tell you hello," called Toby, hoping it was a code to let the loner know he could share his information with the orange tom.

The master cat swiveled his head in their direction. Terence glanced from the large gray tom to Toby, his whiskers twitching. The little gray and white patched tabby's ears swiveled outward. Toby ignored his friend's anxious looks, willing the large tom to return. Master Antwan turned around smoothly. Silently sitting down, he curled his tail around his paws.

"Master Antwan, did you know my father?" asked the orange tom.

"Possibly," said the tom. "Why do you ask?"

Toby glanced at his friend. He wondered how the little cat would react to knowing the real reason Toby wanted to meet this particular teacher. He wasn't sure he should let Terence in on the mission, but he couldn't see any way to avoid it now.

"He disappeared last spring, just before Master Ribaldy was imprisoned for treason. I'm trying to find out anything I can about the special mission he was on."

Terence's head snapped around toward Toby. The little gray and white tom's eyes were wide.

"You said you wanted to find out what your father was like before your folks were mates. You lied to me," the little cat hissed.

"I'm sorry, Terence. I was afraid you wouldn't take me to see Master Antwan if you knew the truth."

"But I don't understand. Why wouldn't I help you?"

"Because some of the information I have so far might cast a bad light on your sponsors. I thought you might want to protect them."

"Protect them? Why would I need to protect them? They haven't done nothing wrong."

"I don't know if they have or not. I just know something's going on in Hielberg County and Lorn and I have been asked to find out what we can about it."

"Just 'cause somethin's going on in the county doesn't mean the gravin and Chivato are in on it. It's a big place and bad 'un's are just as likely to be workin' there as anywhere without some noble's go ahead."

"That's true, trainee," interrupted Master Antwan. "Apprentice, what makes you think I have any information about your father's disappearance?"

"I'm not sure, sir. Master Meredith suggested speaking to you and Master Natsumi about it. She said you may have been classmates with my father."

Master Antwan cocked his head to the side.

"None of my classmates were bright orange. Loners are chosen for their special abilities, but even the best must look like any ordinary cat. I'm afraid Master Meredith is mistaken."

Toby sighed. He felt cursed.

"I'm orange because my mother was involved in a magical accident. Both she and my father are black."

"What's your father's name?"

"Victor."

The loner's eyes narrowed. He looked from Toby to Terence and back.

"Come with me. Both of you."

The two young cats looked at each other. Terence still looked miffed, but he turned to follow the loner instructor anyway. Toby followed along beside the little cat. He stole a glance from time to time at his friend. The tom's stiff-legged gait reminded him of times he had been angry with his mother. He wondered if his friend would ever forgive him. Master Antwan ushered the two cats into an office about the size of a broom closet and closed the door behind them.

"What we say here is not to be repeated, is that understood?" barked the loner.

"Yes, sir," answered Terence.

"I can only promise not to tell anyone beyond my mage and the head masters. They need this information as much as I do."

"So be it."

The loner reclined on a large cushion, tucking his paws under his chest, and motioned the two young cats to do the same. He fixed a steely gaze on Toby.

"Your father wanted to know if we had someone inside the shadow arts marketers with information on a particular trade going on in Hielberg County. We've been tracking the dragon willow trade on the shadow arts market for some time and have a few reliable informants, so we told your father how to contact one. A few weeks later Victor started sending us letters and packages containing valuable information that helped us shut down several major operations. They stopped arriving just before Master Ribaldy was discovered planting explosives beneath the High Council chambers."

"How can I contact the person my father talked to?"

"This is not a game, son. These are dangerous people. They don't let you walk away just because you're young and stupid."

"I didn't think they would, sir."

Master Antwan licked his ruff. His gaze remained hard when he looked back at Toby.

"I see you won't change your mind. Your father was the same way," said the loner. "You can find the man you need to talk to at the White Dog in the village down the road. Tell the bartender you need 'a pick me up because you've been dragon all day.' Sounds ridiculous, but crooks aren't especially bright."

"Thank you, Master Antwan," Toby said, dipping his head as he stood up.

The two young cats left in silence. The little gray and white cat padded lightly next to the orange tom. Toby considered how he and Lorn were going to sneak off campus to visit a pub on a school night. Going into the village wasn't prohibited during the weekend, but it was frowned upon on a weekday. Leaving campus at night was grounds for dismissal – if you were caught, that is.

"I'm comin' with you," declared Terence.

"What? No, Terence, it's too dangerous."

"Oh, please," snarled the little cat. "I've probably seen more danger than you could imagine."

"That's not what I meant. If we get caught you could be dismissed from the academy."

"Yeah, well, it'd be worth it if we could get our paws on more stuff to shut down those thugs. Gravin Arturo don't need that lot makin' trouble for him." Terence stalked alongside Toby until they reached the Commons.

"Let me know when you plan on leavin'."

Without a backward glance, the little gray and white patched tabby trotted back toward the loner side of campus.

The wind rattled the windows as the three bickered over how to execute the night's escapade.

"Absolutely not," argued Toby.

"But disguisin' ourselves would keep the nosey's outta our business," said Terence.

"I agree, but I will not let Lorn cast a spell. We could all end up looking like something from Erlgarth's Book of Mythical Beings, only not as pretty."

"Oh come on. That was just an accident and it wasn't

all my fault," Lorn pointed out.

Although he knew Lorn was right, he wasn't about to admit it. They'd been working on one of the basic transforming spells for class. While bringing an ingredient to the young mage, Toby had accidentally tipped a bottle over. The contents oozed into a puddle over his paws, making him dance backward just as Lorn upended another bottle into the potion they were stirring. As a result Toby had to endure having duck feet for the rest of the day. The itch alone made Toby think he would go mad, but it was mild compared to what Lorn suffered.

The potion exploded, covering his head in brown goo. The young mage panicked, tried to reverse the spell and managed to set his hair on fire mid-transformation. The young boy's mousy brown hair was beginning to grow back, though it hung in uneven clumps. The elfin points on the lad's ears had finally disappeared, too. Not even the head master mage could figure out just what the boy had done, so Lorn had been forced to wait for the spell to wear off. That took several days. It was one of the rare times when they had received a score of excellent, as well as a reprimand.

"Fine," growled Terence. "Lorn won't cast the spell. I will."

"Can you do that?" asked Lorn.

"I'm a loner trainee, remember? We have to know how to do it all."

"But isn't that dangerous?" asked Toby. Terence sighed.

"As dangerous as doin' any magic alone. 'Sides seems to me it's the only way we're gettin' outta here tonight and, if you're tellin' the truth, it's gonna be safer than havin' Lorn do it."

The partners looked at each other. Terence was right. This would be safer than having Lorn try to transform them, but it would still be dangerous. It seemed their only choice. Looking back at the little gray and white patched tabby, Toby gave the go ahead. The young cat closed his eyes.

A moment later Toby felt his skin begin to tingle. The pins and needles feeling grew until it felt like he was being clawed by hundreds of mice. The mice turned into rats and the rats into cats. The orange tom squinched his eyes against the pain. A moment more and a scream would rip itself from behind his clenched teeth. It stopped. The table beneath him jumped. There was a thud, followed by a low moan from the floor. Toby's eyes flew open. He stared down at a large bearded man and a small brown dog. He looked down at his own paws to see the same brown hair and paws as the dog on the floor.

"Oh," groaned the man, holding his head as he sat up. "So this is what it's supposed to feel like."

"Yep. Awful ain't it?" barked the little dog on the floor.

"Better than when we tried it," barked Toby. The man glared at him.

"At least it worked right," he said, still glowering at the little brown dog on the table.

"Okay, so how we gonna get into town?"

"There's a coach stop down the road a bit. A coach comes by every couple of hours. The academy teachers come and go at irregular intervals day and night," said the man.

"How do you know that?" asked the little dog on the floor.

"Don't ask," answered Toby from the table, thinking about the narrow escapes his mage had experienced with his quick trips into town for necessary supplies, all of which were never teacher approved. He hopped down and joined Terence on the floor. They trotted to the door.

"Wait," called Lorn, standing up. "How am I supposed to tell you apart?"

"Won't matter. We're just dogs. Won't no one expect us to say much 'cept 'Bark. Bark.'"

"I'm afraid Terence is right. I've never heard a dog speak, though Master O'dorn has said there are a few who do. I'd rather not be remembered as one of those rare breeds. Lorn this is going to be up to you."

Lorn paled. He ran a meaty hand through dark curls and shifted his considerable weight from one foot to the other. The boy turned man inhaled. Letting out a loud exhale, he straightened.

"Let's go then. We're wasting time here."

To anyone else, Toby knew he looked like an ordinary border terrier, though perhaps a little better groomed than some of the others in the White Dog, human and animal alike. Like trained beasts he and Terence walked on either side of the miniature mountain between them. Lorn had traded his merchant-styled clothes for a pair of grubby breeches and a shirt that Mariam wouldn't have used for rags. They didn't ask where Terence had found the clothes when he produced them. The smell of years' worth of sweat and rotten food was enough to stop any questions.

The three shuffled to the end of the bar closest to the door. Lorn crammed his shoulders between a little rat-faced man and the wall. He gestured politely toward the bartender. A boisterous shout came from the other end of the room where a game of chance was taking place. The barman thunked several mugs of ale onto a platter and shoved it into the waiting hands of a serving wench.

"Excuse me," said Lorn, making another small wave toward the barkeep.

"That ain't gonna work," whispered Terence. "You gotta act like you belong here."

"And exactly how do I do that?" Lorn whispered back sharply. Terence peered around. He fixed his gaze on the barman.

"Hey, ugly, you gonna let a man die a' thirst?" he shouted.

The bartender's head snapped around. He stomped toward the man and his two dogs. Lorn's hand trembled on the counter.

"Wadda ya wan'," growled the barkeep.

"In-in," stammered Lorn. He cleared his throat to try again.

"Information," he said.

"We ain't sellin'."

The bartender turned to walk away. Toby's heart leapt. Terence barked sharply, catching the man's attention.

"Yer dogs is noisy," he said, pointing a finger at the door. "Shut 'em up 'r git 'em out."

The barman turned to walk away again. Terence dropped back to the floor, growling as he tugged at Lorn's pocket. Lorn pulled away with the sound of ripping cloth. In an instant Terence had his paws back on the counter, dropping a cloth bundle in front of Lorn with a clink. He barked again.

"I said—"

The barkeep strode back to them and eyed the little bundle. He reached toward it. Two brown paws, one on either side of the man, slammed down on the money pouch. Both dogs uttered a low growl, showing their formidable teeth. The man looked from one dog to the other.

"I don' 'ave no infermayshun," he said, licking his lips. "Jus' got good drinks is all."

"In that case, I need a pick me up because I've been dragon all day."

"Wa'cha be needin' then is some ale an' a bit 'a comp'ny. Rachel," he hollered. "Show these fine gen'lmen to our best table."

A voluptuous young wench in a low-cut peasant's dress sauntered up to them. Lorn placed his hand on the bar to heave himself off his stool. The bartender's fingers snaked out and grabbed his wrist.

"That'll be two silvers."

The young mage gulped. He dug through the money pouch, then shakily dropped two silver coins into the barkeep's open palm.

"This way, gen'lmen," purred the wench.

The three followed the young woman to an empty table at the back in a darkened corner next to the huge fireplace. Rachel prodded it with a long poker, then flounced away. Lorn crammed his large body into a chair behind the table, facing the rest of the room. Toby and Terence took up a stool to either side of the boy turned man.

"She didn't ask if I wanted something to drink," said Lorn.

"You're only here for information. She don't expect you to want a drink. Now listen up. Our snitch'll be here any moment."

Toby listened intently as Terence hastily whispered instructions to Lorn on what to ask and how to act. A wiry man approached their table, his rolling gait making it clear he was more comfortable on a boat than on land. He yanked out the chair opposite the small group, spun it around and landed on it to straddle the back.

"I 'ear tell ya lookin' fer a pick me up," said the man as he leaned on the chair back.

"Aye," answered Lorn.

"Bin drag'n?"

"Aye."

"May hap I got wot ya need, 'cept there's this thing. Gotta terrible thirst 'n got no coin, see?"

"I believe this'll buy you a drink or two," said Lorn, pushing two silver coins toward the man.

"Tha's a start, but, ya see, I gotta real pow'rful thirst."

Lorn dug another silver coin from the money pouch. The man reached for the coin, eying the pouch. The boy turned man closed his meaty fist around the coin.

"You get it after you talk."

The man ran his hand over his shaved head, scratching a spot just above a dragon tattoo. He glanced behind him. Licking his lips he leaned in closer. Lorn leaned in too.

"How much ya wan'?"

"How much do you have?"

The man glanced at the money pouch again. He leaned across the table, his hand snaking out. Toby caught a whiff of marigolds and wet metal. He sneezed. The man jumped. Lorn seized the ruffian's wrist.

"You see my friend here?" asked Lorn in a low voice. He jerked his head toward Terence, who gave a feral grin. The man tried to wrench away. Lorn squeezed tighter.

"He doesn't take kindly to thieves."

Terence growled. Lorn let go of the man's wrist with a shove.

"Now," said the boy turned man, "I think we were in the middle of making a deal."

"Cap'n's gotta boat load headin' out t'marra."

"Does he have a buyer yet or do we have a chance at it?"

"Oh 'e's always gotta buyer afore he sets out. But if'n the price is right?"

The man licked his lips and lifted an eyebrow. Toby's lip lifted in an instinctive snarl. He snapped at the air and huffed, wondering what price the captain would place on his own mother. Lorn scratched the dog's ear.

"That's good. Still, I don't want an angry buyer tracking me down because he thinks I stole his property."

"Aye," said the man, darting glances at Toby. "Don' think you'll have that 'appen, though."

"Oh?"

"Bloke's attached to a House. Don' think 'e'll wan' his Master to find out 'e's runnin' goods."

"Which House?"

"Hielberg."

Lorn leaned back in his chair and pulled at his beard.

"So we gotta deal 'r nah?"

"Too risky."

"Jus' like th' other 'un." He spit on the floor, then sneered at the mountain man and his dogs.

"The other one?"

"Big black tom like tha' ya think's 'e got balls, but nah. No guts. Backed outta th' take when 'e 'eard who 'e's stealin' from."

"Did he have a name?" asked Lorn. Toby glanced at his partner from the corner of his eye. He recognized that predatory look. It was the same one Lorn got every time he thought

141

he was on to a way no one had thought of to twist a spell.

"Don' take names, jus' coin," replied the ruffian, tapping the table next to the two silvers. Lorn tossed the third coin next to its mates. The man scooped them up and left.

The walk to the coach stop felt longer. The streets leading away from the White Dog to the more civilized areas of the town were shadowed and crowded with heaps of cloth that sometimes moved. Toby jumped as a shadow separated itself from the surrounding gloom. A woman in filthy rags sauntered toward them, her large breasts sagging beneath a thin layer of cloth. She smiled a come-hither smile, revealing missing and rotten teeth. Terence growled. The woman took a step back, studying the brown dog. She looked back up at Lorn. She reached a hand toward the boy turned man. Terence barked sharply. The woman made a shooing motion toward the dog. Toby stepped up beside his friend and growled at the woman. Casting a glare at the three the woman shuffled away.

The group hustled down the dark streets. Lorn snagged the clothes he'd left bound into a bundle in the alley a couple streets away from the stop. Once they reached the academy and the coach had driven away, Terence reversed the transformation spell.

"I hope I never have to do that again," said Lorn, stripping off the foul linens he was wearing and exchanging them for his own clothes. "I was sure that old woman was part of some trap."

"She might have been. That's why I made Toby 'n me dogs. Figured less likely to mess with a man with two dogs."

"Great thinking," said Toby. He felt a glow of pride creep over his skin.

142

"Just part of the trainin'."

"Let's get back to the room and discuss what we've found out."

The three hurried toward Toby and Lorn's building, putting the largest hedgerow between themselves and the administration building's illuminated windows. Toby wondered who was serving detention tonight. A robed figure stepped in front of them, the light from a nearby lantern post throwing the dark figure's shadow across them.

"Stop right there," said a stern female voice.

The little group halted. Toby's tail fluffed to twice its size. He recognized the voice from their history class. Master Hedy was the one instructor who gave them detention every time they were tardy, which happened to be every fifth week. *Is it fifth week already?* Toby wondered if the night's adventures had made Lorn bold as he took a step toward the teacher, straightening his back and lifting his chin.

"Master Hedy, we were just –."

"You were on your way back from being off campus. At night."

"But, Master Hedy, we can explain," said Toby.

"I'm sure you can and you will. You are hereby confined to your quarters until a proper hearing tomorrow in which your status will be reconsidered. That includes you as well, trainee."

"Yes, ma'am," said the three.

The master mage stood aside as the youths slipped past. Toby glanced behind them as they left the shelter of the hedge. Master Hedy was glaring at their backs. Just on the other side of the hedge, hidden from the master mage's sight, sat a spot of pure white fur with glowing yellow eyes and a smug expression on his face – Reginald.

Chivato watched the black tom saunter into the work room, his glittering green eyes scrutinizing the room.

"Is it ready?"

The gray tom bowed his head.

"Almost. I invited you here to see its final test."

He thrust his chin toward the waiting test subject. A man in ragged clothes sat shackled to the floor across the room. He glared at the cats.

"Ye said I'd get fed, cat. Fed and warm. Didn't say nothing about taking no test."

"Not to worry, friend. This is a test you cannot fail even if you try." Chivato motioned a young cat to take a bowl of lumpy white gruel to the human. The small feline nodded and nudged the bowl with his paws toward the man.

"Now that's more like it."

The man snatched the bowl from the cat's paws before he'd completed the distance, bringing the bowl to his lips and slurping the gruel. A magic shield snapped up around the two. The young cat whirled around, his eyes wide, fur standing on end. He looked back over his shoulder as the man began choking.

"As you can see, a full dose ingested by mouth has almost instantaneous results."

The man's eyes began to bulge. The sound of wheezing breath filled the work room as he slumped to the floor. He stretched a feeble hand toward the young cat. The tom backed away, the hair along his back standing up in a ridged spike, his tail fluffed. He bumped into the shield. He whirled around and clawed at it.

"Let me out!"

The man coughed and retched. Blood-filled vomit ran across the floor, stopping inches from the young cat's feet.

The cat screamed and clawed at the shield. The man lay upon the floor, his labored breath stilling. The shield vanished. The tom ran past the older cats to hunch himself, shivering, in a corner on the opposite side of the room. The black cat padded forward to peer at the dead human. He looked toward the trembling young feline in the corner.

"What of him? Is he infected as well?"

"No. If he had been, he would have died the same as the human."

"Impressive."

"Thank you. I believe this is my finest work yet."

"And what of its rate of infection?"

"Depending on how the subject is infected, it could be anywhere from a few moments to two weeks."

"Is there any way to even that out?"

The gray tom stared at the corpse on the floor, his eyes narrowed.

"If I narrow the ways of infection and alter the potency of the initial ingredients, maybe add a time release agent..." Chivato ignored the sound of the black tom's tail thumping on the floor.

"Can it be done?"

"I'll need to consult my human to be sure, but, yes, I believe it can be done."

The black tom's eyes narrowed, the hair around his neck bristling.

"Do you need his help?"

"I can make the adjustments myself, but I cannot be certain of the results and it will take more time before it will be ready for distribution."

A growl rumbled from the cat. Chivato sat with his tail wrapped around his toes, his chin lifted. A moment crept by.

The black tom lashed his tail.

"Do as you must. I want it released in two days time."

"It will be done." The gray tom looked over his shoulder toward the door.

"Arturo, we have work to do."

The man, dressed in rough woven peasant clothes, strolled into the room, glancing at the dead human on the floor. Grabbing a leather apron from the wall by the door, he nodded at the gray cat. He side-stepped the bloody vomit and reached toward the corpse.

"You will need the gloves."

Arturo snatched back his hands, glaring at the gray tom. He stomped to the work room shelves and yanked a pair of elbow length leather gloves from a cupboard. After jerking the gloves on, the gravin hefted the dead body onto a small cart and rolled it away. The black tom watched him through narrow eyes until he disappeared beyond the door.

"I do not trust him."

"He is harmless, nothing more than a domesticated beast as he should be."

"So you say, but even a domesticated beast can turn on its handler."

Chapter 6

A dragon announced the hearing after the morning bell. Lorn and Toby arrived outside the conference room to find Terence already pacing in front of the closed doors.

"They've been in there an hour already," he said, looking up as the partners entered.

"Who's in there?" asked Toby.

"Looks like all the teachers who didn't have a class this mornin', plus the head masters. My sponsors are in there too," said the anxious young cat. "Oh. And your mother, Toby."

"Mother?" Toby's heart sank.

"Are my parents in there, too?" asked Lorn.

"Not sure. I didn't see 'em go in, but if they were here early they may have been in the room before I got here."

"Have you heard anything?" asked Toby.

"There was some yellin' when I first got here, but nothin' for the last little while."

Toby stared at the solid oak door, wishing he could see through it. He strained his ears forward. Not even a mumble. Lorn collapsed into an overstuffed armchair, cradling his head in his hands. Terence returned to his pacing. The three students waited. A woman in kitchen whites, laden with a tray of finger foods, went into the conference room just as the lunch bell sounded and returned empty handed. They heard the faint thump of an adjoining door close.

Toby hopped to the arm of Lorn's chair. He watched the door as the shadows in the room grew longer, stretching toward it. The dinner bell rang and Lorn's stomach growled. Terence curled up on a couch opposite the partners, wide eyes glowing in the orange sunlight fading from the window. The door latch clicking open made the three jump.

"If you would join us, please," said a master mage from the doorway.

Toby trotted in behind Lorn, finding it disconcerting to see the number of robe covered legs gathered around the enormous conference table. Just inside the door were three stools. The orange tom leaped onto the one to Lorn's left, leaving the one to the mage's right for Terence. Sober faces peered at the students. Toby forced himself to look only at the head masters as they entered from the opposite side of the room and seated themselves across from the students. The orange tom could feel his mother's heated gaze raking his fur.

"I believe, gentlemen, you are aware of the severity of the situation you are in," said Master Jalen. The three nodded.

"Ordinarily," continued the head master mage, "this hearing would be conducted solely by Master Meredith and myself. However, given that Trainee Terence is being sponsored by the gravin of Hielberg County himself and the circumstances surrounding the choosing of Apprentice Lorn Ribaldy, we have decided to include your teachers and guardians as well.

"During the time we have sequestered here, we have discussed academy guidelines and rules, as well as each of your performances to date. Your guardians have made assurances as to your characters and desire to continue your education."

Toby's fur prickled. His paws felt numb. He wrapped

his tail around his toes to still its trembling.

"We've taken everything into consideration as we deliberated and have come to a decision. Apprentices Toby and Lorn and Trainee Terence will remain at the academy to continue their studies for the time being," said Master Jalen.

The gathered mages erupted in sighs of relief and grumblings. Toby closed his eyes and exhaled. He heard the rustle of cloth as Lorn relaxed as well.

"But," said Master Meredith, raising her voice to be heard, "there will be restrictions."

Everyone quieted. Toby kneaded the stool beneath him, his breathing rapid. Master Meredith gazed sternly at the three students as she continued.

"You are confined to the grounds at all times unless accompanied by a teacher or with special written permission, which you are to keep on your persons at all times. Do you understand these requirements?"

"Yes, Head Master," the three answered together.

"At any time, should you choose to disregard these restrictions, you will be dismissed from the academy without another hearing. Do you understand these consequences?"

"Yes, Head Master."

The head master cat looked to her companion. He nodded. The head masters stood together.

"Thank you, ladies and gentlemen, for your cooperation and aid in this matter," said Master Jalen, nodding to the gathered teachers and guardians. "This hearing is adjourned."

The instructors followed the head masters from the room, leaving the guardians to speak with their students. Toby wished he could scurry between their feet and out the door. He leaped from the stool, doing his best to make his fur lie flat.

"I hope you're satisfied," growled Adele. He heard the soft tear of carpet fibers from claws as she paced toward him.

"Just what did you think you were doing?"

Toby looked away from her piercing yellow eyes. There was nothing he could say. He watched as Lorn's father guided his son from the room by the shoulder, the man's fingers causing deep indentations in Lorn's clothing. The young mage's mouth was a grim line. Toby wondered where Lorn's mother was. Across the room sat Gravin Arturo, hands folded upon his cane's head and a frown upon his face. Chivato's stern expression mimicked his companion's. Both were listening closely to whatever Terence was telling them.

"Well?" asked Toby's mother.

"I was following up on something someone told me about father," answered Toby, still watching Terence and his sponsors.

Chivato was saying something. Terence looked down at his paws, then glanced at Toby. Chivato looked over at the orange tom, too. When he looked back at the little gray and white tom, his features softened. He moved closer, placing a fatherly tail across the little cat's shoulders and murmuring something in his ears. Terence nodded.

"Not that you care," Toby added under his breath.

Pain exploded from his ear. He gasped. A drop of blood fell upon the carpet. The young tom gaped at his mother. Her fur was fluffed, her teeth bared in a silent snarl. Toby barely registered the others exit as he stood staring at his mother. She shook her fur flat, gave one last glare at her son, and left without another word.

Several weeks passed. Lorn and Toby did their best to abide by the restrictions handed down by the head masters, even working harder to be on time to their classes. Toby wanted to meet with Terence again. He hoped the young tom would be able to help them discover who in the gravin's household would be trafficking in dragon willow. There never seemed to be enough time to locate the little trainee.

Sitting on Lorn's shoulder, Toby watched the lunch line snake toward the front of the dining room. He let his gaze meander over those already shoveling their food in. Mages and cats alike sat in small groups, each to their own kind just as they had during orientation. As he continued to look around he saw a lone tom seated near the large windows. The little gray and white tom was engrossed in a large book, his untouched plate of food beside him.

"Fix me a plate," Toby said, jumping down from the young mage's shoulder.

Toby wove his way between tables toward the young patched tabby. The little cat's ears were pricked toward the book, as if he could hear the words being spoken. He twitched his tail to turn the page. Toby leaped to the seat opposite the tom.

"Hey," he said.

Terence jumped and squeaked, his eyes wide.

"That must be some scary book," said Toby with a chuckle.

The young cat licked his ruff, then glared at the orange tom. Without a word he bent back to his book. Toby blinked in confusion. He waited, thinking maybe Terence was trying to find a good stopping spot, but the little tom continued reading. Toby glanced around to see where Lorn was. The young mage was just finishing their selections.

"We were wondering if you had any ideas who might be getting that shipment," Toby whispered.

Terence said nothing. Another page flipped. Toby glanced around the room, looking for his companion. Lorn was walking toward them now. Toby turned his attention back to his feline friend. The little gray and white tom's whiskers were clamped together, his ears at half-mast.

"Terence?"

The little tom sighed. He gave Toby a pained look.

"The shipment?"

"You know, the one that – person – told us about."

"I know what you're talkin' about," he snapped.

"Well, do you have any ideas? Has – he – said anything about it?"

"No. Now leave me alone."

Toby drew back as if bitten. Terence went back to reading. The orange tom eased forward to look the young cat in the eye.

"Is something wrong?"

Terence growled, glaring at him. Toby felt his stomach clench. The hair on his spine rose.

"Wrong? What could be wrong?"

"You just seem so angry. I thought –"

"I don' care what you thought," snarled the young cat. "In fact seems to me you don' think. You're just like all the rest of 'em. It's just like Chivato says. You been given cream all your life so you don't know what it's like to have t'fight for what you need. You haven't had to think about no one else but you, so when someone feeds you a lie you swallow it and take everyone down with you."

"A lie? Terence, I don't understand."

"For all you know that man in the pub was a set up. There's a hunt goin' on, or didn't you know that."

"Yes. Gravin Arturo said as much."

"An' you didn't think it was weird that a scum like that would be pointin' fingers at a great man like the gravin?"

"But the evidence –"

"What evidence? Everythin' points to Lorn's uncle. It always has and you know it. Now the High Council's just tryin' to poke around t'see if Ribaldy had any help an' if they can take down the gravin along the way that'd be just peachy. Everyone knows he's always said the High Council pokes its nose into our business, tellin' us how we gotta do things, never lettin' us rise above where they think we oughtta be."

"Terence, I didn't know you felt like that."

"You never asked."

Plopping down in the seat next to the orange tom, Lorn set both plates on the table.

"Hey, guys."

Terence swung his heated gaze toward the young mage. Lashing his tail, he slammed the large book closed. He looked back at Toby.

"Maybe you oughtta think about your situation a bit before you start slingin' muck," the little cat said, casting a sidelong glance at Lorn. Leaping from his seat, Terence floated the large book and his plate of untouched food behind him. Toby watched him leave.

"What was that about?" asked Lorn.

"I think we've stirred up a dragon's nest."

"He's not going to help us anymore, is he?"

Toby watched the doors close behind his friend, wondering what Chivato had said after the hearing.

Toby and Lorn managed to be in their seats for Basic Health and Wellness moments before the class bell rang. Terence's words still blazed in Toby's ears. It wasn't until Lorn poked him in the side that he realized two newcomers were addressing the class instead of the regular instructor.

"Thank you for allowing us to speak with your class," said the short, round man, bowing his tonsured head toward the teacher. As he turned back toward the class, he clasped his hands and bowed his head. A few moments later he looked up to gaze around at the students. Toby began to wonder if the man had forgotten what he had planned to say.

"My fellow travelers, for that is what we are," said the man. Toby had to perk his ears forward to hear him.

"I am Brother Jason and this is my companion in The One, Brother Yannis."

Toby craned his neck to see a shaggy long-furred cat sitting on the floor beside the rotund human. The yellowing fur had been shaved in a rough circle on the old cat's head.

"We come to you today in need."

"I thought The One supplied all your needs," jeered Reginald from the front row.

"Indeed The One does. Blessings to you, my friend, for correcting my direction," said Brother Jason with a smile. "In truth we are here today to ask you to join us in The One's harvest. In the First Book of The One it is said that our Divine Creator will bring up a bountiful crop, but there will be few to harvest it. Our fellow brethren in the Temple of The One are experiencing this verse first hand. Our hallowed halls are filled beyond capacity and we are sending out as many Brothers and Sisters as we can spare into the Lower Districts, but we are too few to give more than meager comfort. Many souls are being lost because we cannot reach them in time."

"Reach them in time? What do you mean?" asked a young girl in the class.

Brother Jason's smile faltered. He looked down at his

companion, his eyes crinkling as if in pain.

"There is a great sickness sweeping through the Lower Districts," said the old cat in a voice that reminded Toby of rusty hinges.

"Many are dying," added Brother Jason.

"Wait a minute. You're asking us to risk getting sick, maybe even dying, to help you save a few souls? That's madness," said Reginald

"Perhaps it is," said Brother Yannis, "but The One gave us The Priceless Measure as our guide. Whatever we would want someone else to do for us we must do for others. We cannot turn our backs upon the sick and dying just because we fear death."

"Is this required to pass the class?" asked another student.

"No, this is strictly voluntary," answered the teacher, stepping up to pat Brother Jason on the back while looking at each student in turn.

"Anyone moved to help our friends at the Temple may petition the head masters for special permission to be a part of the relief group sent to the Lower Districts. You will need to give the head masters a written release signed by your parents or guardians and a brief explanation of why you believe you should be allowed to participate in the group no later than next week. The head masters will choose who will go from those petitions."

The silence broke into murmurs. Brother Jason shook hands with the teacher, then left with Brother Yannis.

"Okay, class, I know you have a lot of questions, but they'll have to wait until after our session together to ask them. For now, we need to tackle how the body works."

Toby couldn't concentrate on the subject. He was

struck by what the old cat had said about risking his own life because of something he had read in an ancient book. Loathe as he was to admit it, he agreed with Reginald. It made no sense to put himself into a situation that would likely end up killing him just to make someone else happy for a few moments.

Trying to uncover the secret Victor was digging up was dangerous, yes, but it was something that needed to be done for the sake of the entire kingdom, not just a few souls who might die before hearing about The One. No, Toby decided, he felt badly for those in the Lower District, but his time would be better spent retracing his father's mission.

"What do you think about all that?" whispered Lorn.

"I think it's terrible."

"Think we should volunteer?"

"Why?"

"Isn't the Lower District where Terence is from? Maybe that's why he's been so edgy."

"I never thought about that."

Terence's words rang in Toby's mind. The orange tom spent the rest of class weighing the choice between volunteering for the relief group and continuing on the special mission they'd been given by the head masters.

Master Meredith sat at the desk, studying the papers she had in front of her. Toby wondered if it was her habit to always complete one task before moving on to the next — the next being him. He tried not to fidget.

"Okay, Toby, what have you learned?" asked the head master cat, looking up from her paperwork. "I assume it has something to do with your recent disobedience."

The orange tom searched her face, wondering what

she was thinking.

"Yes, it does. Lorn and Terence and I went to the White Dog to speak with the man my father had talked to."

"And what did this man tell you?"

"There's a shipment of dragon willow going out sometime soon to someone connected to the gravin in Hielberg County."

"How large a shipment?"

"According to the man, it's an entire boat load."

"Are you sure?" asked Master Meredith, her eyes narrowing.

"Yes, ma'am."

The tortoiseshell queen turned to stare out the window. The fur rippled down her back.

"You took a big risk going to that pub. Did you eat or drink anything while you were there?" she asked, turning back around. Toby blinked. He remembered Lorn being surprised that they weren't served anything, but it didn't seem like a big deal.

"No, ma'am."

"Did anyone recognize you?" asked the head master cat, leaning forward.

"I don't think so. We were in disguise."

"What kind of disguise?"

"Lorn looked like a man from one of the outer reaches and Terence and I were two plain brown dogs."

"You mean you used an illusion spell?"

"No, ma'am, we transformed ourselves."

"You used a transformation spell?" she asked, eyes widening. "After what happened the last time you two tried changing your appearances I would have thought you would have been more careful. I'm surprised you weren't changed into something unsavory."

"Terence did it."

"Ah, I see. It seems you were correct in your assessment of the young cat's talents. Still, that was a dangerous thing to do."

He ducked his head to hide his smile. Terence might not want anything to do with him anymore, but Toby couldn't help feeling proud of the little cat. He glanced up at Master Meredith through his eye whiskers, noticing her whiskers twitch. Her gaze softened.

"I'm glad none of you were harmed. I assume you had the presence of mind to keep your mouths shut while you were dogs."

Toby raised his head and nodded.

"Good. That alone may keep you from being targeted. It may have been why you weren't offered anything to eat or drink, as well. A good disguise is worth a king's ransom when the stakes are this high."

"Excuse me, ma'am, but why would our disguise keep us from getting any food or ale?"

"Be glad it did, Toby. Many have tried to do as you three did and ended up poisoned for their trouble."

He shivered.

"What would our mysterious person connected to Gravin Arturo want with an entire boat load of dragon willow?" murmured the tortoiseshell queen, looking back down at the desk.

"The gravin did say it would fetch a good price on the shadow arts market," offered Toby.

"That is true, but there aren't that many assassins out there who would need a large supply, especially one this large."

"Assassins?"

"Yes, Toby, dragon willow is most often used in assassinations – poisonings to be precise. A talented shadow arts mage can create a poison from the bark that mimics many diseases and is difficult to detect."

"Is there anything else it could be used for? Anything good?"

"Yes. Dragon willow is the best known aid for many diseases. That's why it's such a popular choice amongst assassins. Turn a cure into a poison, then, when the target is given a second dose of untainted dragon willow, the effect is doubled, leading to a very painful death. I just can't see why anyone would need such a large amount."

Toby considered what the gravin had said about trying to deal with shadow arts marketers and of Terence's insistence that he was a great man.

"Ma'am, is it possible Gravin Arturo has his own relief plan for the Lower District? Maybe he's going to give the dragon willow to them."

"That would be a very noble thing to do, but if he were going to do that why use the shadow arts marketers to ship it?"

"Well, I suppose he could be planning to capture them first," Toby said.

"That wouldn't be out of character. It seems he has worked with the loners to shut down a number of trafficking rings."

Toby couldn't shake the feeling that they were missing something. Master Meredith sighed, closing her eyes. Her whiskers drooped and her shoulders sagged. The orange tom thought she looked tired.

"I will have to discuss this with Master Jalen. In the

meantime, apprentice, please remember that you are under restrictions. Under no circumstances are you to continue digging into this matter without first consulting myself or Master Jalen. Is that understood?"

"Yes, ma'am."

"Good."

The young cat jumped to the floor and left. As the door shut behind him, Toby continued to ponder the meaning behind the large shipment of dragon willow. He would have liked to ask Terence. His thoughts were going nowhere until he remembered. There were two other people he had yet to talk to about it – or more precisely a person and a cat.

After making a mirror call to the Office of the High Council, being transferred to several different secretaries and then back to the first person they'd talked to, Toby and Lorn had managed to find out the academy liaisons were out of the office for the rest of the week. They could, however, leave a message and someone would get back to them as soon as possible.

They left a message.

"That was helpful," said Lorn sarcastically.

"I suppose we can't expect them to be available just whenever. Still, it's frustrating." Toby paced the length of their work table.

"Well I'm all out of ideas." He sat down to face Lorn.

"Yeah. Me, too."

The silence lengthened as they tried to think of anyone else they could ask for information. The young cat stared at the pile of textbooks perched on the edge of the table, hardly touched since the semester began. Toby could almost hear his mother's growl coming from those books.

"We could always study."

Lorn groaned and reached for the top book, stretching his arm toward the pile as if it lay beyond a deep chasm. Toby grimaced at his companion's melodramatic flair. The mirror chimed. Their gazes shot to the shimmering surface. Scrambling away from the work table, they leaped to answer the incoming call.

"Hey, guys," said Alie.

"Hey," said Lorn. "We thought you were going to be gone all week."

"We are. I just happened to check our messages before leaving," said Dora.

"So what's up?" asked Alie.

"We were wondering if you'd be free for a visit here sometime soon," said Toby.

"We're scheduled to stop by the academy at the end of the month to pick up some paperwork for the High Council. Wanna have lunch?"

"You're not stopping by anytime sooner?" asked Lorn.

Toby shot him a reproachful look. Alie and Dora glanced at each other.

"We're not scheduled to be there until Last Day. Why?"

"Is there any way you could sneak in a visit this week?" asked Toby.

Dora looked down at something beneath the mirror's view. Alie hunched over the little cat and pointed to something. The little calico cat shook her head and tapped a delicate paw against what Toby assumed must be a schedule. Alie studied it, shaking her head. Her face brightened and she pointed to another spot to the left. Dora's whiskers splayed into a grin.

"Would Fifth Day be soon enough?" asked Alie.

Virginia Ripple

"Perfect," said Lorn.

"Great," said Alie, snatching a charcoal nub from thin air and writing on the schedule. "You can tell us all about what's so important then. See ya later."

Fifth Day came slowly. Toby and Lorn were shivering at the coach stop as soon as the sun was up. The cold breeze found its way under Toby's orange fur despite its thickening layers.

"A warming spell would be nice right about now," said Lorn through chattering teeth.

"Do we know any?"

"I think I remember one my tutor had me try." Lorn cupped his trembling, pale hands. He opened his mouth to speak the incantation.

"Before you say anything, are you sure you have the words firmly in mind?"

"Yes."

"And you're sure you know the correct inflections to use."

"Yes."

Toby jumped down from the bench and trotted away a couple of paces. The orange tom sat down, curling his tail around his toes. Lorn glared at him.

"Why are you sitting over there?"

"I don't want to get singed when you burst into flames."

The young mage rolled his eyes. He cupped his hands again and stared intently at his palms, his brow furrowed. Toby felt his fur crackle as the boy whispered the spell. A small orange ball swirled into existence in Lorn's cupped hands. The young man grinned at his friend. Toby paced forward. The orange ball remained steady. The tom leaped onto

162

the bench. Lorn sat down beside him and lowered the globe to the cat's eye level. It was giving off warmth that made Toby grin.

"Good job," said the orange tom, looking up at the young mage.

The sound of horse hooves made the friends look toward the road. In a flash the orange ball sizzled and grew white. Lorn dropped it, cursing as he shook his blistering hands. The ball bounced off the walkway. It shot past Toby, scorching the fur along his side, and up into the sky. Toby watched in horror as the white ball of fire arched through the air and plummeted toward the prize herb garden outside the Common.

"Ecks PLOden dis PERsal," shouted Lorn, waving wildly at the impending disaster.

The ball burst into showers of red, yellow and orange sparks, dissipating before they reached the garden shield. Toby sighed in relief. He wondered if he'd ever get used to things like this happening. As he blinked the afterimages away, he heard Chivato's dire suggestion about being partnered with Lorn in his mind.

"I've never had anyone set off fireworks for me before."

Toby turned to see Alie grinning at them. Dora hopped up beside the orange tom with a little chirp.

"Sure. The academy liaisons deserve the best," said Lorn with a smile.

He glanced at Toby, his eyes pleading with the cat not to say anything. Toby forced his whiskers apart to mimic the young mage's smile. He managed to flatten his fur, but his tail remained twice its normal size. The tom dangled it out of sight behind the bench and hoped the little calico wouldn't notice.

"So, would you care to tell us what was so important we had to schedule an extra stop in our rounds?" asked Dora.

"Couldn't you just tell us whatever it is over the mirror?"

Toby glanced at his companion who gave a small nod. The tom looked back at the young woman and then to the she-cat.

"Let's go somewhere quiet."

"How about the tearoom in the library?" asked Dora.

"There's a tearoom in the library?"

"Yep," said Alie with a chuckle. "It's strictly for teachers and visitors, but I'm sure it'll be fine as long as you're with us."

The group hurried across the campus. The warm, musty smell of old books was a welcome relief from the bitter cold, as was the hot tea and milk.

"I'm assuming you didn't freeze yourselves just to enjoy a nice hot drink with us," said Alie.

"No, we didn't," said Lorn, looking at Toby.

"We were hoping you knew something about the dragon willow trade on the shadow arts market."

"Other than the general information we send out to the public," said Dora, "there's very little we can tell you."

"Journeymen aren't privy to the specifics. It's a security issue since we're only in the High Council Liaison Program for three years. After that who knows where we'll end up."

Toby's ears flattened in frustration.

"I don't suppose you could tell us anything about my uncle's case, then."

"According to what little information we have, it's pretty cut and dried. I'm sorry, Lorn, but every scrap of evidence we've seen points straight to your uncle as being a traitor," said Alie, leaning forward to put a gentle hand on the young boy's. Dora looked from Lorn to Toby, eyes intent.

"You already knew all that, though. What's this really about?"

Toby glanced around the room, then leaned forward.

"We're trying to find out what my father was doing just before he disappeared. He was on the trail of someone connected to Gravin Arturo's House who was buying large amounts of dragon willow on the shadow arts market. Somehow Lorn's uncle is another piece to the puzzle, but we don't know how and we can't get access to any of his notes."

"We were hoping you might be able to find out something. You know, keep your eyes and ears open."

Alie captured her bottom lip between her teeth and looked toward Dora.

"We can do that, but I don't know how much we could help."

"We hear a lot of gossip and rumors, but that's about it."

The young calico's fur shivered, her eyes wide. The young woman cocked her head to the side.

"What about the records we're shelving all the time? There might be something in one of those."

Dora licked a paw, her tail twitching. When she looked back at the partners, her whiskers were drooping.

"I don't know. It's a long shot."

"A long shot is more than we had a moment ago," said Toby, ears perking up. The calico's ears swiveled outward as her brow furrowed.

"We'll see what we can dig up. In the meantime you two be careful."

The she-cat cast a sidelong glance at her companion.

The young woman studied her hands, sliding them below the table. When she looked back at Toby, she wore a thin smile, her dark eyes shining from a face that had paled. The tom turned his gaze back to the she-cat. Her whiskers were clamped tight.

"If there is someone in the Hielberg House into dragon willow trafficking, you can bet they won't find it hard to track down two nosy apprentices."

Chapter 7

Sitting on the top of the stairway, Toby marveled at the extravagance of the Fall Harvest Festival. The celebration after the partnering ceremony seemed like a thrown-together gathering by comparison. The banquet hall was adorned with everything from horns of plenty to tepees of cornstalks and mountains of pumpkins. Large tables laden with treats surrounded three sides of the large room. Dignitaries and students mingled amongst smaller tables bearing fall-colored table cloths. A few couples danced at the end of the room to the music of a small quartet.

"Lovely, isn't it?" asked Lilith, sitting beside him.

"It's absolutely amazing."

"Yes. It's not as grand as last year, but considering one-third of the kitchen staff left I'd say they did a wonderful job."

"Why did so many leave?"

"Most of them have family in the Lower District to care for. Others went to help friends."

Toby was speechless. The Brothers had said there were a lot of people dying, but he thought they had been exaggerating. He stared across the crowd and tried to imagine what it must be like in the Lower Districts now. He wondered again if he should volunteer to be a part of the relief group working with the Brothers. Would that make things better with Terence?

Lilith cleared her throat, making the young tom turn his attention back to her.

"How are you enjoying your apprenticeship?"

"It's harder than I expected, but not as difficult as my mother made it out to be."

"I'm sure you're doing fine. Just remember to ask for help when you need it."

Lilith splayed her whiskers and laid a gentle tail over Toby's shoulders before pacing down the stairs. Toby scanned the crowd for a familiar gray and white shape. He spotted Terence making his way toward one of the small tables, a plate piled high with food floating behind him. Toby raced down the stairs and wove his way around groups of visiting humans and cats. He wanted to ask after the little tom's mother, find out if she had the sickness and if he could do anything to help.

"Hey there," said the orange tom, hopping onto a stool beside his old friend. "What are you up to?"

"Well I was gonna enjoy a nice plate of food, but I just lost my appetite."

Toby's ears flattened to half-mast. He looked down at his paws.

"What do you want me to say?"

This wasn't the conversation he'd intended to have with his friend, but if he had to apologize for getting Terence in trouble to save their friendship, he'd do it. The orange tom looked up at his friend. The little gray and white cat's eyes were cold.

"You could apologize for the lies you've been spreadin' about Gravin Arturo."

Toby blinked.

"What lies?"

"You know what lies."

"I don't know what you're talking about."

"You've been tellin' everyone that Gravin Arturo is sellin' dragon willow to shadow arts mages. So now the gravin's tied up answerin' a lotta stupid questions instead of workin' on changin' the way the High Council is run so us cats can have a real chance at a good life."

"I haven't said anything to anyone about anything. And what do you mean a chance at a good life."

"You know what I mean," said Terence, raising his voice to just below a yowl. "We cats are second class citizens. Always have been. But Gravin Arturo and Chivato are gonna fix that."

"Fix what how?" asked Toby, raising his voice to match.

The toms faced each other, fur fluffed, claws extended. This was crazy. He knew things hadn't been good for Terence and his mother, but he'd said that was just part of living in the Lower District. Had the gray tom said something that changed his mind or was it that Terence's mother was suffering from the sickness? Terence showed his fangs.

"They gotta plan that'll get cats a paw up into helpin' run the government. 'Bout time we showed those stupid humans that cats are just as smart."

"Terence, I don't understand what you're talking about. Cats and humans have always worked together."

"Just go away, Toby. You don't know nothin'."

"That is very rude, young trainee," said Gravin Arturo, striding up behind Terence.

"Might I suggest you lower your voice, as well. Your argument is beginning to draw attention," said Chivato.

Toby looked around. They were the center of a wide

circle of staring humans and cats. He licked his ruff and forced his fur to flatten, then focused his attention on the gravin and his companion, glancing at the crowd.

"Sorry."

Terence continued to glare at him. Chivato floated a stool beside the gravin and hopped onto it as Arturo pulled a chair from a nearby table. He sat down, frowning at the two cats.

"Now, then, would someone mind telling us what this little dispute is about?"

"Toby's the one whose been tellin' lies about you an' gettin' the High Council all stirred up," said the little tom. The gravin raised his eyebrows.

"Is that true, Toby? Have you been spreading rumors about me?"

"No, sir. I asked some questions about the shadow arts market in Hielberg County, that's all."

"I see."

"There's no harm in asking questions, though questions about the shadow arts market tend to be a hot issue these days. It's a problem when those questions lead others to wonder about their governing leaders, especially when those leaders are doing everything in their power to bring criminals to justice. Do you understand what I'm saying, Toby?"

"Yes, sir."

"And, Terence, you've accused your friend of lying," said Chivato. Terence turned his head away from Toby.

"He's not my friend."

"Friend or not, accusing anyone of slander is very serious. It is nearly as detestable as spreading those lies yourself."

"But he *is* lying."

"Do you have proof?" asked the gravin.

"Yes. No. I guess not."

"Until you can prove otherwise, we must assume Toby is telling the truth."

"Now that that's settled," said Gravin Artuor, slapping his knee. "There are a few people here I would like to introduce our trainee to. If you will excuse us?"

Toby watched as Terence fell in behind the gravin. Chivato turned to leap to the floor.

"Sir, may I ask a question?" asked Toby. The gray tom looked over his shoulder at him.

"Of course. I'd be surprised if you didn't have any questions."

"Terence said you and Gravin Arturo were working on trying to get cats into government roles. Is that true?"

"As a matter of fact, we are. You know about the terrible epidemic in the Lower District, correct?"

"Yes. Two Followers of the One came to our Basic Health Class to ask for volunteers."

"Ah, yes. The Followers do what they can, but their efforts are ineffectual. They believe everyone adheres to The Priceless Measure. What they do not realize is that preaching we should treat each other as equals will not make it happen."

"What would?"

"A stronger government."

Toby watched the large gray tom flow to the floor and melt into the forest of legs and tails. Hadn't Toby's own thoughts been similar? He remembered his orientation interview and wondered just how different his ideas were from Chivato's. A stronger government could make a difference in the lives of those living in the Lower District, but at what price?

The orange tom looked around for his human friend.

He spied Lorn several tables away talking with his father and a woman who alternately dabbed at her eyes with a large handkerchief and patted her bosom, all the while beaming at the young mage.

Lorn shifted from one foot to the other, clenching his hands together behind his back. When the young man's eyes locked on Toby, they pleaded for rescue. Toby smiled. He turned to leap to the floor and spotted Reginald and his cronies at the next table.

The white cat stared back, his whiskers splayed and eyes narrowed. He turned his head just enough to whisper something into the ear of a haughty looking she-cat. She narrowed her eyes as she looked at him, then smirked. Her tinkling laugh made Toby shiver. Trotting toward Lorn, he pretended not to notice as their stares bored into his fur.

"Hey, Toby," said Lorn, his teeth gritted in a smile. "Where have you been?"

"I've been speaking to a friend."

"And who might this charming young feline be?" asked the woman, fluttering her eyelashes.

"Mother, Father, this is Toby, my partner and friend."

"A pleasure to meet you," said the young cat, dipping his head to each.

"Toby, my dear, if you don't mind my asking, were you born such a striking shade of orange?"

"Elsabeth," scolded Lorn's father.

"It's quite all right," said Toby. Elsabeth nodded sharply at her husband.

"My coloring comes from a magical accident. When mother was pregnant with me she was helping Master O'dorn mix a remedy and someone burst into the workroom, startling mother and causing her to inhale quite a bit of glow beetle powder. Needless to say she insists on a "do not disturb" sign on the workroom door now."

"Then I would say you may be the perfect cat to work with my son, since he is prone to accidents," said Lorn's father.

"Henry," scolded Elsabeth. Lorn rolled his eyes.

"I'm sure the head masters had many good reasons to partner us. Speaking of whom," Toby continued, turning to face Lorn, "Master Jalen would like to see us."

"Oh dear. You're not in trouble again, are you?" asked Elsabeth, clutching her giant handkerchief to her breast.

"No, ma'am, I believe the head master has some people he would like us to meet."

"Oh how wonderful." Elsabeth fussed with Lorn's collar and sleeves and straightened his hair. Toby clamped his teeth on his laughter and did his best to keep his whiskers from betraying him. The young mage shifted from foot to foot.

"Mother, please," the young man hissed.

"Indeed, Elsabeth, let the boy alone. The head master is waiting."

"Nonsense. The grand master mage himself can wait for a moment to make sure Lorn is presentable."

"There is no grand master mage right now."

"Well, even if there were, he could still wait. There. Nobility itself," she declared.

Lorn walked away, legs and arms stiff. Toby trotted beside him. When they were surrounded by a crowd, the young man relaxed. He scanned the room and then looked down at the tom.

"*Does* Master Jalen need to see us?"

"No. I thought that was the best excuse to rescue you from your parents."

"Good thinking. So now what?"

Toby gazed around at the sea of legs.

"Could I get a lift?"

Lorn bent down so Toby could hop onto his shoulders. The tom wondered if his mother had ever had to ride on Master O'dorn's shoulders. As if the thought had summoned them, he saw his mother and the master mage sitting at a table across the banquet hall.

"Over there. The red table with the elderly mage and black queen. That's Master O'dorn and my mother," he said, turning to look at the boy carrying him. Lorn chuckled and batted at Toby's whiskers.

"That tickles."

"Sorry."

"Should we go see them?"

Adele's sharp gaze zeroed in on them and she beckoned with a tail twitch. Toby sighed.

"I don't think I have a choice."

Lorn weaved through the groups of mages and cats toward the master partners. The tom could feel the young man's shoulder muscles tighten the closer they came to the table.

"I was wondering if you were going to make an appearance," said Toby's mother. "I'd hoped you might be locked away in your room studying, but I suppose socializing could be beneficial."

Toby bit his tongue.

"I trust you've been on your best behavior."

"Yes, mother."

Lorn bent toward a stool, allowing Toby to flow from his shoulders. The young mage pulled out a chair and sat on the edge.

"You must be Lorn Ribaldy," said Master O'dorn, leaning across the table to shake the young man's hand.

"Yes, sir."

"A pleasure. I worked with your uncle for many years. He had an unusual way of looking at things."

"You're very kind, sir. Most people would call Uncle Hecktor a crackpot."

"A cracked pot can serve well as a watering can in the right situation," countered the old mage with a wink. Lorn smiled.

"So tell me, have you decided what you'll specialize in yet?" asked Master O'dorn.

"It's a bit early for that, sir."

"Come, now. Surely there's been something that's intrigued you."

Lorn raised his eyebrows and glanced at Toby. The tom blinked and shook his head, wondering what the old mage meant. When he looked at the human, Master O'dorn's mouth was quirked in a lop-sided smile. He chuckled.

"Ah, well, as you said. It is a bit early to plan your entire future, though I do hope you've been enjoying your classes."

"The ones you make it to, anyway," said Toby's mother.

The young tom stared at her. How did she know they were still getting to classes late? He glanced toward a mirror at the end of the banquet hall, then back at Lorn. The young man's eyebrows were raised and his eyes were wide. Toby looked back at his mother. She was eying Lorn as if he were a sleeping viper. She turned her gaze on her son.

"No, I haven't been spying on you."

Master O'dorn shifted forward in his seat, capturing Toby's attention.

"What your mother is saying is that you are not known

to give up solving a puzzle, especially when there is aid to be found."

Toby's thoughts shattered. He couldn't think of anything to say that wouldn't make his mother snarl. His skin felt alternately cold and hot. Adele's piercing yellow gaze never wavered.

"Don't bother trying to lie. You were never good at it anyway."

"All right, yes. We're still trying to find out why father disappeared."

"Why can't you just leave this alone?"

"Because no one else cares," said the orange tom, his fur rising. Adele glared at her son. Her tail appeared momentarily above the table as she lashed it to and fro.

"I care about you. I don't want to see you expelled. Concentrate on your studies. It's what your father would have wanted."

"We don't know what father would have wanted, do we, Mother. He's not here to tell us."

The black queen hissed, hunching down as if to spring across the table.

"Adele, my friend," said Master O'dorn, "would you be so kind as to fetch me something to drink? This conversation has left me rather parched."

She turned her glare on her old friend. Clarence frowned at her and made a small circle in the air with his index finger. The queen turned her head toward the nearby crowd. A few cats and humans were staring at them. Others were giving them furtive glances while pretending to be engrossed in conversation.

Adele turned narrowed eyes back on her table mates, then dropped to the floor and disappeared among the crowd.

Master O'dorn watched her stalk away. He shook his head and turned to look at the young tom.

"You really shouldn't bait your mother, Toby. It's in poor taste."

"I know, Master O'dorn, it's just she always seems to rub my fur backwards."

Closing his eyes he heaved a sigh, letting his fur flatten. He knew the old mage was right. Toby felt Lorn's hand on his head. He opened his eyes and looked up at his friend. When he turned his attention back to the master mage, the man was smiling again.

"Given that you're obviously going to continue searching for more information regarding your father's disappearance, perhaps I can help."

Toby's ears perked forward.

"It's not much, but after our little discussion last time I went back through everything I had received during the time Victor was on his mission. There wasn't much outside of normal High Council business, but I found a single letter from Victor to your mother. At the time I thought the old cat had decided to pick up penning bad poetry, some romantic fantasy for Adele or something. Now I wonder."

"Bad poetry?" asked Toby.

"Yes. Several parts of it are quatrains that seem to be nothing but nice words put together. I suspect the poetry may hold clues to his disappearance, but I have no way to decipher them."

"When did you get the letter?" asked Lorn. "We're trying to retrace Victor's steps in order."

"I think it was about a week or two before we found out he was missing."

Toby kneaded the stool. His focus narrowed to the

mage sitting across the table.

"Is there any way you could get that letter to us?"

The old man glanced away. Toby followed his gaze, spotting his mother at the punch bowl. She was filling the cup with the frothy pink liquid, her tail straight as a rod. Master O'dorn cleared his throat.

"I will send it by dragon messenger at the first opportunity."

"Thank you," said Toby.

"Oh don't thank me. I may have just pushed you into the eternal abyss. Your mother thinks I've been warning you against further investigations, you know."

"She won't hear otherwise from me."

"Nor me," agreed Lorn.

"That's good to hear. Now, you two best be elsewhere before she returns."

The partners stood to leave.

"And, Toby, do be careful. You're father was a skilled loner, not an apprentice, and he still disappeared."

The orange tom nodded to his old friend, then leaped onto Lorn's shoulder. Together they left.

Toby trotted toward the building housing the offices of the loner instructors. He felt rather conspicuous with Lorn jogging beside him. Few humans came to this side of the academy, though Toby had never wondered why until now.

"Are you sure it's okay for me to be here?" asked Lorn.

"I don't remember any rules against humans coming onto the loner campus."

"Me either, but I feel like everyone's staring at me."

Toby glanced toward a group of trainees gathered with their books in a sunny spot. They looked up from their studies as the partners passed by, then returned to their books.

"You're imagining things. If you want to go back, fine, but I want to know if Master Antwan knows anything about why my father would have started writing bad poetry while he was on this mission."

Lorn didn't say anything more as they entered the building. The walls echoed with the sound of the young mages footsteps. Toby cringed, hoping the sound wouldn't disturb anyone as they made their way to the office Master Antwan shared with Master Natsumi. Toby scratched at the door.

"Enter," said a soft feminine voice.

The partners squeezed into the small, dimly lit room. A sleek silver tabby she-cat sat on a cushion upon a high shelf with her eyes closed. Nearby a half dozen sticks of incense smoldered in a small pot of sand. Toby lifted his nose, inhaling the smoke. He sneezed. The young tom peeked up at the tabby. The she-cat didn't move. Toby motioned for Lorn to sit on the floor next to him and wait. The young mage braced himself against the door jamb and scrunched himself into something resembling a seated position, knees touching his nose.

"What can I do for you?" asked the feline on the shelf as she stretched first her front legs, then her back.

"We're here to ask Master Antwan some questions about some information he recently gave us," answered Toby.

"What information might that have been?"

Toby tried to think like his father. He didn't know this cat. Could he trust her? His paw pads prickled.

"I would prefer talking to Master Antwan. Would you know where we could find him?"

"I'm afraid Master Antwan is away on holiday this week," said the she-cat, jumping from shelf to shelf until she was sitting on a cushion in front of the apprentices. Toby grimaced, flattening his ears to his head. The she-cat cocked her head to the side, her eyes narrowed to slits as she stared at the orange tom.

"You have your father's determination, though it seems you also have your mother's temper," said the she-cat.

"Excuse me?"

"Antwan wasn't exaggerating your color, either. If you're ever sent on secret missions you'll have to be able to use the art of disguise better than anyone I've met."

"I'm sorry. Have you two met?" asked Lorn, raising his head enough to be heard over his knees.

"No. Not until now," said the she-cat.

"You must be Master Natsumi."

The tabby nodded.

"I'm Toby and this is Lorn."

"Yes. I know. I understand young Trainee Terence has been helping you on a special case. I'm a little surprised he's not with you today."

"We, uh, had a disagreement," said Toby.

"I see. Nothing serious, I hope."

"Yeah. So, Master Antwan really isn't going to be around for the rest of the week?"

"I'm afraid not. He's visiting some friends in the Middle District. Is there something I can help you with?"

"I'm not sure," said Toby, glancing at his friend for some guidance. Lorn gave a minuscule shrug.

"If it's about your father's last mission," offered Master Natsumi, "I know as much as Master Antwan. We worked several cases together in conjunction with your father."

The young tom relaxed.

"I was hoping Master Antwan could explain something about what my father wrote in a letter to my mother. Maybe you can help?"

"I can certainly try. Do you have it with you?"

"Well, no. Master O'dorn is supposed to send it to me."

"In that case I'm not sure how much help I can be."

"Actually, I was just wondering if father had said anything in his letters to you about taking up writing poetry."

"Poetry?" asked the silver tabby, sitting back as if Toby had hissed at her.

"Is that weird?" asked Lorn.

"Victor was certainly a romantic, but it would be highly unusual for him to wax poetic in the middle of a mission. What else do you know about this letter?"

The silver tabby leaned forward. Toby felt like a hunted mouse. He fought the urge to hunch himself into a ball.

"Nothing, except that it was sent a week or two before we were notified of father's disappearance."

Master Natsumi sat back, licking her ruff. The young tom shivered as he tried to shake the hunted feeling. The silver tabby squinted at Toby, then looked away toward a wall. Toby followed her gaze to a large medallion hanging from a leather thong. It's triangular shape was at odds with the circular red stone set in its middle.

"I wonder," whispered the loner. Toby held his breath. The rustle of fabric as Lorn adjusted his position sounded loud to the young cat.

"That medallion was the last thing Victor sent us before we lost all communication with him. It and nothing else. When we tested it we found only two magical signatures, your father's and Master Ribaldy's, overlaid by a trace of blood magic. It was the only real evidence we had that Master Ribaldy was involved in Victor's disappearance."

Lorn groaned. Toby put a paw on the young man's knee. Master Natsumi straightened and let her piercing gaze rest on the boy.

"I'm sorry, young man. To all appearances your uncle master minded the entire thing. If we hadn't received a tip about his plan to blow up the High Council chambers while it was in session, he might have succeeded in throwing society into chaos."

"I know. It's just..."

Toby patted Lorn's knee again. The boy was ashen. The tom looked back at Master Natsumi.

"You said "I wonder." What did you mean?"

"If your letter arrived when you think, then it's possible there's something more to this medallion. We wondered why Victor hadn't sent more information about it. We assumed either he hadn't had time to write them or they'd been intercepted along the way. Perhaps we never received them because he sent them somewhere he knew they'd be safe — to your mother."

Toby waited anxiously for Master O'dorn's letter to arrive. A week passed and then another. The young tom was about to mirror call the old mage to find out what was keeping him from sending it when it arrived. No sooner had the door closed than Toby and Lorn were hunched over the pages.

My dearest Toby,

My apologies for the late arrival of this package. When I promised to send it I did not foresee the outbreak of the disease ravaging the Lower District among those inhabiting the Middle District. I've enlisted the aid of the Temple as the disease is spreading

182

rapidly and appears to be similar – if not exactly the same. At the current rate of infection, it is all I can do to keep up. There have been few fatalities, thank the One as my Temple friends say, but they assure me more will follow unless we figure out a way to slow the disease's progress. To that end I am devoting all my time, as is your mother. That being said, I must return to work now.

I wish I had more pleasant news to pass on, or even an idea of where to begin in solving the riddle of your father's letter, but I have none.

Your mother sends her love as well.

Sincerely,
Master C. O'dorn

"Things must be worse than Master O'dorn is letting on," said Toby.

"Why do you say that?"

"My mother would never say that."

Lorn slid a piece of paper out from under Master O'dorn's letter. It was blank. The young mage shuffled the two pieces of paper, then looked inside the packet. Toby checked the floor from the door to the table. Nothing.

"Why would he send a blank piece of paper instead of your father's letter?"

"He did say he was busy. Maybe he was distracted?"

"Or maybe someone else got this before we did."

"But why replace the letter with a blank sheet? Why not just keep everything?"

"You've got a point."

Lorn got up to fetch the kettle of hot water and saucer of spiced milk he'd left on the hearth to warm. He placed the saucer beside Toby, then poured the hot water from the kettle into a cup he'd borrowed from the kitchen weeks ago.

"Do you ever plan to return that?" Toby asked, nodding toward the cup.

"I hate to send it back to the kitchen only to have to borrow another one."

Lorn cut a slice of lemon for his tea, held it over his cup and squeezed. A seed flew across the table, bouncing off Toby's cheek and landing on the blank sheet of paper.

"Watch it."

"Sorry."

Toby patted the seed across the paper toward Lorn, leaving a trail of tiny black dots and dashes. He sniffed the trail, opening his mouth to draw the scent across his glands. There was another smell under the powerful aroma of lemon. Silvery images zipped across his mind, leaving a salty aftertaste. It reminded Toby of the stomach remedies Master O'dorn sometimes drank on stressful days, something he'd done a lot just before the tom had left for the academy.

"Look at this," said the tom, patting the paper.

"What's that?"

"I'm not sure. It appeared where the seed touched the paper. Smells a bit like a stomach remedy. Do you think this really is my father's letter?"

"Maybe. You said the dots formed just where the seed touched the paper?"

Toby nodded. Lorn stared at the page, then looked off to his right. He closed his eyes and frowned. He grinned and grabbed the lemon, then rubbed it over the paper. Toby gasped.

"What are you doing?"

"Something Uncle Hecktor taught me. See, if you use a certain kind of ink, it will disappear after it dries. When you

184

rub a lemon slice over the page, the ink reappears."

"Why not just use a spell?"

"Because that's the first thing a mage will think of," said Lorn, frowning.

As Toby watched, writing began to appear on the blank page. The orange tom gaped. When Lorn finished, the entire page was covered in writing.

"I don't think this letter was written by your father. At least, not entirely."

Toby recognized his father's sharp lines at the top of the paper, but the poem was written with a number of flourishes very unlike Victor's efficient penmanship.

"I think you're right. But whose handwriting is that?"

Lorn looked at the lemon, then back to the page.

"It's Uncle Hecktor's."

"How is that possible? Master O'dorn worked with your uncle a lot. Wouldn't he have known his handwriting?"

"I doubt it. Uncle Hecktor was a master at copying other people's handwriting. He told me it was important to learn how to tell the difference between a person's real writing and someone else's copy of it."

"So, if your uncle copied someone else's handwriting, whose did he copy?"

"That's a very good question. Without having a sample of the original, I'm not sure I could figure it out."

"Well, I'm sure we can't get samples of everyone's handwriting in the entire kingdom just to compare them with this. Have any other ideas?"

Lorn shrugged.

"We could always read it."

Toby rolled his eyes. The partners leaned over to read the newly revealed letter. While Victor's paragraphs seemed pretty straight forward, the poems were just as Master O'dorn had said, pretty words strung together. Toby stared into the fire, letting the words play in his head. Lorn stood up, crossed his arms and snorted.

"That was helpful."

Toby shushed the young mage. He continued to stare into the fire. For some reason the image of the medallion on the loner's wall kept surfacing when he concentrated on the words of the poem, but try as he might he couldn't make the connection. The tom sighed and looked up at the boy.

"You're right. There's not much here that makes sense."

"Aside from Uncle Hecktor's love of lions who have won golden medals, the only other thing that sticks out is the number three."

"And don't forget Captain Fi Bonah of the Nahchee Clan. He was mentioned several times as well."

"But what does it all mean?"

Toby watched as the young mage began pacing. He wondered how long it would take before their floor wore through to the room below as Lorn retraced his steps again.

"This is hopeless," said the young mage, throwing his hands up.

Toby didn't want to agree, but he couldn't see where the boy was wrong. They weren't trained for this. Not yet, at any rate. He considered taking the letter to Master Natsumi for help. The sleek silver tabby had seemed eager to see it. Toby shivered as he remembered her hunter's gaze. He looked down at the letter and re-read the first paragraphs written by his father. It felt like the last link he had to the large black tom. He wasn't ready to give it up yet.

"Maybe we should take it one piece at a time."

"What do you mean?"

"There are four things in this letter that stick out to us, right?"

"Yeah, so?"

"Why don't we do some research on each of those and see what we find?"

"What if they're dead ends?"

"Maybe they will be, but it's a place to start, isn't it?"

Chapter 8

"Having any luck?" Lorn rubbed his eyes. Two stacks of books rested at this elbow, a cup of untouched tea within arms reach.

"No. I know all kinds of great trivia now about lion racing in Kella, but nothing about any special golden medals. How 'bout you?"

Toby arched his back in a spine popping stretch, then sat down, wrapping his tail around his toes.

"Well, I could tell you the history of every major clan in the last hundred years, but there's no mention of any NahChee Clan anywhere, let alone anyone named Captain Fi Bonah."

"Looks like I was right. This is a dead end."

Toby lashed his tail.

"I'm not giving up."

"I didn't say we should."

"Then what are you saying?"

"I need a break." The young human took a sip of tea and grimaced.

"Want me to warm that up for you?"

Lorn glared at the orange tom.

"I can do it."

The boy placed his hands around the cup and stared into the brown liquid, muttering under his breath. Toby's ears began to itch. He sighed and leaped under the table. A moment later he heard the sound of shattering porcelain followed by Lorn's cursing. The young tom stayed under the table until his companion stopped dancing around holding his hands to his chest.

"When are you going to take care of that?"

"I have a special tutoring session with Master Baqer first thing in the morning. He seems to think he can help me 'tame the wild beast that is your magic.'"

The young mage's voice quavered and he gestured wildly in imitation of his teacher. Lorn grimaced. Toby kept still though he wanted to laugh. It was a perfect imitation. The only thing missing was the wild white hair and bushy eyebrows.

"Would you like me to help you with your hands?"

The young man shrugged and held them out. Toby floated the healing salve and cloth strips from a shelf to the table. With practiced efficiency, he moved some of the white goo from the container onto the human's outstretched palms. A couple twitches of his tail completed the wrapping process.

"I know he's weird, but I've heard his methods work — if you use them."

"Whatever."

Lorn uprighted his overturned stool and stared down at the tea stained pages of the open book he'd been reading. Toby looked at them, too, wondering what kind of punishment one gets for mutilating a library book. Probably lifetime detention with the librarian. A shiver ran down the young tom's spine.

"Look at this." The young mage pointed to a paragraph. The cat craned his neck to read a passage about transferring magical signatures between objects.

"So?"

"I didn't know you could do that."

"It's amazing what you can learn when you actually read a book instead of just copy spell ingredients and incantations."

Lorn glared at Toby again.

"It says here that while this kind of spell can be done by any master mage it's usually used by those who practice the shadow arts. Huh. I wonder why."

"Maybe it's because most mages don't need to hide their signatures."

"That makes sense."

"Interesting as that is, though, it doesn't help us figure out these code words."

The young mage sighed, flopping down onto the stool. He shut the book, placed it on one stack and pulled another from the other pile. Toby did the same.

"Look on the bright side," the young tom said, forcing his whiskers into a cat grin. "We still have a few more books to go through. Maybe there's something in one of them."

"Yeah, maybe."

As the boy began to read, Toby glanced at the two stacks of books. The read pile was far larger than the to-read pile. His whiskers drooped. Yeah. Maybe.

Two weeks later, Toby and Lorn were no closer to breaking the code, although they had several interesting theories. A knock at the door interrupted the partners as they pored over more volumes on codes they'd borrowed from the school library. When Lorn turned from closing the door, the young tom noticed he was carrying a large package.

"Whose it from?"

"There's no name on it." Lorn opened the package.

"It looks like copies of some official documents. Look, that's Uncle Hecktor's handwriting. These must be some of the records that have been locked away."

"Way to go girls," said Toby, batting the air.

"There's a letter, too." Lorn placed the stack of papers on the table next to the tom with the letter on top.

Dear Lorn and Toby,

As you know, we could get into big trouble if anyone finds out we gave these to you. D. made the copies herself, so hopefully no one will notice. We didn't see anything in them that was helpful, but a couple of them were rather unusual, as if M. R. was already losing his mind.

Don't let anyone know where you got them if you're found with them. And be careful. Any mention of M.R. here is like playing stick ball with a bee hive.

Sincerely,
Us

Toby patted the letter to the side. As they read each document, they saw what Alie was talking about. Several pages seemed to contain gibberish and odd phrases, much like Victor's letter. There was another mention of Captain Fi Bonah and the number three was a prominent theme on one entire page.

Toby's whiskers splayed as he looked at Lorn. The young mage grinned in return. They may be no closer to cracking the code, but they were sure they were on to something. The last page was nearly blank with only a paragraph of information on how the human body was different from the feline body. Toby leaned close to the page. A whiff of stomach remedy entered his nose. He turned to Lorn.

"Do we have another lemon?"

Lorn snatched a lemon slice from the saucer under his cup and rubbed the blank areas of the page. Faint lines appeared written in the same handwriting with the same flourishes as on Victor's letter. Toby's skin rippled from his shoulders to his tail as he read the lines.

> *So dark the time of man doth come*
> *When Sneak doth death decide to run*
> *And charge upon the willow's sun*
> *That blood be cold and change be done.*
>
> *The Spider finds the widow's peak*
> *A cat doth spin his will to seek.*
> *Should will define, the day be bleak*
> *And hell upon mankind doth wreak.*

"Either your uncle was truly mad, or there's a lot more going on than we thought."

"I vote for mad. None of this makes sense."

Toby re-read the poem. Lorn was right. It looked like the gibberish of an addled brain. Yet, it felt like there was something more to it, something Toby just couldn't quite get his claws into. He looked at the shuttered window, latched against the cool fall wind. The young cat lashed his tail, feeling as frustrated as the wind. The shutters rattled again. Toby blinked and cocked his head.

"The only way to open a window is to unhook the latch."

"What?"

The young tom turned his gaze on his companion. Lorn was frowning.

"You have to unhook the latch to open the window or you can't get in."

"Are you okay? Do you need a break or something?"

Toby shook his head until his ears made a popping sound. He stared at the window again as the wind continued to rattle the shutters.

"I was just remembering the time I got locked out of Master O'dorn's house. It wasn't until I stopped trying to force the window open that I was able to get it open." The young cat looked back at Lorn. The young man's brows were puckered in confusion. Toby nodded to the piece of paper on the desk.

"We're trying to force the poem to make sense as a code. What if we think of this as a poem instead?"

"What do you mean?"

"Remember in Basic Incantations we learned about crafting spells into poems so they'd be easy to remember?"

"Vaguely."

Toby sighed. He'd thought Lorn had been taking notes on the lecture, but later he'd seen Lorn's notes were a list of ingredients for a spell he'd found further on in their textbook. So far, the young mage hadn't had time to try the spell out, much to Toby's relief.

"Okay, so the easiest way to remember something is to make a rhyme of it. Rhymes are often formed into poetry. Poetry includes symbols, which lead back to the rhyme. The rhyme leads back to the thing you're trying to remember. Do you see where I'm going with this?"

"So what you're saying is if we do some research on the symbols in this poem, we might understand what Uncle

Hecktor was trying to say?"

"You got it."

"Then let's go," said Lorn, snatching the page from the table and heading toward the door.

"Wait. The girls asked us to keep these secret. We can't just go flashing them around the library."

"Well, how are we going to know what to look up if we don't take this with us? I know you have a terrific memory, but I think we need to be able to compare the whole poem to whatever we find."

"What if we make a copy?"

"A copy of a copy? Would we be able to read it?"

"We would if we made a handwritten copy. Look, the ink is already fading again. If we hand write it out, you won't need to carry lemon wedges in your pocket."

"Hadn't thought about that. It would look suspicious if we had to keep rubbing a lemon on a piece of paper, wouldn't it."

Lorn grabbed a pen and copied the poem in the same handwriting on a fresh sheet of paper. The young tom cocked his head as he watched.

"Why are you copying the handwriting, too?"

Lorn shrugged and stuffed the poem in his pocket.

"Habit."

Toby blinked, wondering just how alike the boy was to his uncle. He glanced at the original papers, then flicked his tail and sent them into the hiding hole they'd created under a loose brick on the hearth. The young tom hurried out the door behind his partner, pausing only long enough to reset the dampening field on the room.

"You know the rules, apprentice. Until you return the

books you've borrowed, you may not borrow any more."

The librarian glared at the partners over the mountain-ous desk, her beaky nose wrinkled as if they'd been dipped in manure. Lorn slumped away toward the stack of books they'd left on the table. Toby clung to the boy's shoulders as the young mage balanced another stack in his arms.

"I told you we should have brought those with us," whispered Toby.

"Now what are we going to do?" asked Lorn, drop-ping the books on the table and earning a harsh shush from the librarian. "Good thing we made a copy. It looks like we'll have to do our research here for now."

"Let's at least take these to a back table."

Toby floated several books and followed the young man toward another table in a dark corner. Lorn had yet to manage floating anything larger than a paper weight without turning it into a blazing fireball, but he was showing progress. They both agreed library books were probably not the best things to practice on. The boy carried as many as he could, while trying to see where he was going. He tripped, sending everything flying, including the poem.

"Well, well, well," purred a familiar voice. "Look who dropped by."

Snickers filled Toby's ears. His skin felt hot. Lorn scrambled to pick up the books, casting apologetic glances at the librarian. Toby turned to face the white tom.

"What do you want, Reginald?"

"What could I want from probates?"

Toby glared at the tom, wishing Lorn would hurry up.

"Here, let me help you with that," said the white cat, swishing his fluffy tail at the piece of paper. It rose into the air and floated toward the small group of cats.

"What's this?" he asked.

"None of your business," said Lorn, snatching at the paper as it flew past.

"Ooo. What a touchy human," said one of the females.

"Could it be a love note, perhaps?" said another and giggled. Reginald peered down at the paper. His ears twitched. He looked up at Toby, then at Lorn. The mage's ears looked as if they would burst into flames.

"Nothing so fun, I'm afraid," said the white tom, flicking his tail at the paper to make it fly toward the partners. "It's only the boy's attempt at bad poetry."

"Pity," said the first female.

"Oh, I don't know," said Reginald. "If they don't succeed in magic, at least they have something to fall back on. I hear the Lower District is in need of minstrels now with so many having died."

"That's true. And we all know they have no discerning tastes," another tom said.

Reginald cut his eyes at the orange tom, a sneer on his lips. Without another word, he lead his chortling group away. Lorn crammed the paper into his pocket and finished picking up the rest of the books.

He stomped to the corner table, dropped the books on it and slumped into a chair facing the rest of the library. Toby let his books settle onto the table. Irritated he may be, but he didn't want to face the librarian because he damaged one of her precious books.

"That cat burns my hide."

"Agreed."

"Ever met his human?"

Toby shook his head. Lorn glared at the white cat's retreating back.

"Two of a kind."

"Not surprising."

The friends stared out a window past the librarian's desk. Lanterns lit the paths to the other campus buildings.

"Shall we keep going?" asked the orange tom.

"What's the use? We're never going to find anything."

"We won't if we stop trying."

Lorn glanced at Toby, then went back to staring out the window.

"You know, Toby, times like this make me wonder about whose really in charge. If the Temple guys are to be believed, then this all-knowing, all-powerful, loving Being must be asleep or something."

"What makes you say that?"

"Well, look at what's going on. Why would a loving Being let manure chewers like him have a golden life and let decent people live in poverty and die a horrible death? It just doesn't make sense. I mean, Brother Yannis talked about that thing being our guide—"

"The Priceless Measure."

"Yeah. That. So what about it? Do you see anyone helping someone in need just because that's what we should do?"

"The Brothers are."

"Yeah, but they have to. They take vows about that kind of thing."

"What about Master O'dorn? He doesn't have to help anyone with the great sickness. He could turn them away."

"I guess. It just seems to me the only way to get anywhere in this world is to look out for yourself."

Toby was silent. He joined Lorn in staring out the window. Leaves scurried across the paths. The wind moaned. Students wrapped in scarves hurried past, clutching hats over ears, looking only at the path in front of their feet. The orange tom's whiskers drooped as he pondered what Lorn had said.

"Let's go back to our room."

Lorn nodded. Toby leaped to the boy's shoulders and fluffed his fur in anticipation of the cold beyond the door. The wind buffeted the cat, who clung to his companion's shoulder, trying not to pierce the soft flesh under the boy's clothes. His companion shielded his eyes with one hand and kept his head down. Although the tom would have liked to close his eyes against the debris blown about he feared losing his balance if Lorn ducked or made a sharp turn, so he kept them narrowed to mere slits.

Neither noticed the shadow looming in front of them. The young man ran head-long into it. The shadow staggered a couple paces, then darted into the surrounding hedges, disappearing from sight. Lorn bounced back and landed with a thud. Toby was thrown to the ground with the sound of tearing cloth as his claws stuck into the human's clothing.

"Who was that?"

"Don't know, but it felt like a bony wall."

Toby pulled at the bits of string caught in his claws. He looked up at Lorn who was pressing his fingers to the shoulder Toby had been riding on.

"Sorry about that."

"Not your fault. That guy should have watched where he was going."

"He could say the same to us."

Lorn scowled at the orange tom. Toby blinked in return. The young man sighed and shrugged, wincing as he raised his injured shoulder.

"Do you think it was a teacher?"

"Doubt it. Only desperate students would be out on a

night like this."

"You mean like us?"

Toby blinked again. He turned his gaze toward where the shadow had disappeared. A flutter of something white caught his eye. He flattened himself to the path and crept toward it. A twig snapped nearby. He paused, ears swiveling to catch any sound. The wind moaned through the trees.

He crept closer. A rustle of cloth. He stopped, listening. Nothing. Another step. He paused, adjusted his weight. The thing fluttered again. Toby sprung onto it. The scent of parchment and ink flooded his nose as he bit down on it. The young tom sat back, staring at the scrap of paper he had just captured.

"What is it?"

"Looks like a note." Toby picked it up and carried it back to Lorn. The mage opened it, flattening it over his knee. Lorn gasped. He thrust the piece of paper under Toby's nose.

"This is a note to Reginald. It says he should carry on his duties to the House and look at the handwriting."

The flowing handwriting meant less to Toby than the faint smell coming from the paper. He drew the scent over his glands. The image of a field of bloody marigolds unrolled. He sneezed. The young cat's eyes widened as he looked at his friend, a grin spreading across the young man's face.

"I bet whoever wrote this is the same person who bought the dragon willow and Reginald is somehow involved."

"I knew there was something about him I didn't like."

"You mean other than he's a bully and a snob?" asked Lorn, shoving the note into his pocket. The young cat's whiskers splayed.

Suddenly they heard a rustle of cloth, followed by

footsteps running away. The partners stared into the cold night. Friend or foe, the shadow was gone.

"What do you mean you have new information? I thought I made it clear you were not to investigate this any further without our express permission," Master Meredith said. She clamped her whiskers and flattened her ears to her head.

It had been several days since they'd received Master O'dorn's letter and the package containing Master Ribaldy's notes. They'd looked through every library book on poetry and symbols they could find with nothing to show for it except a better respect for those who could write a good poem. Toby suggested they ask the head masters for help.

"Yes, Master Meredith, you did, but we didn't think it would do any harm to see if someone at the High Council had any information and Master O'dorn volunteered the letter from Toby's father."

"You asked someone at the High Council for classified documents?" The calico's neck fur bristled, her eyes wide. She looked toward her companion who was frowning and tapping an index finger on the desk. Toby shifted from foot to foot on his stool.

"Not exactly."

"What exactly did you do, then?" asked Master Jalen.

"We asked an acquaintance if they had heard or seen anything about Uncle Hecktor's case."

"An acquaintance," repeated the head master mage.

"A friend," said Toby. His fur was beginning to feel too thick, his skin prickling under the head masters' stern gazes.

"And did you tell your friend why you wanted this information?" asked Master Jalen.

Toby's ears flattened to half-mast. Lorn grimaced.

"I'll take that as a yes. You do realize that was a foolish risk."

The young apprentices looked at the floor. Toby sucked in a breath and wondered if they'd just jeopardized the thin cord keeping them in the academy. It would be fair. After all, Master Meredith had been very specific about what they should and shouldn't do after their infraction. He could hear his mother's growls already.

"Still," said Master Meredith, "they did manage to get more information than we have. Perhaps it would behoove us to look at it."

Toby let out the breath he'd been holding as Lorn reached into his robe to extract the copies they had made of all Master Ribaldy's documents and Victor's letter.

"Have you shown this to anyone else?" asked Master Jalen, taking the package and untying the string.

"No, sir," said Lorn.

"I did mention my father's letter to Master Natsumi, but at the time we were still waiting for it to be delivered."

"How did she react?" asked Master Meredith, eyes narrowed.

"She seemed very interested. She wanted to see it right away."

"Naturally," said Master Jalen, glancing at the she-cat from the corner of his eye.

The apprentices sat still as the head masters spread the papers across their desk and studied them. The crackling fire had burned low by the time the older partners looked up. Master Jalen sat back in his chair, rubbing his eyes with the fingers of his right hand. The she-cat stood on her toes and arched her back, stretching muscles held still while studying the documents. Toby clenched his jaw shut. Although he was perched on the edge of his stool, he didn't want to interrupt whatever conclusions the head masters were mulling over.

"I can see why you had no luck with your research," said Master Jalen.

"Both your father and your uncle were very clever. The poem in your uncle's documents appears to be a dire warning, but of what I have no idea," said Master Meredith.

"Nor do I. You're correct in believing there is a code hidden within the documents. In fact, it appears there are several, which must be broken in a particular order, before we can understand the real message Master Ribaldy and Victor were sending us."

"Can you figure it out?" asked Lorn.

"No. Even with as much information as you have here, there are pieces missing. Without those pieces we have no way of deciphering any of it," said the head master mage. He turned to Master Meredith, letting his hand drop to the arm of his chair.

"I think we must include Master Natsumi in this."

"Is that wise?"

"What other option is there?" asked Master Jalen, lifting his hands, palms up. "She is the best decoder we know. She's also familiar with the case."

The she-cat closed her eyes, head drooping onto her chest. Toby glanced at Lorn. The young human quirked an eyebrow, but said nothing. The tom returned his gaze to the head master cat. Her eyes snapped open and she looked up at her companion.

"What about the Temple? They have a library that dates back centuries. Some of these quatrains remind me of old prophecies I read as a kit."

"That may work," mused Master Jalen. He stared into space, eyes unfocused.

"The question is, how do we go about getting the information we need?" he continued. "We can't ask the Brothers to search their library for vague references. I hesitate to share any of this information with even them."

"One of us could go," said the head master cat.

"That may call too much attention to what we're trying to find out. Neither of us can claim to be going on sabbatical nor are either of us involved in a class that would necessitate a trip to the Temple library."

"What if we went?" asked Toby, fur standing on end. He kneaded the stool, trying not to overbalance and fall.

"Yeah. We'd have a good idea what to look for and nobody else would have to know why."

"The problem with that is you are both restricted to the grounds," said Master Meredith.

"Not to mention that it would appear odd for two apprentices to go on a field trip to the Temple by themselves for no apparent reason."

Toby's whiskers clamped together. They were right. Their jaunt to the White Dog had looked like a couple of younglings out on a dare. This would make no sense outside of the head masters' office.

"Wait a minute," said Master Meredith. "I have an idea. Toby and Lorn are correct. They are the best candidates for finding the information we need from the Temple and I think I know how to get them there without raising suspicions."

"How?" asked Toby and Lorn together.

"Leave that to Master Jalen and I. The less you know, the safer it will be. In the meantime, keep thinking about possible ways to get at this puzzle and be ready to go."

Chapter 9

Reginald gazed around at the plush velvet chairs and couches. He kneaded the soft purple dyed rug under his paws, a purr rumbling in his chest. Someday this would be his. He'd been promised.

"I see you like the rug."

The white tom spun around, catching a claw in the ornamental rug. Chivato scowled at the young tom as he tried to tug his paw loose.

"What news do you have?"

Reginald eyed Arturo as he entered with a tray with bowls of milk and treats. The man laid the tray on an ornately carved table near a couch, then placed a bowl of milk beside each cat on the floor. The white cat's fur bristled along his spine.

"How dare you insult me, human."

A gray paw slammed into his head, making his ears ring.

"Idiot. Do you think I want milk stains on my furniture?"

The young cat lowered his eyes, giving his ruff a quick lick, watching the human from the corner of his eye. Arturo acted as if he hadn't heard anything. He laid a white linen cloth on the floor in front of the gray tom and turned to dish the cat's meal. Chivato's tail twitched, recapturing the young tom's attention.

"What news?"

"The partners are still digging into your affairs, Master. They were in the library doing research on a poem Master Ribaldy wrote."

"How do you know he wrote it?"

"I recognized the handwriting as yours and assumed you would never allow either of those two to make a copy of something you wrote. The poem seemed like something he would write, as well."

The human placed the gray cat's meal upon the floor on porcelain plates Reginald could almost see through and then turned to begin dishing out another plate of the same treats for the young tom. Chivato bent to take a dainty bite of meat.

"Do you remember what it said?"

Reginald sat tall, gazing over the gray tom's head.

"So dark the time of man doth come;
That blood be cold and change be done.
Should will define, the day be bleak
And hell upon mankind doth wreak."

"Are you certain that is the entire poem?"

The white tom returned his gaze to his master. Chivato's yellow eyes stared intently at him. Reginald could feel his gaze burning into him even when Arturo leaned between them to place another white linen cloth on the floor in front of the him.

"Yes, master."

The gray tom looked toward a fireplace large enough to roast a whole deer.

"Not much to go on. Doubtful they can figure out the old man's nonsense. Still…" Chivato turned back to the young tom in front of him, watching him shift from paw to paw. The gray cat's whiskers splayed wide.

"It seems you are taking my missive seriously. Well done."

"Missive, sir?" Reginald cocked his head, blinking in confusion. He glanced at the human as the man finished placing the white cat's meal on the floor and backed away. Arturo bowed his head toward the master cat.

"Will there be anything else?"

The gray tom waved his tail in dismissal. Reginald watched the human turn to gather the tray and leave, his lips quirked in a sly smile. The young cat turned his attention back to Chivato. The master cat's eyes were narrowed.

"I sent you a message regarding what to do about our spies. You must have received it."

"No, sir. I didn't."

Chivato turned toward the human.

"Arturo, did you deliver my communique to young Reginald here?"

"As you commanded, I took it to the academy and delivered it to the appropriate party."

The master cat looked back at the white tom, ears laid back. Reginald felt his fur begin to rise. He stared wide-eyed at his master.

"I swear I never got it."

"It is beneath a cat of your breeding to lie. If my human says he delivered it, then you must have received it. I can only assume from your adamant denial that you somehow lost it and are trying to cover that fact up. An unfortunate thing."

Reginald lashed his tail, glaring at the human and

growling. Arturo stood, looking down his nose at the white tom. Chivato hissed, swiping a paw through the air.

"That will be enough. It seems you are still too young to comprehend the burden of this mission. I will have to call upon another to send a stronger message to our spies."

"I can do it. I've been making things difficult for them since they moved into their quarters. I know how to get past their shield. Just tell me what you want done."

Chivato narrowed his eyes at the young tom and shook his head.

"This is not a job for a novice. Arturo, please show our young guest to the door."

Toby dug his claws into Lorn's shoulders, shifting his balance as the young mage was jostled by classmates in the small entry of the Temple library. The smell of musty old books and wood polish tickled the orange tom's nose. He opened his eyes wide to catch every bit of light as he strained to see the end of the bookshelves marching down the hallway.

"Master Meredith wasn't kidding. This place is huge," he whispered in Lorn's ear.

"Shhh," said a striped cat who didn't seem to have any ears. Toby looked at the she-cat, wondering how she could have heard his whisper until he realized her ears folded forward toward her face. The tom turned his attention back to their history instructor.

"All right, ladies and gentlemen, the head masters and I thought it would be a great idea to bring you to the Temple library for a little project, just to see how well you've been paying attention in class," said the instructor with a smile. "I'm sure you all remember your lessons on what the past can teach us about the present and how both will affect the future.

To that end, each of you will be assigned a specific topic for a research paper. Keep in mind you will only have the run of this library today, so take advantage of this opportunity. Temple librarians and dragon aides will be available to assist you."

The students formed a line and filed past the history masters to get their assignments. Lorn darted down a nearby aisle so they could read it in relative privacy.

How are heraldric symbols, poetry and magical incantations related? What were their past and current uses? How could those uses be modified for the future?

"Clever," said Toby.

"I wonder how they made sure we got this assignment and not something else."

"Who knows. Let's get started."

"Fine. Where would you like to start?" asked Lorn, waving toward the expansive library.

"Did you bring a list of those symbols?"

"Yeah," Lorn said, patting his pocket.

"Then let's start with those, then move on to poetry."

"Sounds like as good an idea as any."

Catching the attention of a nearby dragon, the apprentices requested volumes on symbols, specifically those used in secret messages, and commandeered a secluded table halfway down the hall. They'd only made it through one stack when another dragon quietly exchanged the candle stub on their table for a new candle, breathing a small flame onto the new wick. Lorn sat back from the large book he was searching through and rubbed his eyes. Toby stretched his front legs, then his back ones.

"This is ridiculous. I'm not finding anything helpful and we're running out of time," said Lorn. "It would help if we could ask for references on just those words we're interested in."

Toby's ears perked up

"Why can't we?"

"We're not supposed to let anyone know what we're doing, remember?"

"Yeah, but what if we simply ask for a cross-reference of those words within poetry, magical incantations and prophecy?"

"That would certainly narrow the search."

"We could also expand that a little and ask for references within religious numerology, couldn't we?"

"If we did that, we'd be sure to catch the number three and maybe something we missed in the documents."

Lorn flagged down a passing dragon and explained what they needed. In a matter of moments, their table was swarmed with small dragons who took away most of the books they had and left a new pile of books in their place. A larger, green dragon, hovered over their table. With a voice like tiny chiming bells, the dragon began singing at the books. Toby watched in fascination as one book after another floated into the air, pages turning in a blur of motion. They gently drifted back into separated piles on the table, each open to the pages the apprentices had asked for information on. After every book was back on the table, the dragon disappeared with a pop.

"Well that was easy," said Lorn.

Their pens raced across page after page of clean paper as they took notes on the treasures they discovered in each book. Just as Toby closed the last open book, a dragon popped in to tell them their class was gathering at the door to leave. Lorn rolled their notes into a thick cylinder and shoved them into his robe pocket along with their list. Toby jumped to his shoulders.

"From what I read, I think the number three means picking out the third word in each line or something like that," said the orange tom.

"But is that the first thing we're supposed to do?"

"I don't know."

"I say we compare our notes to the documents as soon as we get back, then decide what to do."

"Agreed."

As Lorn hurried toward their building with Toby riding on his shoulders, they saw several students scurrying out the door covering their mouths and noses. Yellow smoke billowed from the top windows.

"What happened," demanded Lorn, catching the arm of a fellow student as she stumbled by.

"Explosion," she said. A coughing fit stopped her from saying more.

"Top floor," gasped the feline at her feet.

Toby stared wide-eyed at the smoking building. The front lawn was becoming crowded as more students gathered to watch. Dragon grounds keepers zoomed around the building, darting in windows and out again carrying smoldering furniture. Scanning the crowd, Toby spotted head masters Jalen and Meredith speaking to a medium-sized blue dragon who could only be the head housekeeper. As he watched, the dragon turned and pointed directly at them. Master Jalen glanced at them, nodded to the head housekeeper and walked in their direction.

"It seems, gentlemen," said the head master mage, "that the explosion came from your room. Do you have any explanation for this?"

"Our room?" asked Lorn.

Master Jalen nodded, the she-cat on his shoulder looking at the partners through slitted eyes. Toby's fur raised at the implication.

"Head masters, I know we've had problems in the past, but –"

"Like setting off fireworks in your room?" asked Master Meredith. Master Jalen raised a questioning eyebrow. Lorn stared at the ground, nudging a pebble with his foot.

"That was an accident."

"As I'm sure this was," said the master mage.

"That's just it, though," said Lorn, looking up at the head masters. "We didn't do this."

"We weren't even here," added Toby.

"That's true," said Master Jalen, rubbing an index finger across his chin. "Still, it is possible to leave a potion brewing for an extended time, causing it to explode."

Lorn's shoulders slumped. Toby dug his claws in to catch his balance, making the young mage flinch. Master Jalen grasped the young man's arm.

"We believe you."

"There will have to be a formal investigation, however, so I would suggest you go through everything you own carefully. If there's anything missing or anything amongst your things that doesn't belong to either of you, let us know immediately."

The head housekeeper trumpeted the all clear from the front of the building. Toby stretched to look over Lorn's head, then turned back to the head masters.

"Won't it be suspicious if we go through our stuff and find something that doesn't belong?"

"The housekeepers cataloged everything as they did a search and clear. We'll have a list shortly of everything each student in the vicinity had in his or her rooms."

"They'll most likely include diagrams as well. They're very thorough."

"Better get to it," said Master Jalen, patting Lorn's arm.

Toby watched the head master mage stroll away, Master Meredith perched on his shoulder. As he looked over Lorn's head at their building, he felt the young man take a deep breath. Wisps of yellow smoke were still escaping the windows. Scattered across the lawn where the dragons had left them were their belongings. Toby looked down at his companion, who blew out the air he was holding in a large gust. Together the pair made their way to their room. Lorn pushed the door open.

"By the One that stinks," exclaimed the young mage, clapping a hand to his nose.

Toby wished he had hands to cover his nose, too. It smelled as if someone had thrown a basket of rotten eggs into the room during the summer break and left every window sealed tight. Sulfurous tendrils of yellow smoke drifted up from a blackened star burst shaped hole in the center of the work table. A handful of ingredient bottles lie scattered on the lopsided shelves across the room, the rest laid shattered upon the floor.

The young cat's eyes were drawn to the fireplace. Chunks were missing from the large mantel. Some had lodged in the ceiling beams, while others lay in fragments on what was left of the hearth. All but a couple hearth stones were smashed. Toby heard Lorn suck in his breath. The young mage was staring at the hearth, too. He darted to the hiding place. The stone was missing. A pile of ash and paper fragments were the only things in the hole. Toby leaped down and sniffed the ashes. A familiar lemony scent drifted from the scattered remains. Lorn looked at the orange tom who shook his head. The mage collapsed onto the floor. He picked up a stone fragment.

"How?" Lorn asked, turning the fragment over in his hand. "How could someone get in here and do magic? We had a dampening field."

The young cat paced slowly away, alternately pushing his nose into cracks in the stonework and lifting it into the air.

"They didn't get in. They rigged it from the outside."

"How is that possible?"

"It's something Terence told me. As long as you're outside the field you can move whatever you want inside."

"Great. So whoever did this probably used our stuff to create the explosion."

"Most likely."

The smell of sulfur permeated the air. Hidden underneath, Toby could just make out a few scents he recognized from Lorn's personal stash of special ingredients for spells he wanted to try. The young tom squeezed his eyes shut. Thinking about what those combined ingredients could do made the hair along his spine stand on end. *Can't think of that now.* He lifted his nose again, opening his mouth to let the air filter over his glands. Nothing.

"We're doomed, then. All an official investigation is going to turn up is that everything used in the explosive came from our supplies."

Toby stuck his nose in the small space under the cupboard by the door. A hint of something exotic tweaked his curiosity. Sleek gray shadows padded through Toby's mind, disappearing into ribbons of smoke, as he let the smell wash across his scent glands. Reaching as far as his paw could go, he snagged something small and stick-like.

"Maybe not," he said, batting the little stick across the floor to Lorn, who picked it up.

"It's a stick."

"Not just any stick. Notice anything odd about it?"

Lorn peered at the pinky length piece of wood. He rolled it between his fingers, a frown on his face. His eyebrows rose as he gaped at the orange tom.

"This is an incense stick. We don't have any of those."

"Exactly."

"You don't think…"

"I don't know. Master Jalen seemed to think she might be involved. What matters most now is that we have something to show the head masters that could at least throw doubt on us being responsible for the explosion."

"Let's hope they see it that way, too."

Toby and Lorn searched off and on the rest of the week between classes, hoping to find anything that would point to who created the explosion. Toby discovered several odd scents he was positive were not there before, but nothing else. They brought the scant evidence they had to the head masters who now sat frowning across Master Jalen's massive desk. The master mage's eyebrows were furrowed as if he were in pain.

"I'm sorry, Toby, but unless one of those smells leads to an object we have to assume it was either there prior to the incident or was introduced into the room during the evacuation."

"But why?" complained Lorn. "With Toby's sensitive nose, wouldn't he have smelled those things before now?"

"Unfortunately there is no way that we know of to test smelling abilities as there are to test magical abilities. As far as the other arbitrators are concerned, Toby's unique talent has been exaggerated. Any mention of them now would cast even more doubt upon your credibility," said Master Meredith.

"All we have is this," growled Lorn, waving sharply at the offending stick laying on the desk.

"And that is even questionable, am I right?" asked Toby, kneading the stool he sat on.

"I'm afraid so," said the head master mage. Master Meredith sighed.

"Had you found it out in the open, it might be a different story. As it is, anyone could dismiss it as a piece of flotsam missed by housekeeping."

"It looks as if whoever did this wanted to make sure you were both expelled and to destroy the documents. It's just a good thing you left them with us."

Toby's fur prickled. He hoped neither head master could feel the heat emanating from him as he looked at his companion.

"Um, yeah."

Lorn's lips compressed and his eyes widened. The young man gave a tiny shake of his head, but Toby ignored it. He turned back to Master Jalen who raised an eyebrow. Master Meredith's slitted gaze raked the orange tom's hide.

"What are you not telling us?"

"We made some copies," said Toby.

"But they were destroyed in the explosion," Lorn added in a rush.

"Are you sure?" asked the head master cat.

"Yes. There's nothing left but ash," Lorn said.

Toby's pads felt sweaty. He wrapped his tail around his toes to still its trembling. Was this the kind of thing Master Kiyoshi had dealt with with Master Ribaldy? Was this what his mother had worried about? Toby glanced at the human he'd been partnered with. The young man sat on the edge of his chair, leaning forward in apparent earnestness. Only he could see the slight tremble in the boy's hands. The tom looked back at the head masters, wondering if they noticed Lorn's odd behavior.

"That could work in our favor. If our adversary believes the documents have been destroyed, it may give us more time to decipher the code," said the head master mage, tapping the desk.

"Were you able to find anything useful in the Temple Library?"

"We did a cross-reference between all the symbols, ancient prophecies, poetry and codes and came up with a lot of information, but we still don't know where to begin."

"Did you bring your notes with you?" asked the tortoiseshell she-cat.

"It took us most of the day to hunt down the right books. This is everything we could get in the time we had left."

Toby watched Lorn produce a cylinder tied with purple ribbon from his robes and drop it next to the stick. The boy clasped his hands in his lap, his knuckles going white. Toby looked back at the notes. When had Lorn had time to tie the ribbon on it? Master Meredith pawed the notes closer.

"Master Jalen and I will take it from here. You two have done more than we could have expected in the short amount of time you've had."

"In the meantime," said the head master mage, "it's going to be up to you to clear your names. If you can bring us some solid physical evidence, we may be able to forego a hearing. Otherwise you'll be facing the arbitrators with just your word against apparent facts."

"How much time do we have?" asked Toby, his voice quivering.

"We've managed to delay the hearing until after mid-winter break, but that's all."

"Will we be able to stay on campus during break so we can search?"

"I'm afraid not."

"But, that only gives us a few days," gasped Lorn.

The head masters nodded. Toby watched the young man's face pale, knowing if anyone could see his skin it would be doing the same. A few days to search their old quarters. That's it. And if they couldn't come up with more evidence, who would believe they weren't responsible? No one. The young tom's ears lowered to half-mast as he thought about what his mother had said about Master Ribaldy's relationship with Master Kiyoshi. He glanced at his companion and wondered if he'd made the right decision.

Beads of sweat coursed down Lorn's face, dropping onto Toby's head. The orange tom scarcely noticed as he concentrated on focusing the young mage's will upon the pile of ash on the table in front of them.

Ash motes drifted into motion, swirling into a miniature tornado. Piece by minuscule piece, the tornado grew until every bit of ash and paper fragment whirled in a blur. Carefully, Toby spun out his own will, forcing the tiny motes to combine until they resembled blackened shadows of the papers they had been.

Minutes ticked by as Toby fed his memories of the documents into the magic they were creating. Each paper took shape with agonizing slowness. Lorn's hands on either side of Toby began to tremble. Toby wished for just a little more strength, just a little more endurance. *Almost there,* he thought. A gasp. The papers disintegrated. Toby sighed and closed his eyes.

"Did we do it?" asked Lorn between heaving breaths.

"No."

"Blast!" Lorn pounded the table with his fist and rose from his stool. Toby arched his back, watching as Lorn began to pace the room they'd been temporarily assigned.

"Okay, so what happened?"

"The same thing that happened last time and the time before that and the time before that."

"Anything different?"

"I'm getting faster."

"All right, so that's some progress. Just give me a couple minutes and we'll try again."

"Lorn, we're both exhausted. There's no way we'll be able to do any better in a few minutes."

Lorn spun around, glaring at the orange tom.

"Are you just going to give up?"

"I'm not giving up. I'm being reasonable."

"You're being a wimp."

Toby's hackles raised in an instant. Stalking toward Lorn, he lashed his tail and hissed.

"Say that again."

Lorn lowered himself to Toby's eye level, glaring at the tom. He leaned closer, inches between their noses.

"Wimp."

Toby leaped, screeching. Lorn stumbled back. He screamed as the tom's claws dug into his cheeks. The young cat felt the boy's fingers digging into his sides, grinding into his ribs. He hissed.

Stretching his mouth wide, he aimed for the human's nose. Lorn's hand gripped his head, covering his eyes. The tom bit the finger over his mouth. Lorn screamed again. The young man pounded the cat's head. Toby's vision swam. He couldn't hang on.

Lorn hit him again. With a thump, Toby came to rest against the far wall, breath heaving in and out. He scanned the room for the young human. Lorn lie on his side, facing away from the tom. Toby closed his eyes. He took a deep breath, then another. He opened his eyes and padded toward the boy.

"Hey," he said softly, gently prodding Lorn. The young man rolled onto his back and stared at Toby.

"I deserved that, didn't I?"

"Yeah."

The young man groaned as he propped himself onto his elbows.

"You okay?"

"I think I bruised my hip when I hit the wall, but otherwise I'm fine. How about you?"

"I'm pretty sure I won't win any beauty contests any time soon, but I think I'll live. Man, your claws are sharp." Lorn gingerly touched his bleeding wounds.

"They're supposed to be."

"Yeah. Remind me next time not to call you names."

The young mage levered himself into a sitting position. He looked around the room. The table was on its side. The stool had been knocked into a corner next to the bed. The ceiling lantern was swinging, casting crazy shadows everywhere.

Lorn reached toward a piece of cloth hanging from a hook nearby. He let his hand flop to his side. Toby flicked his tail at the cloth. It wiggled as if it wanted to obey, but remained steadfastly on the hook. The tom sighed. He shuffled to the wall and stood on his hind legs to snatch it between his teeth. He dragged the thing to Lorn who smiled as he took it and pressed the cloth to his cheek.

"Should we clean this up?"

Toby flopped onto the floor.

"I'm too tired."

The partners sat in silence. Toby began cleaning the blood and skin from under his claws. He glanced at Lorn who had scooted back to recline against the wall.

"Mind telling me what that was all about?

"All what was about?"

"Besides calling me a wimp? Let's see, there's the lie about giving copies to the head masters and keeping the originals for ourselves. Then there's the fact that the cylinder you gave them was about half the size it should have been, not to mention tied with a purple ribbon. And what about not telling them that we asked a reference dragon for help to get the information you obviously didn't give them?"

"Caught that did you?"

Toby stared at the young boy, waiting. Lorn tightened his lips into a thin line. He took a deep breath and blew it out through his nose.

"All right," he said, resting his head against the wall, "you want to know the truth?"

"No. I want you to lie to me. Of course I want the truth."

"I need to solve this myself."

"Why?"

"Most of my life I've been a nobody. Uncle Hecktor tried to tutor me when he could, but it just wasn't enough to make a difference. Mother thought putting me in a class for gifted students would help. Father said it was too expensive for someone who wasn't showing more than rudimentary skill."

"Ouch."

Lorn managed a strained smile.

"Father's solution was to bribe the local mage school to add one more student to its already over crowded class. It was a nightmare. Stolen homework. Hide and seek with the school bullies. Projects that would self-destruct moments before the teacher could grade them."

"How did you manage to make it to the academy?" asked Toby, staring wide-eyed at the young mage.

"One night Uncle Hecktor caught me trying to do an invisible spell on my notes. I was trying to keep the bullies from stealing them again. He not only told me it was better to do it the non-magic way, but showed me how to do it. A few days later, he took Father aside and convinced him I should have a personal tutor instead of being in an overcrowded school."

"Did it work?"

"Sort of. Father thought maybe the old man was right — that it would look bad for his business if his son had to go to a public institution, but he didn't see the need to hire a first rate mage. After all, as far as he could see I wasn't showing any promise."

"So you ended up with a second rate tutor," surmised the orange tom.

"Third rate, more like. We'd be doing a lesson and the old coot would fall asleep. In the middle of a sentence, no less."

"Wow."

"Yeah. Anyway, I did my best, but it was never good enough. Then Uncle Hecktor turned traitor. Father was dead set against me following in his footsteps after that. If Mother hadn't seen to it that I was shipped off to the academy before Father returned from one of his business trips, I'd still be there, likely being apprenticed as a merchant instead."

Lorn fell silent. Toby stared into space, trying to imagine what the young man had gone through. He shook his head, making his ears flap.

"We can't do it, can we?" asked Lorn softly.

"No."

"Then it's over."

Toby stared at the scattered ashes. They didn't have the skill or the energy, but he couldn't just give up. He glared at the ashes.

"Help me gather this up and put it in a box or something."

"Why? What are you thinking?"

"*We* can't do it, but I think I know someone who can."

Chapter 10

It had been easier than Reginald had thought to lift the items he needed from the academy storage. Making the camouflage potion had proven more difficult to do by himself, but he'd managed. He could have asked his companion to help him, but he wasn't about to share the glory with a human. No, if he was going to get back into Chivato's good graces, he was determined to do it on his own. Reginald padded to the Commons and waited by the door for his quarry to come out.

"Are you sure he'll help us?" asked Lorn, holding the door for the orange tom.

"No, but it's worth a try."

"What about your mother?"

Reginald fell in behind them, doing his best to move smoothly while staying just within earshot. Toby trotted alongside his human like a well-heeled dog. The orange tom snorted.

"She'll probably strip my fur from my skin for this."

"But will she help us?"

"If we can convince her of what's at stake, maybe."

"Maybe?"

"Maybe."

The invisible tom was thankful the path to the residences had been cleared of snow. An extra set of paw prints following his quarry would have ruined everything.

"Do you think she knows about the explosion yet?"

"I wouldn't be surprised."

"That's not likely to make her want to help us."

"Nope."

"So how do you plan on explaining it?" Lorn tugged his worn overcoat tighter, then shoved his pale hands into his pockets. Reginald sneered at the gap between the sleeve and the pocket edge. Toby ruffled his scruffy orange fur and sighed.

"I doubt I'll get the chance. She'll know everything is connected."

"Won't that make her want to get involved?"

"You'd think so, but I think she's scared."

"Of what?"

"I wish I knew."

Toby stopped, glancing over his shoulder. Reginald held as still as he could. He cursed the snow that was beginning to fall. He watched as the orange tom scanned the area around them. Lorn waited quietly, a quizzical look on his face. The young tom began walking again, his companion falling into stride beside him.

"What about Master O'dorn? Do you think he could talk her into it?"

"Maybe."

"There you go with the maybe's again."

"Yeah. I know."

"Well, let's say they both agree to help and we get the — stuff — put back together again. Do you think we'll be able to get it all figured out before the hearing?"

"I hope so. The head masters weren't very hopeful that finding that stick of incense would be enough to sway the arbitrators."

"I wish there were a way to prove you can smell things better than any other cat."

"So do I."

The orange tom stopped again and scanned the area. Reginald froze, wanting to growl with frustration. Lorn sighed.

"What's the matter now."

"You ever get the feeling you're being watched?"

The white cat's whiskers clamped tight. How could that tom guess he was a tail length away? He glanced up at the human, trying to gauge his reaction to Toby's question. Lorn narrowed his eyes. He looked around, turning in a slow circle.

"I don't see anyone."

"That's the problem. Neither do I, but I can't shake the feeling that someone is spying on us."

Toby's skin shivered. He turned and stared back down the path they had taken. Reginald prayed the snow wouldn't cling to his fur at that moment. He didn't dare shake it off and reveal a tell tale shimmer. The orange tom raised his nose to sniff the air.

"I smell Reginald."

"Where?"

"Somewhere close. Give me a moment. The wind is making the smell shift around."

The young tom closed his eyes, his nose working. The white cat's heart began to beat faster. Toby took a step closer. Reginald could almost feel the heat coming off the orange tom. A group of young humans and their felines raced by on a connecting path. The partners watched them run past.

"There's Reginald's companion."

"Do you see Reginald anywhere?"

The white tom jumped behind a hedge, said the incantation to reverse the camouflage spell and raced after the group. He glanced at the partners from the corner of his eye as he sped past. Lorn was pointing at him, smirking. Toby's eyes were narrowed. Too close. That was way too close. The white tom wondered what stuff they were planning to put back together. Chivato would know. Whatever they were doing he was sure it wasn't what his master wanted them doing.

If it weren't for the head masters' leniency they would have been expelled already. They should be expelled. They didn't deserve to be at the academy. But what else could he do about it? Reginald continued pondering that question as he ran toward the group standing outside his residence. The white tom's fur bristled as he thought about what Toby and Lorn were trying to do. To smear the name of a House should be considered treason. Reginald slowed his pace. He saw a young girl lean toward the others in the group he was heading for.

"Did you hear?"

"Hear what?" asked another young man.

"The Dastardly Duo have gotten a reprieve. The head masters have pushed their hearing back until after break."

"What rot. They should have been expelled immediately."

"Indeed. It's not as if they belong to a House."

Reginald trotted up to his human, who bent down so he could leap to the young man's shoulder. An idea sparkled into existence. Perhaps his comrades could aid him in his quest to get the partners expelled.

"That's not the half of it. Wait until you hear what they're claiming."

Chivato sat, watching the black tom wash himself before the fire. It was a shame to spoil such a beautiful winter day with bad news, but Reginald's message had to be passed along. Lifting his chin, he decided to get it over with.

"It seems our little spies are getting outside help."

The black cat looked up at the gray tom, narrowing his green eyes.

"From whom?"

"They're taking what's left of the documents to Victor's mate and her human in hopes they can put them back together and solve the riddle of Ribaldy's poem."

"That is not good. Adele and O'dorn have been a thorn in our paw before, always shifting the sentiments of the High Council at the last minute before an ordinance for our freedom can be passed."

The black tom stared into the blaze. His tail lashed to and fro. In an eye blink he raised himself to a hunter's crouch, his gaze intent on whatever it was he saw in the fire. He looked back at the gray tom.

"When you first began your work, didn't you create something that killed both human and cat?"

Chivato cocked his head to the side.

"Yes. I lost a good many servants during that time. It became difficult to explain why they went missing."

"Do you still have it?"

The gray tom's whiskers clamped together as he bared his fangs. The black cat shifted forward, his eyes narrowing as he leaned closer to Chivato. The master cat closed his mouth on the unvocalized hiss and drew back. The fire crackled and popped as the two cats stared at each other. The black tom turned his gaze back to the fire and returned to his crouch. Chivato exhaled quietly and curled his tail around his toes.

"I always keep the various stages of my experiments. One never knows when one might need a previous version."

"Very good." The black tom relaxed again, flowing back into a reclining position with liquid grace. Chivato narrowed his eyes at the black cat.

"What would you like to do?"

Slowly, the tom turned his eyes back to the gray cat. His whiskers were splayed wide, his eyes narrowed to mere slits. A purr rumbled in his throat.

"Adele is such a lovely queen, don't you think?"

"I suppose."

"So clever. So regal. And to think she's had to raise our little spy all on her own."

Chivato was silent, watching the black tom's tail twitch rhythmically. He turned back to the fire.

"We should send her a gift."

"A gift?"

"Yes. I think you should alter your designs just for her."

"It will take time."

"You have until tomorrow morning."

Four days had passed. Winter-break was here and the partners still had found nothing beyond the odd stick of burnt incense. They'd resigned themselves to facing the arbitrators as they waited for the city coach.

Toby huddled close to Lorn's feet. He considered suggesting the young mage try making a small fire ball, but thought better of it. Several other students were gathered nearby waiting for their carriages, hopping from foot to foot and rubbing hands together. No need to give them a show. Snow fell softly around them, making it difficult to see beyond a few feet.

Although he'd fluffed his fur as much as he could, Toby was still shivering. Melted snow dripped onto his head and ran into his eyes. He shook his head and hunched himself into a smaller ball. Hands grabbed him around the middle.

Before he could object, Lorn popped the shivering tom into his fur-lined wrap. At first he stiffened, thinking he should demand to be put down. As the warmth of the fur and the young mage's body soaked into his skin, though, he began to feel grateful. Toby wriggled around until he could poke his head out under Lorn's chin.

"By the One! It's hideous!" said a nearby mage.

"What is it? A two-headed golem?" asked a cat in the same group.

"It must be. They'd never allow anything like that to be a student here," said another mage.

"No, wait, I know what that is. It's only the Dorky Duo."

Toby's fur rose along the ridge of his back. There could be only one cat with that silky voice.

"We know Master Ribaldy was a crackpot traitor, but tell us, Toby, was your father as inept at creating magical bonds with a human as you are? Was that why he was a loner?"

Toby growled. He braced himself against Lorn's arms to spring at the white tom.

"Ignore him," whispered the young mage. "Remember what'll happen if we cause any more trouble."

"I'm not the one making trouble."

"Yeah, but do you see anyone here who'll agree with that in front of the arbitrators?"

Toby growled again, but settled back into the young man's arms. He purposely kept his eyes and ears forward as they continued to wait for the city coach.

"I hear they're claiming that someone else set up the explosion in their room," said a young woman in the group.

"I wager they'll say this mysterious someone dropped a stick in their room and Toby's excellent nose just happened to sniff it out," said Reginald. Toby's ears twitched. He wanted to demand the white tom tell them how he'd come up with that idea, but Lorn's grip was tight enough to squeeze the air from his lungs.

"Likely it would be a stick from one of the bushes outside the building. I wouldn't put it past them to suggest one of the teachers was in on the whole thing," added the white cat.

"Sounds like something a traitor and a coward would come up with," said a young tom with a snort.

"Indeed. So long as they don't start accusing the Houses, I say let them bury themselves in their lies."

The orange tom thought he'd die soon from lack of air when the family carriages began to arrive. The Hielberg carriage arrived first. Toby breathed a prayer of thanks as he watched Reginald leap into the dark interior. Lorn loosened his hold.

"I bet he's the one who created that explosion," growled the orange tom.

"I wouldn't put it past him, but how do we prove it?"

"I wish I knew."

"Was it just me or did that last bit seem like a threat?"

"You mean about accusing one of the Houses? I think it was. It makes me wonder how far Gravin Arturo is willing to go to keep the reason behind my father's disappearance a secret."

A dark shadow loomed out of the snow followed by

the muffled sound of horses hooves moments later. Two black horses appeared from the thick falling snow pulling the worn-out city coach. Sitting in the driver's seat, the dour man was wrapped head to foot in a large black cape. Toby shivered.

"Do you believe in omens?" he asked as the coach pulled beside them and the driver slid the door open.

"Nope. You?" Lorn replied, gripping the cat a little tighter.

"Nope."

Neither friend moved. The driver turned slowly to look at them. He motioned sharply toward the cavern-like opening with his whip. Taking a deep breath, Lorn grabbed his bag and hurried to the coach. The driver's bone white hand was the last thing Toby saw before they were enveloped in darkness.

"Honestly, I don't mind sleeping on the floor," said Lorn.

"Nonsense. What kind of hostess would I be if I made even a half-trained mage sleep on the floor," said the black queen, casting scathing glances at her son.

"It really isn' no trouble, lad. Th' Master keeps a spare cot 'round jus' in case," said Mariam as she bustled about the cats' quarters making Lorn's makeshift sleeping arrangements comfortable.

"I'm just sorry we haven't better accommodations for the former grand master mage's nephew. Had we been informed *earlier*, I'm sure we could have had something more suitable prepared."

Like a bed of nails, thought Toby as he watched his mother's claws soundlessly knead the rug. He kept his mouth shut.

"Adele," said Master O'dorn from the doorway, "once

you're satisfied the boys are settled in, I would appreciate your help with that new remedy. The last of the supplies have just arrived."

"I'll be right there."

The black queen watched the housekeeper finish tucking the bedding on the cot. She nodded approval, dismissing the housekeeper, and rose unsteadily to her feet. As she neared, Toby caught a whiff of the sickness clinging to her fur. The young tom stiffened, alarm zinging through his body to his paws. He opened his mouth to draw the smell across his glands, wanting to be sure.

"Close your mouth," snapped the queen. Toby obeyed quickly. He stared at his mother.

"It's just fatigue and the smell of someone who works with sick people. Nothing more." Without another glance, she strode past the orange tom. Toby stared after the black queen.

"Do you think she's lying?" whispered Lorn.

"I don't know. I don't remember her ever smelling like that before, but I don't remember there ever being a sickness this bad either."

"Master O'dorn would know, wouldn't he?"

Toby watched the young man dig his night clothes out of his bag.

"Maybe."

"What's the harm in asking him?"

"Other than mother finding out?"

Lorn stood, holding his night clothes loosely and stared at the young tom.

"Toby, don't pretend you don't care. Go ask him. I'll even come with you."

"No. You go ahead and get some rest. I'm sure mother will have more barbs to throw at you tomorrow. Best be well rested for that," said the orange tom lightly, forcing his whiskers to splay in a cat grin. Lorn tossed his clothes on the cot, then bent down. Placing a gentle hand on his friend's head, he stroked it.

"Let's go."

Toby blinked at him gratefully. Turning, he led the way back down the hall toward Master O'dorn's work room. A soft knock at the outer door made the friends pause out of sight around the corner. They heard the soft footsteps of the master mage. The door's hinges creaked.

"Come in, my friends," said Master O'dorn.

"We're sorry to bother you at this late hour," said a soft male voice, "but we received news."

The door hinges creaked again. More soft footsteps accompanied by a set of paw steps retreated into the master mage's work room. The door opened and closed. Toby looked up at Lorn. The young man's brow was furrowed, a frown on his lips. He gave the orange tom a sharp nod. Together they tip-toed to the door and pressed ears to the wood.

"What news," came Master O'dorn's muffled voice.

"The sickness has spread to the other counties. The Temple has been attempting to contact the King to aid us in our fight against this tragedy, but we've been stone walled by the High Council," said another raspy male voice.

"That's odd. I should've been notified about this by the High Council itself."

"Oh dear. We were hoping you had more information on what was going on," said the first male.

"I'm afraid not. It seems someone has seen fit to keep me out of the loop."

Toby could imagine the old mage's scowl as he drummed his fingers on the table. He turned his head to smile

at Lorn. The young man was standing rigid, looking at something in the room. Toby turned to see what had captured the
boy's attention.

"Eavesdropping? I thought I taught you better than
that," growled Adele, tail lashing.

"Mother, I –"

"I don't want to hear excuses. I want you to march in
there and apologize."

"But, Master Adele –"

"Now!"

Adele lashed her tail and flung the door open behind
them. Toby jumped. He looked over his shoulder to see Brother Jason and Brother Yannis standing with mouths hanging
open. Master O'dorn quirked an eyebrow, straightening slowly beside the table.

"Usually you scratch first, my little friend. To what do
we owe this display?"

"Spying," said the black queen between gasping
breaths. Master O'dorn hurried to the queen's side. He ran a
practiced hand over her sides. Lifting her chin, he gazed into
her eyes.

"Adele, you know you shouldn't tax yourself like this."

"What's wrong with her?" demanded the orange tom.

The old mage gathered the black cat into his arms. He
strode into his work room and gently laid her on the table.
Grabbing a bottle of liquid and an eye-dropper from a nearby
shelf, he walked back to the table. With the ease of one used to
making reticent patients take their medicine, Master O'dorn
forced Adele to drink the remedy. Toby leaped to a nearby
stool. He watched as Adele's sides shook with each labored
breath. He could count her ribs. Her dull fur seemed to absorb
the light from the fire in the fireplace.

"She has the sickness, doesn't she?" asked Lorn, quietly.

"Yes," said Master O'dorn.

"Clarence, no," said the queen through a wheezing breath.

"He deserves to know the truth."

Toby jumped to the table and sniffed his mother. It was true. He stared into the old man's face, seeing the new worry lines for the first time. He looked back down at his mother. Her eyes were closed. Her breathing shallow, but easier. Feeling drained from his limbs. He looked from one face to another, searching, though for what he didn't know. Silence. He dropped from the table and slunk to his nest.

When Lorn arrived later, Toby was curled into a ball, tail over nose, pretending to be asleep. He heard the young man ease onto the cot. A few moments later there was nothing but the slow steady breathing of sleep, something he wished he could have.

Toby ran. The black coach careered toward him. Faster. Faster. He could feel the fetid hot breath of the black demons pulling the oversized coffin. The harder he pushed his legs to run, the slower he moved. He glanced back. The skeletal driver's cape whipped in the wind. His bony hands reached toward the orange tom.

Toby jerked awake. He lay in the silence, panting. He swallowed the bile rising in his throat. There'd be no waking from the real nightmare. He wanted to just curl into a ball and pretend reality didn't exist. He settled for numbness instead.

The young cat heaved himself to his feet. His legs felt wooden as they carried him down the hall toward the kitchen, a ritual he'd performed every morning he'd lived here.

He wasn't hungry. He wondered if he'd ever be hungry again.

Without knowing how or why, he found himself at Master O'dorn's work room door. He reached a leaden paw up to scratch. The door swung open at a touch and he peered inside. He could hear the wheezing breath of his mother accompanied by the gentle snore of the master mage. He turned to leave.

"You may as well come in," said Adele.

"I don't want to intrude," Toby said, squeezing through the narrow opening. The black queen snorted. A coughing fit seized her. Toby rushed over. The young cat fervently licked her head.

"Stop fussing," said Adele when she could breath again.

He sat back, studying his mother. He'd hoped his imagination was playing tricks on him last night, but now he could see it hadn't. Her ribs still showed prominently beneath her fur, her coat as dull as cast iron. She stared at him through slitted eyes.

"It's not as bad as you think," she said in a raspy voice.

Toby opened his mouth to reply. A snort from the old mage made them both look up. Master O'dorn groaned and sat up. He stretched his arms forward, fingers laced, then slumped back in his chair.

"Good morning, my friends," said the old mage, rubbing his eyes with the fingers of his left hand.

"Good morning, Master O'dorn. I hope I didn't wake you."

"No. You're fine. Has your mother filled you in on the diagnosis?"

"She says I'm over-reacting."

The mage glared at the queen resting on the hearth.

"That's typical of her."

"She's lying, isn't she."

Adele glared back at her companion.

"*She* is right here."

"Adele, we discussed this already. It's time Toby knew the truth."

"What truth?" Toby looked from one stern face to the other. His mother's wheeze filled the air.

"He won't thank you later for trying to save him. Do you really want to leave it like this?"

The black queen growled. With a sigh she lowered her head to her paws. Master O'dorn smiled sadly. His eyes were full of compassion when he looked at the orange tom.

"How long?" asked Toby.

"At most two weeks, *if* it proceeds like it has in humans."

"Haven't there been other cats who've gotten the sickness?"

"A few, but Brother Yannis says they were already dead by the time they were found."

The young tom looked at his mother's frail form. Her chest rose in shallow breaths through a hot, dry nose. He could see small drops of moisture at the edges of her eyes, the culprits of the darker tracks down her cheeks.

"I've been giving her a strengthening remedy, but it won't keep the sickness from overwhelming her, especially since she refuses to rest."

"You need my help. Without it more will die. We must find a cure."

"What if someone else helped you and mother rested?"

"Assuming that someone was fresh and well trained, it

could cut our discovery time down considerably."

Adele gave a coughing laugh.

"And where do you expect to find anyone qualified who isn't already whisker deep in this sickness?"

"What if this someone had very little training, but was fresh and eager to learn?" Toby asked, ignoring his mother. There was a creak as the door opened wider. Lorn stepped into the room, head held high.

"Make that two someones."

Master O'dorn smiled.

"It'll take longer than it would if they were fully trained, but I'd say no longer than it has thus far."

"Clarence," gasped the black queen, "you can't be serious."

The old mage turned a stern look on his friend.

"I've never been more serious."

Adele looked around at their determined faces.

"No," she said.

"Adele."

"No."

Toby's ears flattened. He glanced at the master mage who slumped in his chair. The orange tom looked over at the young man who had leaned over the work table, hanging his head. He stared at his mother, trying to think of what to say. Adele swung her gaze to her son.

"Not unless you test your remedies on me first."

Chapter 11

Toby sat by the gazing pond. He stared at the frozen patterns, willing their feathered shapes into some kind of message. They ignored him. He watched the gray clouds float past in the sky, hoping for a sign. They refused to cooperate.

"What am I supposed to do?" he asked. A twig snapped behind him. He swung his head around.

"My apologies, my child," said Brother Yannis. "I did not mean to disrupt your prayers."

Toby blinked at the tonsured old cat, then turned back toward the pond. The patterns remained unchanged. He gazed up at the clouds again. Still nothing. He heard the soft pad of paws as Brother Yannis turned to leave.

"Why is she doing this?"

The old Brother padded to the young tom's side. He sat down and stared out at the pond.

"There was a cat on his way to meet his master in the market. He lost his way and wandered into the bad part of the city. A gang found him and when he told them he had nothing of value to give them, they beat him and left him for dead.

"A Church Father happened by, but crossed the road to avoid the half-dead cat. An Apothecary did as well. Later, a man who sold death drugs came down the road. Seeing the wounded cat, the man scooped him up and took him to a nearby mage. He paid the mage enough to see to the cat's needs, both the remedies and his lodging."

The old cat fell silent. Toby waited, glancing at the Brother from the corner of his eye. Snow began falling. The fat flakes clung to the old tom's fur, but he didn't shiver them off, making the young cat wonder if the old Brother's mind was wandering. Toby chirped to bring the old cat's attention back. Brother Yannis turned his sharp yellow eyes on the young tom.

"Do you know what The Priceless Measure is?"

"It's a moral code from one of the Books of the One," replied Toby.

"But do you know what it is?"

Toby blinked in confusion. In the distance he could hear Brother Jason calling his companion. The old tom placed his ragged tail on the young cat's shoulders.

"Once you understand The Priceless Measure, you will understand what it is your mother is asking. Until then, have faith in the gifts the One has bestowed upon you."

The old cat padded away. Toby's mind whirled with questions. He felt no closer to a decision. He stared at the pond, the snow piling higher on the frozen water. Still no answers there.

He had faith in his abilities, didn't he? But what about all those times he'd failed when she was tutoring him? This was no basic transference spell where failure would mean inky snakes under the floors. *What if I do this and screw up? She could die.*

A rock of emotion lodged in his throat. He kneaded the frozen ground, tearing at the dead grass below the snow. He shook his head until his ears made a popping sound. Snow melted on his furry head and ran into his eyes, blurring everything. He blinked the water away. His vision cleared.

He backed up a step. Adele could die if he failed. He backed up another. She would die if he did nothing. He turned and raced back to the house, his decision made.

The apprentices watched as Master O'dorn sifted the ground willow powder into the boiling mixture. Toby mentally cataloged each ingredient and the amount used. He could hear the scritch scritch of Lorn's pen as the young mage made notes. They had all agreed that the apprentices would observe and learn for most of the process, only adding their energy when the time came. Master O'dorn would prepare the remedy and carry the burden of focusing the magic.

"That should do it," said the old mage, giving the brew one last stir. He extinguished the flame under the small cauldron and ladled the mixture into two bowls. With a sigh, he looked at the young apprentices.

"Now comes the challenge. Toby, I need you to spin a very fine thread of energy into a ball just above the liquid in this first bowl. See it as a walnut sized ball of spider silk. Think you can do that?"

Toby nodded, already concentrating on the image.

"Lorn, I want you to watch what I do with your inner eye. After this is done I'll have you and Toby repeat the process on the second bowl to see how well you've comprehended the process. Ready?"

Both youths nodded.

"Then let's begin."

The orange tom spun the energy into a ball. Master O'dorn captured the end of the thread as Toby clipped it off. The old mage wove the energy into something that looked like a shimmering net around the liquid. When the shape was complete, Master O'dorn paused. Toby looked at the man, using his inner eye, and saw that the old mage was examining the warp and weft of the magic. The tom felt a gentle tug on his mind as the master mage pulled them all into the close up examination. He watched silently as the old man shifted strands into better positions until he was satisfied.

Toby felt his mind float back as Master O'dorn released them. He saw the mage focus his will upon the net and tug. There was a flare of light and an audible pop as the net disappeared. Lorn began scribbling like a man possessed.

"When you're ready, you may begin," said the old mage.

Toby kneaded the stool and waited for Lorn to stop writing. The young man put his pen down and studied what he had written, making the tom want to yowl. He'd never seen Lorn take so long preparing to do any spell. Finally Lorn nodded.

The apprentices followed Master O'dorn's example. After Lorn finished weaving the net, he spent so much time fixing it that Toby's neck fur bristled. The young man, sweat beading on his forhead, looked up at the old mage. Master O'dorn nodded for him to finish.

Toby held his breath, tensed to dive for cover, as he felt Lorn tug the shape into place. With a flare of light and a pop the net disappeared. The fire crackled in the hearth. The clock ticked. Nothing else happened. Toby let his breath out in a big sigh. He looked at Lorn, returning the young man's grin. The orange tom hopped to the floor to follow Master O'dorn into Adele's sick room. The old mage knocked before entering, the apprentices close behind.

"Your son and his companion are fine students. They performed the steps for this remedy flawlessly."

The mage placed the bowl of remedy in front of the black queen. Adele blinked at them without raising her head from her paws. Her wheeze had grown stronger. Toby padded closer. He bent to lick his mother's ear as she struggled to raise up to lap at the liquid. The comforting smell of willow wreathed itself around the queen's head, mingling with the stench of sickness.

Toby sneezed. He sat back on his haunches, sneezing again and again. The orange tom turned away, gasping for breath between sneezes. A powerful sneeze rocked him onto his side, then they were gone.

Toby blinked the hazy moisture from his eyes, trying to focus on the astonished faces of his friends. One breath. Two breaths. No more sneezes. *What happened?* The orange tom looked from his friends to his mother, still poised to lap from the bowl. His eyes widened. He shot across the floor and batted the remedy away from his mother, sending it flying into the wall.

"What are you doing?" shouted Lorn, quick-stepping away from the splashing liquid.

"I couldn't—. It would've—," said Toby, shaking.

"Killed her," said Master O'dorn. The old mage bent to stroke the queen's head. She mewed pitifully and laid her head back on her paws, closing her eyes. Lorn sat down beside him and rested a hand on the young cat's shoulders.

"You smelled it, didn't you?"

Toby nodded. He didn't trust his voice. Wrapping his tail around his toes, he continued to shiver.

"You say you smelled it. What exactly did you smell?" asked Master O'dorn, staring hard at the young cat.

Toby gulped. He looked up at Lorn. The young man nodded. The orange tom looked down at his mother, lying so still he almost wondered if he'd failed to keep her from drinking any remedy. Her chest rose and fell, a wheezing breath emanating from her dry nose. The young cat looked into the old mage's piercing eyes. He ordered his thoughts, bringing forward each smell as it had crossed his scent glands.

"First I smelled the willow in the remedy. It was warm and inviting. Then I smelled the sharp tang of the sickness, but..."

Toby squinched his eyes closed, trying to pull the scent memory apart to distinguish the exact smells. The room was quiet except for Adele's loud breathing. What had caused his allergies to appear? He bared his teeth with the effort to remember.

"Relax. Let it come to you," Master O'dorn said. The young cat took a deep breath. Exhaling it he forced his mind to relax. He let the scene play back in his head. His eyes flew open with the memory.

"I smelled a stronger scent of willow, but it wasn't the same as what was in the remedy. And there was a faint scent of marigolds and wet metal."

"Where did you smell that? Was it coming from the remedy?" asked Master O'dorn, turning to look at Lorn.

"No. It was coming from mother. It was hidden under the sickness."

"By the One," gasped the old mage.

The tom searched the master mage's pale face. The man's hand trembled as he stroked Adele's black head. Toby looked back at Lorn, wondering if the young man understood what was going on. Lorn shook his head. They both turned back to Master O'dorn, waiting for him to say something.

"We should go."

They rose to follow the master mage from the room.

"Stay."

"You need your rest. We would only disturb you with our chatter."

"I... want... to know," she gasped between wheezing breaths. Toby saw the old fire in her eyes again.

Master O'dorn waved to someone or something beyond the door, then came back into the room. Two small stools floated in, settling beside the queen's nest. The humans took their seats as Toby hunched into a ball near his mother. She reached out a paw, touching his shoulder. Startled, the young tom looked at his mother. She blinked in return.

"I can't be certain," began the master mage, "but it seems this sickness isn't natural. If Toby's nose is right, then this could be the work of shadow arts masters."

"You mean everyone with this sickness was cursed?" asked Lorn.

"I don't know. All we can be sure of right now is that what Adele has is not naturally occurring."

"How do you know that?"

"It's dragon willow I smelled isn't it?"

Master O'dorn nodded. Lorn shifted on his stool.

"So that means what?"

"Master Meredith told me assassins use a dragon willow poison sometimes to fake an illness. Once the victim receives the normal remedy of willow powder, then he dies faster."

"And in excruciating pain," added the master mage. They all looked at Adele. She glared at the empty doorway. Toby could imagine the scathing thoughts running through her mind.

"But who would want to kill Toby's mother?"

"The person who wants to keep us from discovering

the truth behind father's disappearance," said Toby. "The other smells, the marigold and wet metal, I've smelled those before. During the coach ride to the academy with Gravin Arturo and Chivato. My allergies went crazy when I caught a whiff of those two. They told me that the gravin needed a particular stomach remedy and, since they mix it themselves, I had gotten a double dose of the smell. But that's not true, is it?"

"I'm afraid not. A mage and cat can mix and take the same remedy without the smell ever clinging to them. You should know that from watching your mother and I."

Toby glanced at his mother. She blinked in response.

"What you smelled then, and again just now, is blood magic, one of the darkest of the shadow arts."

"That's what they accused Uncle Ribaldy of using."

"Indeed it is. And it's beginning to look as if your uncle was framed."

Lorn pressed his lips into a fine line and turned toward Toby. The young man's thoughts were plain. Over the next several hours, the apprentices explained the mission they had been on, as well as about discovering information on the large shipment of dragon willow to Hielberg County and their conversation with Master Natsumi.

Toby told them about the explosion and subsequent investigation, studiously avoided looking at his mother. When Lorn took over telling about trying to resurrect the documents, the orange tom glanced at the black queen. She seemed to be studying him as if he were a new herb she'd just discovered.

"Vipers," hissed Adele when Lorn had finished.

"A nest of them," agreed Master O'dorn, "but how many? We can guess who the head snake is, but how many smaller heads does this beast have?"

"That's why we've tried to keep most of the information to ourselves. Lorn and I think Master Ribaldy's documents hold some key to the gravin's plans, but we didn't have time to try to decode them with the information we got at the Temple library."

"We were hoping you could help us resurrect my uncle's documents and Toby's father's letter."

The apprentices looked with hope at Master O'dorn. The old mage stroked his chin and gazed down at his companion.

"You may be right about those documents proving Gravin Arturo's behind your father's disappearance, maybe even that he set Master Ribaldy up to take the fall, but if they're as hard to decode as you say they are that's going to take a lot of time to figure out. I don't know if we have that kind of time."

Lorn looked as if he were about to protest. Toby snagged the young man's pant leg. When the young man glanced down at him, the orange tom nodded toward his mother.

"Do it," said Adele.

"Master O'dorn's right, mother. We need to concentrate on finding a cure."

"Don't... argue.... Time... short."

A coughing fit racked the black queen's body. Toby tried to get close enough to lick her ears, but she scooted away. When the coughing subsided, the orange tom nosed his mother's head. She weakly batted him away.

"No.... You... catch.... Find... cure," she whispered between gasping breaths.

"That's right, mother," murmured the tom, "we'll find

a cure first, then worry about the documents."

"No...."

Adele lay sucking in wheezing breaths, her eyes slits, her whiskers clamped tight. Toby's throat closed. His mother's mind must be fogged by the sickness. He mewed at her, trying again to get close. She batted his nose away. Her gasps slowly returned to shallow breathing. She gave her companion one of her formidable stares.

"I think what your mother is trying to say is that there may be information on a cure in the documents. Am I right?"

The black queen purred brokenly as she settled her head back onto her paws. Within moments she was asleep.

"And that, my friends, would be a dismissal," said the master mage with a chuckle.

Toby watched in fascination as the ash motes rose and danced in the magical wind Master O'dorn was creating. The apprentices lent the master mage their energy, hastening the process, but the old mage was the one in complete control of what was happening.

The tom was both entranced and chastened, watching what a master could do. In the end he was just glad Master O'dorn had agreed to help them. What had taken them several hours to attempt and fail took the master mage a matter of minutes to accomplish. Toby patted at the papers now lying on the work table. He bent to sniff the one Lorn had rubbed a lemon wedge on. Yes, they were all intact, right down to the smell. He gave Master O'dorn a wide cat grin, which the mage returned.

"Now, then, let's see what we can discover."

He spread the documents out according to the dates written on them. Toby leaned over, trying to stay out of the way while also trying to read each page. All three were silent as they perused the riddle.

"May I see your notes?"

Lorn handed over a thick cylinder of paper. The old mage studied each page, asking for clarification on a few items, then put the notes aside and bent over the pages of Master Ribaldy's documents. He shifted a few papers, moving Victor's letter to the beginning and a few other pages further to the end, then stood up straight.

"Your thoughts are correct. I believe if we can decode Victor's letter, we should be able to figure out the rest. Thankfully, it should be the easiest of them all."

"What makes you think it should be first?" asked Toby.

"Well, to begin, it was dated the most recent, which means any information it holds would be most important. Add to that the fact that your father disappeared just days after it was written, and it would seem that it contains information worth doing anything to obtain."

"That makes sense, but why would it be easier to decode than the others?"

"If the answer to our riddle lies within these other documents, then we would need a key. If it is urgent we decode the riddle quickly, then the key must be easy to discover because, as the saying goes, the fate of the world is at stake."

"Then are we also right about the number three being the key to unlocking father's letter?"

"Indeed you are. If we look closely at this poem, we can see that the truly odd words are in the third line of each quatrain."

Master O'dorn picked up a pen and turned over one of Lorn's notes. He scrawled the words lion, medal, NahChee and Fi at the top. They stared at the words.

"I can't make sense of it," said Lorn.

"Perhaps they're out of order," suggested Toby. He concentrated on the words, lifting a copy from the page and shifting them with his will. A moment later he had the re-arranged words settled a little further down the page: medal, lion, Fi, NahChee.

"And your mother was convinced you couldn't do such basic spells," said Master O'dorn.

"Wait a minute. What if those aren't separate words at all?" Lorn asked. He grabbed the pen and wrote: medallion finahchee.

"I see where you're going. It looks like father was trying to tell us about some kind of medallion, but what's a finahchee?"

The apprentices looked at the master mage. He stood, staring at the words, stroking his chin. He leaned over Victor's letter. The old mage looked back at their guesses. A smile crept over his face as he stood up.

"It seems, gentlemen, that Victor was as willing to cheat in espionage as he was at games of strategy. There is a piece missing in our word."

Both apprentices searched Victor's letter again.

"Bonah," they exclaimed together.

"So the last word is actually an incantation, isn't it?" said Toby. Master O'dorn wrote out the spell's words: fiBOnah nahCHEE.

"So we find this medallion, wherever it is, and say that spell and the rest falls into place," said Lorn.

"Something like that, yes," answered the master mage.

"Okay, so where's the medallion?"

"I'm afraid it could be anywhere. There's nothing

in the letter indicating where it could be and this is the last communication we have before he disappeared."

Toby's ears flattened as he stared out the window. Master O'dorn was right. The medallion could be anywhere between here and Hielberg County. For all they knew, Victor disappeared before he could send the last piece of the puzzle. The last bit of information they needed. Their last chance.

The orange tom's ears perked up. He stared at his father's letter. Master O'dorn had said his father had cheated. What if he hadn't cheated, just did the unexpected?

"I think I know where the medallion is."

Both humans looked at him.

"I think Master Natsumi has it."

"You mean the necklace hanging on the wall?"

"Yeah. Listen, father cheated with the code, right? He split the first part of the incantation into two parts. What if he did something like that with the medallion?"

"Split it in two?" asked Master O'dorn.

"No, not exactly. If the only way to decode Master Ribaldy's documents is to have the medallion and the only way to make the medallion work is to use the incantation, it makes sense to keep the medallion and the spell separate, especially if you think someone is on to you. And Master Natsumi said the medallion was in the last communication they got from father."

"But why send the medallion to Master Natsumi if she's in league with Gravin Arturo?"

"Maybe father only knew *someone* was involved. After all, up until he sent this letter, he was working with the loners to stop the dragon willow trafficking."

"May I also point out that all your evidence against Master Natsumi is conjecture? A careless word and a stick of

253

burnt incense does not a case make."

"Yeah, but the head masters seemed to think she was involved," said Lorn.

"That may be, but we cannot fling accusations about without proof."

Toby opened his mouth to protest, but the old mage forestalled him with a raised hand.

"What we need to concentrate on is solving the puzzle before us. I will contact the head masters and have them send the medallion by special messenger. It should be here by morning, if all goes well, and we can see about unraveling this mystery then."

Master O'dorn lead the apprentices out of his work room into the adjoining waiting area.

"In the meantime get some rest. You'll need your wits about you if we're going to figure this out before our time runs out."

Toby glanced across the waiting room to his mother's closed door. It wasn't their time he was worried about.

Chapter 12

Torn's cot was empty when Toby woke up, so he raced into Master O'dorn's work room, thinking the humans had started without him. He found the old mage alone, studying the medallion from the loners' office.

The red gem in the middle of the golden triangle twinkled in the winter sunlight pouring through the window. A note lay next to the messenger tube on the table. Toby jumped to a stool and leaned over the note to read it. Head Master Jalen cautioned that the medallion was tainted by blood magic, but hoped it would be useful in Master O'dorn's research in ancient remedies. The orange tom's brow wrinkled.

"Ancient remedies?"

"Sometimes a cure for a modern illness rests within ancient texts."

"So you lied to the head masters to get the medallion?"

"Not at all. From a certain point of view we are using the medallion to unlock ancient codes in the hopes of finding a cure."

"But Master Ribaldy's documents aren't ancient."

"True, but his use of prophetic-style poetry, symbols and numbers in code form is."

"Do all humans think in circles?"

"Only the brilliant ones," said Master O'dorn with a wink. Toby splayed his whiskers in a wide cat grin.

"Is Lorn in the kitchen?" asked the tom.

"I sent him to fetch Brother Jason and Brother Yannis."

Toby's eyes widened.

"I thought we weren't going to tell anyone else about this."

"Ordinarily I wouldn't, but they are experts in understanding ancient prophecies. I believe we'll need their expertise to unravel this mystery."

"You trust them?"

"The Temple Brothers are prohibited from telling anyone's secrets when they are told something in confidence. Besides that, I've known both of them since before your mother was kitted. They are trustworthy. In the meantime, let's see how far we get by ourselves."

"What about the trace of blood magic? Will it interfere?"

"A very good question. What do you think?"

Toby stared at the medallion, it's gem glittering in the sunlight. Why would Master Ribaldy use blood magic on it if he were truly innocent? A memory tickled his thoughts.

"Does blood magic carry unique signatures?"

"Every magic from incantations to potions to those things done in the shadow arts carries the signature of the mage who casts it."

"What about transferring someone else's signature to an item? Can you do that if the someone else uses blood magic and you don't?"

"I suppose so, though blood magic carries more than just the mage's signature. It also carries that of the victim. Why do you ask?"

"It was something Lorn dug up in our research when we got Father's letter. Something about putting another mage's magical signature on an item. What if Master Ribaldy didn't use blood magic to create the medallion? What if he created the medallion as a key, but wanted to tell us who was responsible for the need of the key?"

"I see where you're going with that. Perhaps we should dissect the signatures on this before we try to unlock it."

Toby nodded. The master mage set the medallion floating within a dampening field, then said an incantation to reveal the various signatures embedded in the necklace. The gem glowed liked molten metal, then spewed an image that looked like a knotted rope. Master O'dorn pointed his index fingers at it, then pulled his fingers in opposite directions. The image split into three ropes, each with different knots. He pointed to the two on the left.

"This one is Hecktor's signature and this one is your father's."

"What about the other one?"

"It is the combined signatures of the shadow arts mage and his victim."

The master mage repeated the pulling apart process on the third rope. It glowed a dull red, its knots throbbing in time to an invisible heart. Toby had to look at the fourth rope from the corner of his eye to see it at all, its pale image nearly invisible.

"Can you tell who they belong to?"

"No. I'd have to access the High Council archives to identify either of them, but I can tell you that the victim was immature in his magic, possibly a human hopeful."

"And the shadow arts mage?"

"A master cat."

Toby glared at the pulsating rope, wishing that slashing it to ribbons would inflict the same harm on the cat who owned it. Master O'dorn cleared his throat. The young tom looked up at the old human's piercing gaze. Mirrored there were Toby's own thoughts. Without looking, the mage waved a hand at the ropes and they disappeared.

"I believe we should unlock the key now, don't you?"

Toby nodded. Master O'dorn said the incantation they had discovered hidden amongst Master Ribaldy's documents. White light shot from each of the triangle's points, curving into a large circle. From the luminous circle more rods of light grew, each looking similar to a skeleton key

"Do you see the pattern?" asked Master O'dorn.

Toby studied each of the eight keys. At first it seemed simple, each key had one more tooth than the one before, but then the orange tom noticed the number of teeth increased beyond just adding one to the next one. The first was just a straight line. The next two had one tooth each. The fourth had two teeth and the fifth had three. Key number six had five. Number seven had eight and number eight had thirteen. Toby shook his head.

"If there's a pattern, I don't see it."

"How familiar are you with mathematics?"

"Mother drilled me in basic numbers, but she said I was too hopeless to try anything harder. She gave up."

"A pity. Perhaps, then, we can approach this problem using history instead. Do you remember reading about Leon the Erabain?"

"Yes, he helped our kingdom evade starvation during one of the worst winters by showing people how to raise rabbits. What does that have to do with mathematics?"

"Leon used a pattern of numbers to predict the population growth of the rabbits."

"And this is that pattern?"

"Indeed it is. Can you see it now?"

Toby studied the keys again. They refused to divulge their secret. The orange tom considered the breeding habits of rabbits and tried to imagine the teeth on each of the keys to be a rabbit. He closed his eyes and watched as the bunnies hopped by in ever increasing numbers. His whiskers splayed as the answer became clear.

"When you add the teeth from one key to the teeth of the previous key, you get the number of teeth on the next key."

"Bravo. I think your mother gave up on you too soon. We shall have to speak with her about that," said the old mage with a wink.

"Then father's letter was a simplified version of these documents."

"Correct again. And now that we know the sequence we can begin decoding the documents."

Several hours later, there was a soft knock on the door. Master O'dorn wrote the final words on their notes as their guests entered the room. Toby watched Lorn's smile fade as he took in the master mage's grim face.

"We came as quickly as we could," said Brother Jason, squeezing his considerable girth through the work room door. Brother Yannis was perched upon his shoulder.

"It's good that you did. It seems our situation is worse than we thought."

"What happened?" asked Lorn.

"We decoded most of your uncle's documents," said the orange tom.

"And?"

"Before we jump into what we've uncovered so far, I

would like for the good Brothers to help us unravel the part that mimics ancient prophetic poetry."

Master O'dorn motioned for the man and his companion to have a seat at the table, then pushed the last page of Master Ribaldy's documents toward them. Brother Yannis recited the poem, the sound of his voice raising the hair along Toby's spine.

> *So dark the time of man doth come,*
> *When Sneak doth death decide to run*
> *And charge upon the willow's sun*
> *That blood be cold and change be done.*
>
> *The Spider finds the widow's peak.*
> *A cat doth spin his will to seek.*
> *Should will define, the day be bleak*
> *And hell upon mankind doth wreak.*

The Brother Cat looked at his human friend, whiskers clamped tight. The portly human brought his trembling fist to his lips and kissed the knuckle of his index finger, then touched it to his forhead. Brother Yannis turned his sharp gaze on the master mage.

"May I ask where you found this?"

"Can you tell us anything about it?"

"It's predictive apocalyptic poetry."

"We figured as much. We were hoping, with your expertise in such things, you might be able to give us an idea what its predicting."

"Well, if I had to hazard a guess, I'd say it's a warning of coming disaster, but that's somewhat obvious, given it's apocalyptic nature."

"Yes, but what disaster?"

"That's the problem with ancient prophecies, especially those declaring the end of time, there's no way to know for certain. Some would look at this and say the poet was predicting the current sickness." Brother Yannis squinted at the old mage. "It all depends on who the poet was."

Master O'dorn leaned back on his stool, stroking his chin. Toby looked from the Brother Cat to his friend. Their cool gazes reminded Toby of the strategy games he used to watch his father play with the old mage.

"The poet was Master Ribaldy," said Master O'dorn.

The answer hung in the air. Brother Yannis' tail twitched. His companion picked up the document, the paper rattling in his trembling hand. Toby watched the overweight Brother mouth the words again as his face paled. Slowly the human returned the paper to the table.

"We must help them, Brother."

The tonsured cat licked his ruff. He turned to nip at his flank. He shook his head, making his ears flap. Finally, he turned toward his human counterpart. Brother Jason returned the old cat's gaze steadily. Brother Yannis looked over his shoulder at the master mage.

"If we are to help you, then there must be no more secrets."

"Agreed."

Brother Jason leaned forward conspiratorially.

"Let us begin first, as a sign of trust. Master Ribaldy came to us shortly after the High Council decided to investigate the dragon willow trade in Heilberg County. He said he believed someone was manipulating the High Council's decisions, but he didn't know who."

"Based upon the stone walling we've received in gain-ing aid for those falling ill, I'd say the mage was right," said Brother Yannis.

"What did he hope to gain by telling you this?" asked Master O'dorn.

"He wanted us to gather information through our various smaller temples and traveling Brothers, anything that seemed out of the ordinary."

"Did you find anything?" asked Lorn.

"There were some murmurings about an unknown cat spreading a message of freedom for cat-kind, but we never discovered who or what the message meant."

"And you delivered this information to Master Ribaldy?"

"Actually, we gave it to Master Kiyoshi. He was supposed to convey it to Master Ribaldy. I don't know if the mage ever received it."

"When was this?"

"Just a few days before Master Ribaldy was discovered setting up explosives under the High Council Chambers."

"That means Master Ribaldy may have figured out who was buying all that dragon willow and known what it was going to be used for before he was arrested for treason," said Toby.

"What do you mean?" asked Brother Yannis.

"Look at the dates on these documents. The first were written soon after the investigation began, leading up to when you said you gave Master Kiyoshi that information. Then the one with the poem and father's letter were written a couple days before the arrest."

"Then, Master Kiyoshi must have told Uncle Ribaldy about the mysterious cat. But that doesn't explain why he'd want to blow up the High Council during Session. That would've been suicide."

"I think I can answer that," said Master O'dorn. "According to what we've been able to decipher from this code, your uncle was betrayed. It seems this mysterious cat has a number of associates feeding him information. Although the High Council, in conjunction with the loners, had been able to shut down several shadow arts marketers, they were always small operations, never anything leading to the snake's head."

"Mystery Cat was also able to feed misinformation back into the investigation, laying a trap for your uncle and my father."

"After Master Kiyoshi delivered your information, he and Hecktor decided to go undercover in the city to see if they could hear what this cat was saying for themselves."

"What did they find out?" asked Lorn.

"Apparently, they overheard several followers talking about a plan to overthrow the "human-run government," which I can only assume had something to do with blowing up the High Council."

"So Uncle Hecktor was set up."

"That's what it looks like."

"And Master Kiyoshi?"

"Bait," growled Toby.

The room was silent.

"Who would do such a thing?" asked Brother Jason.

"That, I hope, is something you can tell us."

Brother Jason raised his eyebrows. His feline companion opened his mouth to protest. Master O'dorn held up a hand.

"We think the answer to the identity of our mysterious cat and his plans lie within this poem, but we need your help to decipher it."

The Brothers stared at the poem again. Heaving a sigh, Brother Jason scooted his stool closer to the table to read over the tonsured cat's head.

"Deciphering predictive apocalyptic poetry isn't a precise magic, like you're used to. It's a matter of interpreting what the poet's message may have been word by word and line by line."

"Go on," said Master O'dorn, waving a hand at the piece of paper.

"Well, take the first line, for example. The word "dark" can mean literal darkness or night."

"It can also mean something bad or evil," added Brother Yannis.

"Certainly, and in this case I think that's what Master Ribaldy was saying based on the rest of the line. He was trying to warn the reader that something bad or evil was coming."

"What about the rest of the poem? Does he say what that evil might be?"

Brother Yannis gave the master mage a hard stare.

"If you're hoping he specifically says, "Watch out for Master So-and-So because he's going to blow up the High Council," you're hoping in vain. Predictive apocalyptic poetry doesn't lend itself to specifics like that."

"No, but he does hint at a couple names," said Brother Jason, pointing at the poem. "Look here. He capitalized Sneak and Spider. It's likely he was using imagery or even name meanings to tell us who we're looking for."

"You're right. If we had our book of names we could easily find out, but it's back at the temple."

"What about the rest of the poem?"

"Basically it says these two persons, one of whom seems to be a cat, plan to use death as a weapon to create a change they want and that whatever that change is won't be good for the rest of us," said the large human.

"That's helpful," snarled Lorn.

"Indeed. It seems the poem is a dead end."

"There's nothing in there about what kind of death the Spider and the Sneak will use?" asked Toby.

"Nothing useful. The closest references are *death decide to run* and *charge upon the willow's sun.*"

Toby looked around the room at the humans and cat, each in various postures of defeat. Lorn had walked to the fireplace and was leaning with his back against the mantle. The young man's lips were compressed into a thin line and his eyebrows were drawn together in a scowl as he stared across the room at the closed door. Suddenly the human's gaze snapped back to the papers on the table. He blinked. He smiled.

"What if Uncle Hecktor is telling us without telling us what the weapon is made from? Master O'dorn, didn't we charge the willow in the remedy we mixed for Adele?"

"Yes," the mage answered hesitantly.

"Could a master mage charge willow in a way to make it a poison instead of a remedy?"

"You're right," exclaimed Toby. "Gravin Arturo said dragon willow could be used in the shadow arts by twisting something benign into something evil and Master Meredith said it was often used as a poison by assassins."

"The sickness is the weapon," said Master O'dorn.

"And I think I know who created it," said Toby. He looked at Lorn.

"Do you still have that note to Reginald we found?"

The young man bolted from the room, returning again a few moments later waving the piece of paper.

"We bumped into someone on our way back from the library one night. He dropped this."

He laid the note on the table next to everything else. Pointing to the poem and to the short note, Lorn grinned.

"It's a match. Thank you Uncle Hecktor."

Toby batted the air, then turned to look at the curious faces surrounding them.

"This note was supposed to go to Reginald, a student from Heilberg House. As you can see, he's supposed to be doing something for someone connected with the House. My guess is spying on us and maybe distracting us."

The young tom turned to look into Lorn's eyes. The young man's expression hardened.

"Like with disappearing supplies and exploding homework?"

"Exactly."

Brother Jason leaned forward on his stool, his eyebrows puckered.

"I'm confused. What does this note have to do with the poem?"

Lorn tapped the note.

"Uncle Hecktor copied this person's handwriting to show us who is responsible for creating the weapon. If we can identify it —"

"We'll have our assassin," said Master O'dorn, smiling.

"Can you identify the writing?" asked Brother Yannis.

"If it was written by a master mage or cat, then it will have his magical signature. Now that we've narrowed the search to Heilberg House, I'll be able to check the High Council Records for any matches. Finding a match shouldn't be too

266

difficult from there."

Toby couldn't help purring. He took a step toward the old mage.

"And I bet whoever wrote that note has the same magical signature as the blood mage's on the medallion."

The mage leaned toward the young cat, placing a hand on his shoulder.

"Then let's not wait."

They'd arrived at the academy yesterday, just in time to debrief their findings with the head masters and crawl into bed before exhaustion claimed them. The meeting hadn't gone well, considering the number of secrets they'd been keeping, but the end result wasn't as bad as they feared.

Other than being ordered to keep silent on what they knew, they were to cease digging into the matter. Master Jalen assured them they would work with Master O'dorn and the High Council to uncover the assassin's identity. Toby wondered if alerting the High Council was the wisest course of action, considering someone there seemed to be leaking information, but he'd had no say in the matter. In the mean time they had been restricted to their rooms until after the hearing two days hence.

That was yesterday. Today Toby was determined to convince Terence that his mentors were devious master minds. Unfortunately, Lorn was standing between him and the entryway.

"There's nothing you can say that'll change his mind," said Lorn, blocking the door.

"I have to try."

"Why? Hasn't he made it clear he doesn't believe you?"

"He's just repeating Chivato. Deep down I know he

has to feel that something's not right."

"Maybe he does, but do you honestly think pointing it out again is going to make him agree with you?"

Toby lashed his tail and growled.

"What are you getting at?"

"Listen," said the young mage, holding his hands out in placation, "how would you feel if your best friend kept reminding you that you're going against your gut instinct?"

"I'd be grateful."

"Would you? Even if you were jealous of how your friend was chosen and you weren't?"

"Why would Terence be jealous? He's a loner in training."

"Yeah, but you were chosen. Being chosen is about as close to becoming noble as many of us get. Terence is from the Lower District, so Chivato's message probably sounds pretty good. What you're telling him is that he's always going to be what he's always been, a nobody."

"But that's not what I'm saying at all."

"I know that, but that's not what it's going to sound like to him."

Toby drew his claws across the wooden floor. He hated to admit that Lorn had a point. The orange tom thought back to when he and the little patched tabby were hopefuls. Terence had been in awe of everyone and everything, though he had plenty of experience with the more practical applications of magic like dampening fields.

Toby flattened his ears and hissed at the mage. Lorn didn't budge. He crossed his arms, staring down at the orange tom. The cat lashed his tail once, then turned and stalked away.

There was a knock at the door. Toby ignored it. He

stared into the fireplace, wishing the human and cat behind everything were roasting on a spit somewhere in the hell some of the Followers of the One spoke of.

"It's a letter from Master O'dorn," said Lorn, closing the door. He walked over and sat beside the tom.

Toby was afraid to ask. When they'd left, the master mage had gone to search through the signature records. He had promised to be quick so he could return to combing Master Ribaldy's documents and his books on blood magic diseases.

The strengthening remedy had stopped working for Adele. Toby knew there were only a few days left before she would die, but he had to return to the academy with the information they'd uncovered. They couldn't risk a special messenger being intercepted. Dragons were formidable, but not invulnerable.

The orange tom waited, listening to the crackle of the fire. His body felt numb. He wanted to know. He didn't want to know. Lorn laid the letter down.

"What does it say?"

"She's holding on, but still no cure. He's created a mixture that slowed the sickness down again. It's working for your mother and the other humans they were treating. Master O'dorn is sure he'll find the cure any day now."

"How many days does she have left?" asked the young tom, still staring into the fire.

His mind replayed each argument they'd had since his father disappeared. Try as he might he couldn't remember any words of love or kindness passing between them. She'd told Master O'dorn she loved him. Why couldn't she have said it to him? Why couldn't he have tried harder, done better, proven he had what it takes? Why did he always have to argue with her? Why couldn't he have kept his tongue behind his teeth?

"She's strong, Toby. She's a survivor."

The cat said nothing. Lorn laid a gentle hand on the young tom's back. They watched the fire burn to embers. *Let her live,* he prayed. He wondered if the One would hear his prayer. He wasn't a Follower. *Let her live and I will follow.* He listened for an answer, but the only sound was the shifting of a few charred sticks as they fell through the fire grate.

Toby and Lorn sat on their stools, waiting for the hearing to begin. Toby's tail twitched as he stared around the conference room at the gathered teachers, surprised Gravin Arturo and Chivato were also in attendance. It was all the tom could do to keep his fur flat when he saw them.

Unlike their first hearing, this time he and Lorn were part of the proceedings. Sitting on one side of the conference table was a balding man in navy blue master's robes, the lines on his face giving the impression of permanent disapproval. On the other side sat a young brunette in dove gray master's robes, her dark eyes reminding Toby of the picture in Master O'dorn's sitting room of a deer nuzzling her fawn. The rustling of cloth and papers quieted as Head Master Jalen rapped the table with his gavel.

"Ladies and Gentlemen, we are here to discuss the veracity of the claim of Apprentices Lorn and Toby that the explosion in their room was perpetrated by someone other than themselves. We have asked Master Leta to represent the students' case and Master Orde to represent the opposing side. Let us begin."

Master Jalen rapped the gavel once more. The balding mage turned in the students' direction.

"What evidence is there that someone other than you had access to your rooms?"

"We found a burnt stick of incense under a large bureau. It wasn't there before," answered Lorn.

"A burnt stick of incense under a large bureau, you say? How do you know it wasn't there before?"

"If it had been, Toby would have smelled it when we moved in."

"And how can you prove that you smelled it? Perhaps you were only looking for anything that could shift the blame to someone else and pretended to find this stick to do just that."

Lorn grabbed his stool as he leaned forward.

"That's not true. Toby's nose is very sensitive. Ask anyone who knows him."

"Friends can be persuaded to lie simply because they are friends."

Master Jalen banged his gavel on the table before Lorn could say more. The young human's face was becoming red. Toby could feel the heat coming off him in waves. The fur between the orange tom's toes prickled. It was all he could do to keep his claws sheathed. The young female mage raised her hand.

"The head master recognizes Master Leta."

"Apprentices, have you been bullied at any time while at the academy?"

There was a rustle of cloth and murmuring. Toby glanced around the room. Several of the teachers from the Houses glared at them. Toby looked straight at Master Leta.

"Yes."

"And what have you done in retaliation?"

"Nothing."

271

"Nothing?"

"No."

"You chose not to defend yourself in any way?"

Toby cocked his head. He looked up at Lorn, who raised an eyebrow. They both turned back to the woman. She sighed.

"Did you or did you not keep your rooms secure at all times?"

"Yes. We put a dampening field on both the work room and the bedroom to keep anyone from using magic against us."

The woman's lips curved in a small smile.

"Head masters, all of us who are gathered here today know that a dampening field is good at keeping magic from being used within the field if the magicians are also within the field. We also know that objects can be moved within that field if one is outside of it."

Master Orde leaned forward, glaring at the young woman.

"Are you suggesting an apprentice knew how to manipulate a dampening field? That's preposterous."

Muttering broke out amongst the gathered teachers, making Master Jalen need to bang his gavel on the table. Master Antwan raised his paw.

"The head master recognizes Master Antwan."

"Actually, we have a trainee who is quite adept at moving items from an area within a dampening field to an area outside of it. It would not be difficult to imagine an apprentice who could do the opposite."

The old mage waved his hands in dismissal. Master Meredith looked from the man to the charcoal gray tom.

"Let us go back to the stick of incense the students

claimed to have found. I think we should interview the head housekeeper to verify if the apprentices' rooms were swept clean prior to the incident."

"Agreed."

Master Jalen motioned to an awaiting dragon. Moments later there was a loud pop as the head housekeeper appeared. The medium-sized blue dragon bowed to the head masters.

"How may I serve you?"

"Mistress, we are in need of details regarding the cleaning of these apprentices' rooms."

The dragon turned golden eyes on the partners. She gave a toothy smile to them, then turned toward the head masters again.

"Their rooms were scrubbed from ceiling to floor before they moved in. Since then we have cleaned them daily top to bottom as is custom. We've also kept a close eye on their special needs."

She turned and winked at them.

"Special needs?"

"Oh yes. These two sometimes need an extra broom or rag on occasion to sweep up their experiments gone wrong. Nothing too demanding. They always clean up their messes best fleshlings can and that's much appreciated."

The old mage leaned toward the dragon.

"So the explosion in their room was nothing out of the ordinary?"

"Oh Dragora bless. That was nothing like ordinary. We're still scrubbing the stench from the walls."

"Mistress," said Master Jalen, drawing her attention back to him. "You said you scrubbed their rooms before they moved in and have cleaned them daily since. Is that correct?"

"Yes, sir." The blue dragon held her head high.

"Would it be possible that a stick of incense could have been trapped under a bureau and been missed in any of that time?"

The head housekeeper glared at the head master. She drew her lips back from her formidable teeth and snapped at the air.

"If one of my helpers missed even a speck of dust I would have her tail as my belt."

Master Jalen nodded, smiling.

"Thank you, Mistress."

The blue dragon nodded, turned to wink at the students again, then disappeared. The head master mage looked around the room.

"I think we can safely assume that had the incense been in the apprentices' rooms prior to the explosion, the head housekeeper would know."

"It also seems that someone might have a reason to cause harm to these students," said Master Meredith.

"Only if you accept their claim that they were being bullied," said Master Orde, rhythmically tapping his fingers on the table.

"I believe their claims are justified given what we know of class rivalries between students," said Master Leta.

"That still does not prove that young Toby sniffed out the stick, rather than planting it there just after the explosion as a means to shift responsibility. We've all had the displeasure of walking past that building since the incident. How could anyone smell anything beyond that stench?"

Master Jalen raised a sheet of paper from the table and cleared his throat.

"If I may, we have documentation from a previous interview with an acquaintance of Toby's stating that the apprentice was able to smell precisely what was being cooked for breakfast during orientation while both hopefuls were on the first landing of the Commons stairway."

"Hearsay," said the old mage.

"Proof." The young woman pounded a fist on the table.

Master Meredith looked from one mage to the other. She stared at Toby, narrowing her eyes.

"Can we not test this?"

Both mages looked at the head master cat. The old mage narrowed his eyes at the tortoiseshell.

"What do you suggest?"

"Choose three humans to select one item each with distinct smells. Hide those items in a large room, say the banquet hall. If Toby can find and identify each item, then we must accept that he is indeed capable of smelling a stick of incense beneath the stench of the explosion. If he cannot, we have no alternative than to expel both students. What say you?"

Toby's eyes widened. He looked first at Master Orde's sneering face, then to Master Leta's wan expression. They both nodded.

"Agreed."

Toby paced outside the doors to the banquet hall. Lorn poked him in the side, motioning to the small group gathering at the door. Gravin Arturo was standing with the head masters and the arbitrators. The young tom wished he could have heard what Chivato had said to Master Orde to convince the older mage that the gravin should be included as an observer to the test.

The partners watched as the head master opened

the door to the hall and waved the others in. Gravin Arturo bumped into Master Leta as they tried to go through the door at the same time.

"Excuse me," he said.

"Not at all. Go ahead."

The gravin motioned toward the opening.

"Ladies first."

Master Leta gave him a bright smile and walked past the door. The man turned, glancing at the apprentices, then entered the room. Toby went back to pacing as soon as the door closed. Lorn shook his head and wrinkled his nose, turning to watch the young cat.

"Nervous?" The young cat stared at his companion. Lorn shrugged.

"Stupid question."

Toby went back to pacing.

"Look. It's not like this is a test over something you learned in class. You were born with this. You can't fail."

"But what if someone does something to one of the objects, makes it so it doesn't have a smell?"

"That would be cheating. The head masters won't allow that."

"How would they know? They don't have super smellers."

"True, but they trust your abilities. If you fail to find an object I bet they'll check it out and then they'd find the cheat."

"I suppose."

The doors opened. Master Meredith stood in the doorway.

"Toby, we're ready for you."

Toby glanced back at Lorn. The young human wasn't allowed in the room. Lifting his chin high, the tom followed the tortoiseshell cat into the banquet hall. They stopped at the top of the stairs. He turned to Master Meredith for instruction.

"There are three objects hidden in this room, each with a unique smell. As you search for them you are to tell us what you smell."

"How will I know I've found them?"

"You will know."

Toby wrinkled his forehead.

"How much time do I have?"

"Thirty minutes, starting now."

The young tom's whiskers clamped tight. He sniffed the air. The stale scent of food hung faintly. He started down the stairs. A whiff of exotic flowers caught his attention. He stopped. Closing his eyes he searched the air around him for its direction. Behind him. He turned, took a step. The smell grew stronger. He opened his mouth to let the scent flow over his glands.

"What do you smell?"

"Flowers. I think they're flowers. I've never smelled it before. It's..." Toby took another step toward the banister. "It's coming from..."

He opened his eyes and stared down at the floor. He cocked his head, looking at the sparkling object. *Rats. Just a pin some lady lost at the last festival.* He batted at it. The object began screaming. Toby's eyes flew wide, his ears flattened to his head. As he tried to back away, his paws skid on the polished wood floor. Master Meredith picked the screaming pin up and placed it on a small table just inside the doors. The screaming stopped.

"He has found the first object."

Master Orde's lips curved in a snarl. He glanced toward Gravin Arturo who seemed intrigued, but nothing more. Toby took several deep breaths as he stared at the two humans. At least now he knew what to expect. He looked toward Master Meredith. She nodded, indicating he should continue. The young tom lifted his nose to the air again.

"I smell stale food."

Toby took a step down the stairs. He turned his head left and right, trying to catch any other unusual smells. There. Over there. What was that? The orange cat opened his mouth again to let the smell caress his scent glands. He closed his eyes. The scent felt like something warm and furry scuttling over his mind. He opened his eyes and looked toward Master Meredith at the top of the staircase.

"There's a mouse in the walls."

The tortoiseshell cat looked toward Master Jalen, then back at Toby.

"Can you show us where?"

Toby nodded and padded down the stairs toward the far wall. He stopped, sniffing the air again. The mouse wasn't moving. The tom stalked his prey, setting one foot lightly in front of the other, wary of any possible vibrations he might make with his pawsteps. The scent was growing stronger. He opened his mouth again. The images playing in his mind of the warm, furry creature became overlaid with visions of flowing metal and the sweet stink of death. Toby ceased stalking the mouse.

"It's dead."

He walked to the wood panel hiding the creature and placed his paw on it. The panel rotated inward, revealing the servant's hidden entrance to the kitchen in the adjoining room. Toby found the mouse two cat lengths past the door. He bent to pick it up by the tail. The short passageway reverberated with the same scream the pin had made.

The young tom flattened his ears against the sound. As he passed the humans at the foot of the stairway, he couldn't help a small splay of whiskers at the look of frustration on Master Orde's face. Master Leta was grinning at him. The screaming stopped when Toby placed the dead mouse next to the pin on the table. This was too easy.

He started down the stairs again. The scent of old perfume wafted by. He sniffed the banister, Lorn's mother must have stood there for awhile. Her perfume seemed to linger on everything far longer than any other scent Toby knew of.

The tom continued on, identifying scents from whatever gathering had transpired recently. Nothing out of the ordinary or recent. He paced the length of the hall, raising his nose to the air at every possible smell.

Nothing. He could feel the stares of everyone in the room. His skin began to prickle. Where was the third object? He turned to retrace his steps around the room. It had to be here. Toby's fears began to twist his stomach. He'd been right. Someone was cheating. Who?

He turned to study the group at the stairs. Gravin Arturo would have the most to gain if he failed, but Master Orde seemed ready to throw both he and Lorn out the moment Toby admitted defeat. The young tom narrowed his eyes. Where would he hide an object he didn't want found?

"May I be permitted to scent everyone here?"

Master Meredith's eyes narrowed. She looked toward Master Jalen who frowned, cupping his chin between a curled index finger and thumb. He looked at Toby, then, taking his hand away from his chin, motioned for him to do as he asked. Master Orde glared at the head masters.

"I will not allow my person to be violated by this apprentice."

"Then you concede that Toby has passed this test and that he and Lorn's records are to be expunged of any wrong doing in regards to the explosion?" asked Master Leta.

"Absolutely not."

"Then what other choice do we have?"

The balding mage lifted a lip in a snarl, but said nothing else. Toby forced his whiskers to remain still, though they wanted to splay in victory. When he reached the man, he lifted his nose and breathed deeply. He closed his eyes and let the scent images fill his mind. Musty visions floated by followed by the tang of a dark blue rivulet and a hint of floral Toby vaguely recognized.

He concentrated on the floral scent. It blossomed into a soft human face with dark eyes and flowing black hair. Toby opened his eyes in surprise, looking up at the master mage. Master Orde's jaw protruded slightly, a steely challenge in his eyes. Toby glanced at Master Leta, who colored pink and dropped her gaze to the floor.

"What do you smell?" asked Master Meredith.

"Only old books and ink."

Toby looked back at the balding mage. The human's face softened slightly and the orange tom blinked in acknowledgment. Turning, he made his way toward Gravin Arturo. Hesitantly, the young tom breathed in the air next to the gravin and let the images play through his mind. Wet stones tumbled past chased by a bitter slime. When he opened his eyes, he stared into the gravin's face. The man cocked one eyebrow, but said nothing.

"It seems Gravin Arturo has recently taken a bath with some very strong soap."

"One can never be too cautious when people are sick and dying at every turn."

Toby opened his mouth to reply, ears laid back and whiskers clamped shut. Master Jalen cleared his throat. Toby turned to continue to the next person, ignoring the gravin's small smile.

Master Leta, bent down to look the young tom in the eye and smiled warmly. Toby's whiskers splayed in response. He closed his eyes and inhaled deeply. He recognized the muted floral scent of her perfume immediately, as well as an underlying scent of old books and ink. He wanted to laugh. He could hardly wait to tell Lorn what he'd discovered.

The young tom was about to move on when a peculiar image zipped past. It was gone before he could catch it. He inhaled again, opening his mouth to let the scents access his glands. To the right. There. Eyes still closed, he stepped closer to the woman. He stretched his neck closer to where the scent was coming from and inhaled deeply.

The rush of marigolds and wet metal overwhelmed his nose. A powerful sneeze pushed him back.

"What do you smell?"

Master Meredith's voice sounded like it was coming from far away down a tunnel. Another sneeze exploded from the young tom. A warm hand touched his side.

"Are you alright?" asked Master Leta.

"Pocket," gasped Toby.

He scrambled away, taking shallow breaths. Halfway across the room, the orange cat found the air easier to breath. He opened tear blurred eyes on the group. The gravin turned to scowl at the young woman.

"It seems Master Leta may have been hiding something."

The woman stood up and reached hesitantly into her pocket. She pulled out a silver charm bracelet, a red gem dangling from one of its links. Her eyes widened as she looked at it in the palm of her hand.

"Is this what you smelled?" she asked, holding the offending object toward the tom.

Toby studied the bracelet. Its red gem glittered in the light from the banquet hall windows. He reached out a paw to touch it, then stopped, unsure of himself. He closed his eyes to replay the images. Wet metal. Marigolds. Anything else? He replayed them again. No. Nothing.

He opened his eyes and looked at the bracelet, his paw mere inches above it. Holding his breath, he touched the object. Immediately it began screaming. Master Leta dropped it. She looked around at the gathered group.

"I don't know how that got in my pocket."

Master Meredith paced toward the screaming bracelet. She picked it up and raced toward the table, dropping it next to the other items. She stared with narrow eyes at the group gathered at the foot of the stairs.

"Although the bracelet was not one of the objects slated to be found, we do have a total of three."

"If the bracelet wasn't one of the original objects, then why did it react like the other two?" asked Master Orde. Master Jalen crossed his arms over his chest. He looked around the group.

"Master Meredith and I cast a spell over this room in which only those items brought in with the specific purpose of being found would emit a scream when our young apprentice touched it. It would appear someone wanted this bracelet found."

"But I didn't put it in my pocket," repeated Master Leta, curling her fists at her side.

Her face was pale, making her dark eyes stand out. She

looked helplessly toward Master Orde.

"We are not supposing that you did, my dear."

The balding mage patted the young woman on the shoulder. He glared at Master Jalen and Gravin Arturo. The gravin gave Toby a penetrating stare, making his fur stand on end. He turned toward the head master mage.

"Does it really matter who brought the object into the room? The fact is that young Toby has passed your test. Isn't that what we are here for?"

The head master glanced at the young tom, then back at the gravin.

"True enough. I believe we can all agree that it is at least possible, given the head housekeeper's statement and the evidence gathered here, that Toby is indeed gifted with a strong sense of smell." Master Jalen looked from one nodding head to the next.

"In that light, I declare this hearing at an end and Apprentice Toby and his companion Apprentice Lorn shall be allowed to continue their studies at the academy. All accusations leveled at the partners in regards to the explosion in their room are hereby withdrawn."

Chivato paced in a stiff circle around Reginald. The fire in the gray tom's fireplace popped and hissed, making the white tom jump.

"It's a good thing Master Orde is such a weak human, wanting to keep his inane little affair a secret, or I wouldn't have been able to get Arturo into that room. Unfortunately, it seems our spies have found a way around our efforts to eliminate them. If I find whoever is responsible for placing my charm bracelet in that woman's pocket..."

Chivato's tail lashed as he tore his claws through the

plush carpet. He turned his gaze on Reginald. The young cat ignored the overwhelming desire to flatten himself to the floor as the gray tom stalked toward him.

"I'm surrounded by idiots and thieves. Do you understand what losing that bracelet means?"

Reginald shook his head, holding his breath as he tried to still his trembling tail by wrapping it tighter around his toes. He could smell the tuna from lunch on the gray tom's breath as Chivato leaned closer.

"It means I have to find another way to do what he wants before he finds out something went wrong. He doesn't take well to having things go wrong."

Reginald saw the gray tom's pupils constrict, his whiskers clamping together. Chivato's whiskers brushed Reginald's face as he turned to pace back toward the fireplace. The older cat sat down, licking his ruff. He stared into the fire for a moment, then turned his gaze back on the young cat.

"We are fortunate that I had something else tucked away that will do just as well. Perhaps even better." Chivato cocked his head to the side as he looked at Reginald.

"Our gracious leader may not like things to go wrong, but he seems to believe in second chances. He has seen fit to allow you one more chance to prove your worthiness in the coming new era."

Reginald eyes widened and his whiskers splayed in a grin. The gray tom's eyes narrowed as he bared his fangs.

"I do not think you are worthy of such a task, but it is his command."

The young cat straightened to his full height, lifting his chin.

"I'm ready. What am I to do?"

"It is dangerous. You must be stealthy."

"I can be night itself."

Chivato snorted and turned away, stalking stiff-legged toward the door.

"If that were true then this would not be your last opportunity." The gray tom called to his human, then paced silently to the fireplace. Reginald opened his mouth to retort, then thought better of it.

"What is the task?"

The older tom sat silently staring into the fire. The white cat's tail twitched and his fur began to prickle. He clamped his jaws tight on the harsh words he wanted to say. Arturo entered carrying a small wooden box. The gray tom turned slowly toward the younger cat, his golden eyes seeming to bore into Reginald's soul. Slowly, Chivato's whiskers parted in a wide cat grin as he motioned the human to open the box for the younger cat to see inside. A shiver ran the length of the young tom's spine.

"You are to deliver the dragon willow disease to the academy."

Chapter 13

Spring came to the academy two months early. At least, the Spring Festival did. The head masters announced the festival would take place two weeks after the students began classes again. No one said why the decision had been made, but Toby guessed it was because the sickness had crept into the noble houses and everyone needed something else to think about.

The large banquet hall echoed with rare laughter. The orange tom scanned the room from Lorn's shoulders. Bright paper flowers adorned the two food tables along with a modest offering of finger foods. A large bowl of punch stood sentinel on the end of each. The number of tables for guests were fewer, leaving a large area free at the opposite end of the room. They'd been told it was for dancing. The musicians had yet to arrive.

The partners made their way down the stairs toward one of the food tables. The human picked up a plate and scanned the fare. He grunted.

"Looks like no one else is hungry."

Toby gazed around at the small crowd. He could count the number of those with plates on his paws and have toes left over. Several humans and cats were gathered around a small table at the back where Chivato seemed to be regaling them with humorous stories.

Virginia Ripple

Toby's stomach squeezed itself into a ball as he watched Terence hang on the gray tom's words. Lorn had been right. Even if the little cat's gut was telling him something was wrong with his mentors, there was nothing Toby could say to make Terence leave them. The orange tom's head sunk to his chest as he balanced on his human's shoulder. Suddenly, Lorn jerked as someone grabbed his elbow.

"We have to talk to you," whispered Dora. Alie lead them to a spot near the dance area.

"Something's up."

"We've been keeping our ears open like we said and there's been some talk about some cat preaching freedom for cat-kind," said Dora.

"Yeah, we've heard of him," replied Lorn. "We think he's tied into the ones responsible for –"

"A lot of bad things," finished Toby, sinking his claws into the young human's shoulder. Lorn winced.

"No kidding. If half what we've heard is true he makes the devil's henchman seem like a sweet kitten," Alie said. Dora nodded, eyes wide.

"There's more. Apparently he's planning something big and it's going to happen tonight."

"Any idea what it is?"

"No, but several members of the High Council were ordered to the palace yesterday and a couple more were sent here to meet with the head masters."

Toby searched the crowd, looking for either of the head masters. He spotted them speaking to somber looking partners. Master Antwan and Master Natsumi, sitting on stools, seemed to be listening intently to what Master Jalen was saying. The orange tom wished he could read the head master's lips.

"They're over there. Are those the council members?"

"Yes," said Dora, stretching to look around Alie's dark curls.

"I wonder what they're talking about," said Lorn.

Master Meredith began looking around at the crowd. When her eyes lighted on them, she spoke to those in the small group, pointing with a delicate paw toward Toby and his friends. The human councilman looked in their direction. He bowed to the head masters and loners, then turned to walk in their direction, his dark furred companion perched on his shoulder.

"I think we're about to find out," said Toby.

"I'm suddenly very thirsty," said Dora. "Why don't we get some punch for ourselves?"

"Wait. You're not leaving us now," said Lorn.

"Trust us, it's better for everyone if no one knows we gave you any information," said Alie, smiling as if Lorn had just told her something amusing.

She nodded and waved, moving away as if she were just another socializer. Toby felt Lorn swallow, his eyes moving from their retreating friends to the approaching councilman and his companion. The tom followed the young man's gaze. The bulky councilman was striding toward them, his green and orange spider pendant bouncing against his gorilla-like chest.

"Apprentice Ribaldy and Apprentice Toby, I presume," said the high councilman, his voice deep and commanding. "I understand you two have recently uncovered sensitive information regarding a mission Loner Victor was on before he disappeared."

Lorn nodded. Toby inched closer to the young human's ear, curling his tail around the boy's neck as he looked up at the sleek black tom. The master cat's green eyes bore into him. Toby wanted to crawl into Lorn's robe to hide. The hair on the ridge of his back stood on end. The orange tom's claws dug into Lorn's shoulder and he winced. The movement allowed the cat to break eye contact.

He glanced toward the food table, watching his friends ignoring them, the councilman's voice fading into the background. He wanted to growl. His gaze slid further down the table where Reginald hovered near the punch bowl. The white cat's gaze darted from one side to the other. He crept two steps closer to the bowl and looked around the room again.

Toby's ears perked forward as he watched his nemesis lean over the bowl. The orange tom caught a glimpse of something silver dangling from Reginald's neck over the punch. The white tom's lips moved as if he were speaking to someone, but no one was around to hear. Sparkles drifted from the silver object into the punch. The white cat glanced around the room again, then jumped to the floor and walked away.

Curious, Toby lifted his nose to sniff the air. The scent of smoked salmon, rare cheeses and fruit drifted to his nose. He drew in another breath, opening his mouth to allow the smells to caress his scent glands. The delicate floral aroma of the punch floated over the young cat's glands. Nothing unusual. He was about to close his mouth and return his attention to what the councilman was saying when a new odor assaulted his nose. Toby felt like he stuck his nose in a garden of overgrown marigolds being watered with blood.

The first sneeze echoed around the banquet hall, throwing Toby to the floor. Sneeze after sneeze wracked the tom's body. Lorn crouched next to him.

"Punch," gasped Toby. "Reginald."

Lorn looked toward the food table. The white tom's

eyes were wide. He whirled around.

"Cea SETH isMOU," shouted Lorn, throwing his open palm toward the fleeing cat.

Reginald shrunk instantly, still scurrying away. Master Meredith pounced on the mouse-sized tom. Carrying the tiny cat, she strolled toward the councilman and placed the squirming bundle at the man's feet.

"I believe this is the criminal you are looking for," said the head master cat.

"An apprentice cat?" asked the councilman. "Surely you're joking."

"Did you not, only moments ago, plan to accuse these two apprentices of criminal activities related to a current investigation?"

"I was merely going to ask them a few questions."

"Indeed. I think you will find, Councilman Damon, that this apprentice is not the snake's head you are looking for, but he will be able to lead us to it."

The room was silent. Councilman Damon stared down at the partners. Toby concentrated on the man's green and orange spider pendant, afraid his heart would freeze if he met the eyes of the cat on the councilman's shoulder.

"Young man, please explain your actions."

Lorn looked to Master Meredith, who only nodded, a paw firmly on the squirming mouse-sized tom.

"When Toby fell off my shoulder sneezing, I knew something bad was happening. He managed to warn me that Reginald had done something to the punch, so I immediately threw an incantation at him to freeze him in place."

The Councilman stared at the young man, then down at the miniaturized tom. He raised an eyebrow when he looked back at Lorn.

"I didn't mean to shrink him," mumbled the boy. The man scowled.

"You mean to tell me you hit your classmate with a poorly formed transformation spell because your partner sneezed? Master Meredith, what kind of absurd reasoning are you teaching these students?" bellowed the councilman.

"I assure you, Councilman Damon, that it is not absurd at all given young Toby's exceptional gift," replied Master Jalen, stepping around a group of onlookers.

"Oh surely you don't believe that nonsense about having the ability to smell bad magic. His father used those same lies to manipulate his way onto the High Council."

"It's not a lie," shouted the orange tom, glaring up at the rotund human.

Damon looked at him with unconcealed scorn. The cat's green eyes continued to bore into him. He felt his fur fluff in fear, his legs stiffened as he tried to wrench his eyes from the dark cat's gaze.

"Toby," said Master Meredith, her voice like a rope thrown to a drowning man, "please tell us what happened before you told Lorn about the punch."

The young tom closed his eyes and tried to relax as he had when he'd explained why he'd slapped the remedy from under his mother's nose. Slowly the scene replayed itself. He was afraid to tell them why he'd been looking at the food table. He could still feel the master cat's penetrating gaze.

"I glanced toward the food table when I caught movement out of the corner of my eye. I saw Reginald creeping toward the punch bowl. He had a silver charm around his neck I'd never seen on him before. He said something over the punch bowl and sparkles fell into the liquid. At first I thought maybe he was playing a joke, spiking the punch, but, when I let the smells go over my scent glands, I smelled blood magic."

"How do you know you smelled blood magic?"

"I've smelled it before. It smells like marigolds and blood. I'm allergic to that smell. It makes me sneeze."

"And this smell, you're certain it came from the punch?" asked Master Jalen.

"Yes, sir, it was hidden under the floral scent."

"I suppose you can prove all this," said Councilman Damon. Toby's ears flattened. The crowd waited, saying nothing.

"We could easily prove not only if blood magic potion was put into the punch, but also who is responsible if there is," said Master Antwan, shouldering his way past several humans toward the table.

The tiny white tom suddenly froze, his eyes wide and whiskers clamped tight. Master Antwan motioned for Master Natsumi to join him. The sleek cat jumped smoothly to the table, glancing in Councilman Damon's direction.

Each loner studied the liquid. Toby watched as their noses worked, barely above the surface. Master Natsumi shook her head and sat up. The large tom narrowed his eyes at his compatriot, then opened his mouth to let the punch's aroma filter over his scent glands. Master Antwan sat up, closing his eyes. When he opened them, he gave a single nod to the head masters.

"Ret URNto oRIG inATE," said the large tom, staring into the punch bowl.

A swirl of sparkles swarmed like bees toward the miniature white tom who squeaked and attempted to pull away from Master Meredith's paw. He cowered on the floor, staring up at the silver mass churning above him.

"He made me do it."

"Who?" demanded Master Meredith.

"Chivato. He told me to dump the vial in the punch and activate it. Please, don't let it touch me!"

"Why?" asked Master Antwan as he stalked toward the mouse-sized cat.

"What does it do?" asked Master Meredith.

"It's the sickness. It brings the sickness." The little white cat's eyes never left the glittering orb.

"Liar," shouted a young voice to Toby's left. The orange tom turned to see who it was. Terence stood stiff-legged, his eyes burning with anger as he stared at Reginald.

"Terence, look at him," said Toby. "He's terrified. Why would he lie?"

"He'd say anything to keep himself out of trouble. He's always tryin' to get someone else in trouble. Even you should know that."

"Yeah, he's done his best to make us do something to get expelled, but he's never tried to poison anyone before."

"How do we know he wasn't just pullin' some kind of joke? How do you know it's poison?"

"You remember when we first met and I told you what we were going to have for breakfast?"

Terence nodded, his eyes narrow slits.

"You asked me if having a strong sense of smell was necessary to be chosen."

"You told me it wasn't."

"Right. Well I found out I can smell blood magic, that I'm allergic to it. That orb is made with blood magic."

Terence glared at Toby, at the swirling sliver ball and then the mouse-sized white tom.

"That still doesn't prove Master Chivato made him do

it," he growled. Toby looked helplessly at the head masters. Master Antwan stepped in front of the young toms.

"Terence, did you see how I made the potion retrace its path to Reginald?"

The little gray and white tom stood at attention.

"Yes, sir."

"Once we put it back in, the person responsible for putting it in the charm in the first place can be found in the same way. I think you should be the one to find out who that person is. Do you agree?"

"Yes, sir," said the little cat, his ear twitching.

With a flick of the loner's tail, the silver charm floated up and away from the white tom still crouched on the floor. The large charcoal gray tom said the incantation to force the potion back in its container. Toby watched in fascination as the sparkling swirling mass was forced into the small container by an unseen hand.

As the vial settled back to the floor, Terence stepped toward it. He glanced at Toby, whiskers clamped tight, ears flattened. The orange tom could smell the anxiety drifting from the young cat.

"Ret URNto oRIG inATE."

Toby held his breath as the silver charm slowly lifted from the floor. In an eye blink it zipped past the heads of the crowd of humans and cats perched on shoulders. The orange tom perked his ears forward, listening for the sound of the metal vial hitting the floor. He stood, ready to charge between legs to nail whoever was responsible for his mother's illness and, most likely, his father's disappearance. Beside him, Lorn stretched as tall as he could, craning his neck to watch as the charm whizzed toward its original owner.

The sound they waited for came an instant later. The

partners shot forward, Toby racing low to the ground, Lorn shoving humans aside. They burst into an opening. Humans and cats alike had drawn away from the gray long-haired tom, the vial spinning on the floor in front of his paws. Toby's thrill of triumph died as he stared at the master cat's bland expression. He felt Terence skid to a halt beside him. The little tom's fur bristled.

"This can't be right. Someone messed with the spell."

"Your spell was perfectly executed, trainee, though your zeal to disprove my guilt gave it more energy than was necessary."

"I don't get it. You... you couldn't have... killed so many."

"Death is inevitable in war."

"What war?"

"The war against humans," said Lorn. "You're trying to take control of the kingdom and you're eliminating anyone who gets in the way. That's why you killed Master Kiyoshi and framed Uncle Hecktor, isn't it?"

"Preemptive strike."

"What about my father? Did you kill him, too?"

The gray tom purred, splaying his whiskers and narrowing his eyes.

"Your father has had a very special role. He's been most helpful in our cause."

"Mangefur! What have you done to my father?"

Toby yowled and launched himself at the master cat. The orange tom slammed into an invisible wall a foot in front of the gray tom, making the master cat laugh. Toby swiped his claws across the shield, ears laid back, fangs exposed in a snarl.

"Take it down and fight me you coward," he hissed.

"It would be my pleasure, but I didn't put it there."

Toby glared at the grinning tom. A rustle of cloth near him drew his attention. The young tom turned his glare on the man standing beside him. The head master had his arms crossed, a frown on his lips.

"I put it there."

The young tom growled and lashed his tail.

"Why?"

"He must be questioned further. We don't know just how many others may be involved in this so-called war."

Toby raked his claws down the shield one more time. He stalked away, lashing his tail.

"What about Gravin Arturo?" asked Lorn.

"We've already sent several mages to the great house to arrest him."

The orange tom continued to glare at the gray cat who sat within the shield calmly washing his paws.

"So what happens now?"

"They will stand trial for murder, treason and attempted genocide."

"And they will be executed," said Master Meredith.

Torchlight flickered on the walls, casting cross-hatched shadows in the cell. The stench of old urine permeated the stone floor. Chivato tried not to breath. He could hear the guards' voices from the end of the hall. Laughter. The gray tom's tail twitched. Footsteps. The jingle of keys. The smell of gruel made the cat's stomach rumble.

"'Ere we are. A feast for 'is majesty."

The guard grinned as he lowered the bowl of lumpy white gruel from the top of the cage. Chivato glared at his gloved hands. The guard laughed and closed the hatch.

"You 'ave a visitor yer majesty."

With a bow to whoever was standing just out of sight, the guard sauntered away, whistling tunelessly. A black tom stepped into view. Chivato bowed.

"Your Lordship."

The black tom stared at him. Chivato returned the stare, his stomach rumbling. He stepped closer to the front of the cage.

"When am I getting out?"

"Eat."

The gray tom turned to stare at the tasteless paste sitting in the bowl. He looked back at the black tom.

"I did what was asked of me. I cannot be faulted for that halfling's weakness."

The black tom stared at him.

"Eat."

The tom looked back down at the bowl of gruel. The cat wrinkled his nose at the lumpy mass, then bent to sniff it, glancing at the black tom from the corner of his eye.

"Your stomach rumblings are loud enough to wake the dead. Eat."

Chivato nibbled at the lumpy gruel, surprised to find it sweetened and spiced. Urged on by his hunger, he began to gobble and slurp up the tasty treat. The black tom watched silently as the caged cat licked the last of the gruel from his whiskers.

"Thank you for persuading them to at least make it taste appetizing." The gray tom began washing his paws. The black cat stared at him.

"Consider it the perfect gift for a noble cat able to complete his task imperfectly."

The gray cat looked through the cross-hatched wall,

his ears swiveled outward.

"Completed imperfectly? I don't understand."

"It's of no concern. Things have a way of working out when you plan ahead."

The black tom's whisker's twitched. Chivato cocked his head, trying to figure out the black cat's strategy. For every decision he made, there were several alternatives waiting. The gray cat narrowed his eyes, wondering how his master planned to release him. He bent to continue washing his paws.

"So when am I getting out?"

"I'm afraid that is impossible."

Chivato stopped mid-lick, staring at the black tom. His stomach clenched.

"What about the inquisitors?"

The tom stared at him. Chivato's stomach constricted again, sending a peculiar burning sensation inching its way up his throat. The room began to waver. The gray tom laid down, limbs feeling weak. He squinted at the black tom watching him.

"That will not be a problem."

"But you just said—"

He wretched. Bloody vomit spilled to the floor. The gray tom stared in horror. The fire in his stomach burned a path into his paws and tail, racing up his neck and into his ears. He looked at the mess in front of his paws then to the bowl that had held the sweetened paste. He could feel the heat turning his eyes glassy as he blinked at the black cat beyond the cage.

"Arturo," he gasped. The ringing in his ears nearly drowned out the other tom's words.

"Ah, yes. I visited him earlier today. The poor man seems to be coming down with something. I do hope it's not the sickness."

Chivato whimpered, reaching a feeble paw toward the door.

"As for you, it looks as if you're not feeling well either. I'll see to it you are not disturbed until the inquisitors come for you."

Rolling on his side, the gray tom closed his eyes, listening to the fading pawsteps.

Toby shivered as the cold wind ruffled his fur. At least it wasn't snowing, though the way the orange tom felt a gray sky filled with a blizzard would have been more fitting than the bright sunshine. A heavy snow might have camouflaged the mounds of earth surrounding them, a grim reminder of Chivato's war. No one knew how far this war had gone, how many others were going to carry on what the heinous cat had begun. Both the gray tom and the gravin were found dead in their cells when the inquisitors had come to fetch them for questioning.

Toby tore at the frozen ground. Aside from the cat's cryptic words, the young tom had no idea what had happened to his father. He'd heard a rumor that Chivato had used other cats for his experiments, maybe Victor had been one of them. For all Toby knew, his father could still be alive somewhere in a cage awaiting someone else's version of torture for the war efforts.

"From dust were we fashioned by the One and to dust we return. Blessed be the One."

Brother Jason pronounced the amen over the open grave, throwing a handful of dirt into it. Toby bowed his head in respect. He glanced to his left to see Terence sitting stiffly, staring straight ahead. Lorn stood to the orange tom's right, shifting from foot to foot. Toby had lost count of how many graves they'd helped fill in today as part of the academy's new relief program. They had been the first students to volunteer, though Toby knew the volunteer part was soon to become a requirement for every student entering the school. Part of the new empathy training every mage and cat would have to take. The orange tom wondered if it would do any good.

At least the number of deaths was coming to an end. Thanks to Reginald's criminal ineptitude, Master O'dorn was able to mix a remedy that worked as quickly as the poison had. Toby's mother had been the first to recover. *If being crippled for life could be called recovering,* thought the young tom. The once proud queen was now sway-backed, her hind legs wobbly and prone to making her tip over. *But she's alive.* The thought pricked his conscience. He'd made a bargain. He needed to fulfill it.

The human Brother nodded for the apprentices and trainee to begin the process of moving dirt from the mound beside them into the last grave of the day. After doing it so many times, they'd become semi professionals, using small amounts of energy efficiently and focusing their combined wills with precision. It was all done in a few moments. The trio stepped around the fresh grave, following the Brothers toward the small temple and a promised cup of hot tea and milk.

"Toby, wait up," said Terence.

The orange tom sat down, watching as his friend kneaded the packed earth. The little gray and white cat glanced around them at the silent resting places for his mentor's victims. He shivered. When he finally looked at Toby, the young tom's pupils were narrow slits, his whiskers clamped and drooping.

"You think I'm stupid," he said, thrusting his chin in the direction of the nearest grave, "trustin' him."

Toby shook his head. Terence looked around the cemetery again, then stared off into the distance.

"Yeah, well, I was. You tried to tell me. Hell, you even tried to show me an' I wouldn't listen." The young cat looked back at Toby again, his eyes haunted.

"What kinda loner am I gonna be if I can't even see the truth when it's right under my nose?"

"You made a mistake. You didn't trust your gut this time, but you'll learn. We all will."

"I'm not so sure, Toby. Look what he did. How many could I have saved if I'd said somethin'?"

"I doubt you could have saved any of them. If you'd said anything, you might be under one of these mounds, too."

"You don't know that."

"Neither do you. Look, we all do things we regret. That's part of life. It's what we do afterward that shows who we are."

"I suppose your right. I just don't know if I wanna continue my trainin', you know? Maybe there's somethin' else I oughta do. Somethin' that'll really make a difference in the world."

"Like what?"

"I was thinkin' of joinin' the Brothers. I see what they've done to clean up Chivato's mess an' they do it without a single bad word said against that mangefur. An' they've been doin' all they can for cats and humans like me as long as I can remember. Maybe I could make a difference like they do."

Toby thought back to his interview. Perhaps being a master cat wasn't the best path to make a difference, but he still felt he could have done what he'd told M'festus. Now, he didn't know if it mattered. He'd made his bargain. His mother lived. He had to hold up his end.

"I was thinking along the same lines. Maybe we should both join the Brothers."

"That would be a terrible waste of talent," said an old tonsured cat, padding toward them.

"Brother Yannis, what are you doing out here?"

"I was looking for you two. Brother Jason has the milk warming by the fire. Sent me out like a mother hen to fetch you." The old cat's whiskers were splayed wide and his eyes twinkled.

"Now, what's this about you two joining the Brotherhood?"

"I been watchin' you an' Brother Jason an' it got me thinkin'. The Brothers were always there for me an' mum when we couldn't find no shelter or fill our bellies. An' the way you been carin' for all the dead an' haven't said nothin' against Chivato even though it's his fault. I'd like to be like that, but I don't know how. I was hopin' you'd teach me."

"Come to me, all you who labor and are heavily burdened, and I will give you rest. Take my yoke upon you, and learn from me, for I am gentle and lowly in heart; and you will find rest for your souls. For my yoke is easy, and my burden is light."

"Huh?"

"It's a quote from the first Book of the One. What we do is follow the One who was the Servant of All. Is that what you want, Terence, to be a servant?"

"I think it is. I wanna try."

The old cat blinked at him and laid his ragged tail gently over the young tom's shoulders. He turned to look at the orange tom.

"And you? Is that your reason as well?"

"Not exactly," said Toby, looking down as he scratched a claw along the frozen dirt.

"Then why are you considering joining us?"

"I made a deal with your One. I promised to become a Follower if my mother lived and she has."

"I see. Son, the One doesn't want Followers just because they try to bargain with him."

"I keep my promises," said the orange tom.

"That's good, but this isn't a promise you're expected to keep."

"What do you mean?"

"It's not that the One doesn't want you to become a Follower. In fact, nothing could make him happier than to bring another lamb into the fold, but if you're only there because you believe it's your duty to be there, then neither of you will prosper from the deal. The One wants more than your fulfillment of a duty."

"Then what does he want?"

"Your heart, son. He wants your love. He wants to be a part of your life, to love and be loved in return. He wants to guide your path, not force you down the road with a whip or a rod."

"So what do I do? I can't just break a promise."

Brother Yannis stared at the young tom a long time. Toby got the impression he was listening to something, or someone, the young tom couldn't hear. The old cat blinked and cocked his head.

"Do you have access to the Books?"

"Yes. Why?"

"If you want to keep your promise — study. Study the Books. Ask questions. Listen with your heart."

"Are you sure that's enough? I mean, the One spared my mother's life and all I have to do is read some books in return?"

"It's enough to begin."

"I don't have to join the Brotherhood?"

"What does your heart say?"

Toby closed his eyes and cleared his mind. He imagined listening to his heart to be the same as listening to his instinct. When he opened his eyes again, he smiled. Brother Yannis smiled back.

"Come, you two. My old bones don't like this cold and we have warm milk waiting."

The young cats kept pace with the old Brother. Toby's mind drifted to his missing father and crippled mother. He was surprised to find his anger at what had happened to them had been replaced by determination to make the world safer by following his dream. He looked toward the small temple and saw Lorn. Putting on a burst of speed, the orange tom ran toward the human. Whatever came in the future, at least he knew someone would be there to help him.

Author Bio

Throughout Virginia's school years she concentrated on her English courses, going on to earn a Bachelor of Arts in English. She was hired as a part-time Christian Education Director after graduating from Northwest Missouri State University and went on to become a seminary student at Brite Divinity, an Associate Minister and a church elder. Virginia re-discovered her passion for writing while in graduate school and with it a new direction for her life. Since then she has balanced her time between her career as an independent author and being a loving wife and mother.

For more information, visit Virginia's web site at www.virginiaripple.com or scan the QR code below to sign up for sneak peeks and special offers in Virginia's monthly newsletter.